THE INNKEEPER ON THE EDGE OF PARIS

J. SCHLENKER

Binka Publishing, LLC

Binka Publishing, LLC

ISBN-13: 978-0-9994278-3-5

ISBN-10: 0-9994278-3-0

To my husband, Chris, and to Carl whom we met on our honeymoon in New Orleans

PART I

1

I don't want to make anyone sad, not even you. Those were the words she opened with, the only words she could think to write. A myriad of excuses flooded her mind before she made herself sit at the kitchen table to draft a note. When she finally mustered the nerve to compose a goodbye letter, she found herself paralyzed, the pen rigid in her hand while she stared out the window, its new transparency beckoning her to the world that lay beyond.

She looked down at her frayed nails, torn and tattered from spending the entire day scrubbing, wiping, dusting, mopping, and cleaning windows—attempting to sterilize what had been. A heavy sigh escaped her lips. All her efforts failed to remove the dark clouds that still penetrated the house's interior.

Like a wax figure, her eyes melted down toward the paper and then to the stack of journals alongside the stationery. There was something so déjà vu about the whole scenario.

So much she had intended to write: about the accident, how it was a wake-up call, how it had inwardly changed her, how she should have acted sooner, about how this pretense of a marriage was doing neither of them any good, and about how they were

3

both still young enough to find happiness. But in front of the blank white paper, she froze. Instead of pouring out her heart to Nick, her own thoughts and feelings, the ones she hid in her locked journal she didn't need to lock or hide because Nick didn't have the least bit of curiosity or interest about what went on inside her head or her heart, she gazed out the window over the kitchen sink in a daze, fixated on the rain now hitting the freshly cleaned pane of glass.

Each word that entered her mind to write dissolved before it reached the pen she grasped between her fingers so tensely. Instead, Nick's words reverberated in her head, the ones he used so often: "Isa, you sadden me." Those words rested like an anvil on her heart each time he voiced them in his usual conde-scending manner. They were the words that came after every argument, and there were plenty.

When she tossed out all the extraneous parts of their marriage, it boiled down to she made *him* sad and he made *her* sad. And although math hadn't been her strong suit in school, she knew two sad people didn't equal happiness. Nick and Isa didn't equal marriage, at least not the marriage she had envisioned. But then, according to Nick, her head stayed in the clouds. She read too many books.

"Life isn't like that," he reminded her only last night. "Mr. Darcy is the figment of a lonely woman's imagination. He doesn't exist."

"Yes, I'm lonely. I shouldn't be married and lonely. Why do we never talk? About anything," she screamed.

"I'm off to the bar," he countered. Going out to a bar to have several beers with his friends was Nick's solution to everything.

"Maybe he doesn't exist, and maybe I'm not Elizabeth, but life *could* be like that," she said as he slammed the door behind him. He either didn't hear or didn't listen. What she should have shouted eked out of her mouth half-hearted and inaudible. There were times she hoped he was off to see another woman. It would make leaving him easier, but either way, her mind was made up.

She stared at the paper on the kitchen table. What was the point in writing a lengthy explanation? She couldn't express herself as an author might. She was a librarian, a reader of books, not a writer. Besides, she and Nick were beyond what words could fix. The marriage was broken. Her life was broken. She wrote two sentences and signed her name.

Nick,

I don't want to make anyone sad, not even you. I will pick up the rest of my things by the end of the week.

Isa

Even though she wrote with a shaky hand and her stomach tied in knots, the note exemplified the perfect penmanship Isa prided herself in.

She left the unfolded note on the kitchen table where Nick would be sure to find it. She then ripped the pages out of her old journals, burnt them one by one, and watched as the ashes disintegrated down the garbage disposal. She cleaned the sink once again and picked up her two suitcases bulging with as many clothes as she could cram in, along with a new journal, one that would record a new life. In a separate bag, she carried her laptop, electronic reader, and two of her most cherished books, *Pride and Prejudice* and *Somewhere in Time*. Where she was going, taking her whole library wasn't an option. The many fantasies scrolled across the hundreds of thousands of pages were already mapped into her brain circuitry like tiny roads. The only question was which road to take. The road she had been on led to a dead end.

Tomorrow she would begin divorce proceedings. She would

return for the rest of her personal stuff, the stuff that wouldn't fit into her suitcases, and figure out her plans. But in her heart of hearts, she had already decided although she had told no one, not even her parents.

They all said she had changed since the accident—her parents, Nick, and even Nick's parents. She had become more agitated, more ruffled. She had become broken.

"What has gotten into you, Isa?" they had all asked.

Hadn't they wanted her to come out of her shell? They couldn't have it both ways. Her shell had been incubating long enough. It was ready to burst. It was now or never. A new Isa was ready to emerge.

Next to the note, she spread out the papers she had printed off earlier. As she examined them, a smile spread across her lips, and a hint of sparkle returned to her eyes. Yes, it was decided. She had been googling Europe for months, in particular, France. She would fix her broken life.

2

*R*eturning from the stable, Dora paused at the doorway of the inn. She held her lantern and gazed down at her likeness in a pool of water on the cobblestone. The reflection showed a woman worn and broken before her time. She pulled her shawl in tighter, warding off a sudden chill in the air that sent a wave rippling across the water. The image changed. Her dark hair was no longer pulled back in a tangled disarray of a bun. Instead, it hung loose and shiny about her face. Her own eyes stared back at her. They no longer looked worn but shimmered with joy. The shabbiness of her attire had transformed into something strange, almost indecent. A sheer material, unrecognizable to her, clung like a second skin. The dress, fitting snug against her waist, bloomed like a garden of splendid colors over her hips and hung freely about her bare knees. She blinked. Her former self returned.

She shut the thick wooden door with a thud, staring at it momentarily, dismissing the temptation to open it again and look out into the night and down once more at the pool of water. What strangeness had she just witnessed?

The sound of the rain grew louder. It was raining on that

night too—the night he came. Many times she had tried to sum him up. She possessed a talent for sizing people up, but the exercise proved sheer folly with him. Every type of soul, from nobleman to laggard, had darkened the door of her inn at one time or the other. He did not fit with any of them. What she knew was that in a matter of hours, he had changed her forever. She lived in a broken world. Most had given up. She had been on the brink of giving up herself before his appearance.

She glided her hand across the uneven ridges of the window. They reminded her of small rolling hills. The glazier had only placed the new glass panes last month. She imagined the man looking back at her through the glass. It was wishful thinking. Her intuition told her he was out there somewhere and that he would return one day. The time was not yet right. Time, no matter how disconnected the world had become, was the one thing that held it all together.

She smiled, recounting his visit in her mind. So often, her thoughts slipped to him.

The tall, slender figure of a man dressed in black except for his indigo cloak stopping just above the heels of his boots had manifested out of thin air, or so it seemed. Making his way across the threshold, his cloak flowed behind him like the ripples of a lake on a moonlit night. His boots, untarnished from travel, glistened. There were no spurs. He dropped his hood back to reveal coils of chestnut hair. It was cropped short enough in the back to expose his neckline. His clean-shaven face, another anomaly, revealed a strong jawline and pale, freckled skin. At first, he appeared young. Upon closer examination, she saw the lines and creases of wisdom mapped across his face. With eyes that sparkled like light blue sapphires, he peered into the farthest reaches of her own dark umber eyes.

"I see your soul in your eyes," he said. "Eyes remain the same from lifetime to lifetime. Eyes don't lie."

He sat with her in front of the fire and told her things she didn't dare repeat—curious tales, unorthodox tales. To this day, she had never spoken of them. Who could she repeat them to? She had no confidantes, no one she could trust. Trust had gone by the wayside, along with innocence, when the Edge came.

It had been three years since he stepped from the steadfastness of time, mesmerizing her like some ancient master descended from the mountains might.

"Might I have a room for the night?" he had asked.

While she sat in a hypnotic trance, he placed coins in her hands, folding his own large hands over hers. They were somewhere between rough and soft, betraying he knew all aspects of life. Then, with one abrupt movement, he grasped an ebony-lacquered walking stick and rose from the chair. The blue crystal handle that matched his eyes glistened in the fire's light, adding to the ambiance of the night and his mysterious nature.

She gave him the key to the library, the one with the feather bed, her private sanctuary off-limits to most. It was the one she retreated to when she considered herself free of demands *or* when she wished to hide from them.

Yes, the rain pelted down hard that night, harder than tonight. It was a sound one could drift off to sleep, with faint thunder rumbling somewhere in the distance. As the back of his cloak disappeared up the stairs, the storm moved in closer. She stood staring at the stairwell. A sudden crack of thunder knocked her back to reality and sucked her back into the constancy of time. She still felt the warmth of his hand on hers as she unfolded her fist to find enough coins for a week's worth of lodging. By morning, he had vanished. No one other than herself had seen the elusive stranger.

She wondered if her memory of him was accurate. Had she built the encounter into something more than it was? Was he a phantom—or a ghost? She didn't believe in such nonsense. Maybe she had dreamed him. She did, however, believe dreams told the future.

The next morning, she found the key in the inside pocket of the bar in its usual place. It made her doubt for a moment he had come at all, but she told herself no, he was real. She had saved one of the coins, the one that differed from the others, hiding it behind a loose hearthstone. On nights such as this, when no one was around, she removed the stone to see if it was still there. She looked at its strange picture, a wheel hovering in the sky among clouds overlooking a serene, peaceful valley. There was an inscription in a language she didn't recognize.

His visit that night gave her hope. She looked toward the door. Dead silence. The man would not return tonight. Perhaps it was for the best. Such tranquil moments as these were rare.

The room exuded a placid calmness except for the occasional snap of the flames and flying sparks in the fireplace. Other than the sound of the fire and the steady rain outside, the throbbing in her chest was the only other sound. It was a strange sound. She concentrated extra hard to drown out everything other than the thump inside her bosom. She couldn't remember when she last had this experience of knowing something was inside her. Perhaps as a child—yes, as a child. She was innocent then. No one ever called her innocent now. Some said she didn't have a heart. But they were wrong. For there it was—a steady thump, thump, thump.

Only an hour earlier, a rowdy, boisterous crowd as undisciplined as any could be on the eve of Sunday worship services had filled the space. Saturdays were always the most rambunctious and sinful of nights, not that she judged this or that a sin. It was easy enough to seek forgiveness the following morn with the jingle of a coin hitting the plate or lighting a candle at Our Lady of Paris. People pretended that's all it took for a week's worth of salvation. Nonsense. Forgiving was one thing. Forgetting was another. Only the onward flow of time made people forget.

The party might have still been going on had it not been for the fiddler's wife. Esther, a portly woman, had burst through the door, entering the room like the rush of a tornado and causing its inhabitants to part like the Red Sea, killing any levity in the air as if the clatter of rain and swelling of mud weren't already enough to depress the spirit. She practically dragged her husband out by his collar. Esther's reputation was known far and wide. The reputation differed among individuals, but it never lacked color. Esther did not fit the Biblical image of her namesake, not that she, herself, knew a lot about the Bible. But Esther did—or at least pretended she knew.

The woman had every illness ever known to man but somehow possessed the energy of Hercules. Loud, obnoxious, complaining—every village had an Esther. She craved attention and drama like an alcoholic craved strong ale, although she had never seen Esther partake of spirits.

It was Esther who pronounced that she had no heart. She heard it not from Esther's mouth but from Esther's gossipy friends, her ladies-in-waiting, the flock of women who followed her around with parrot-like obedience.

She never dared open her mouth in condemnation of Esther to anyone. She vowed in that place where her heart was said to be absent to say no unkind word about Esther, at least not out loud. It would not be good for business for an innkeeper to do so. Nor would it be good for her soul. She worried about her soul a great deal.

In the absence of music, the patrons left either to their own homes or went upstairs, where those who paid extra would crowd against each other in the only three beds. The rest would dream the night away on the many straw mattresses strewn about the floor. Some would scout out the most private place with their own bedroll. Those too drunk would collapse atop others, only to have their bodies dragged off and clumped in a pile in a corner. The rest would find a cozy spot in the stable.

Adding more beds to the inn was one of the many improvements she wished to make. Her husband insisted she open up the library. She proclaimed that was not an option. It was not the extra rent he was interested in but rather the satisfaction of denying her the retreat and privacy she so cherished.

Tomorrow, on the Sabbath, she could sleep in for an extra half hour, at least until the second crow of the rooster. She was not given to churchgoing. Although she would be fined for not attending, it was a small price to pay and one she could afford as her business flourished. Since the Edge, most went, not for fear of a fine but out of dread of something more horrible than the Edge befalling them. It didn't feel right to her, not for a woman purported to have no heart. Besides, there was no time for such things. There was always work, regardless of whether or not it was a day of reverence.

Work—she could not deny it any longer, but her body had become paralyzed to its spot. Paralyzed—that word seemed blasphemous to use considering the circumstances. She froze in thought. After the stranger, she was given to frequent reflections on life's meaning. There was always the mundane, all trivial now. Cleaning could wait until morning. The solitude proved too inviting. Sitting for a brief spell was more luxury than she was used to.

Before she became broken and the world became broken— she was not sure which happened first. It was like the chicken and the egg scenario—there *had* been luxury. Her indulgence in any form of lavishness was with her books. It was on nights such as these she retreated to the library, but duty called—her obligation to her husband. Sitting like this was not normal, not normal at all. She had reconciled her fate to living life in either the standing or lying position. Even the horizontal position could be work, another reason she didn't like showing her face in church.

The walnut chair, polished with wear, rocked back and forth, squeaking on the oak planks with her indecisive posture. She wavered between sitting and standing as there was work that needed tending to, but instead, she sat by the window, admiring its new glass. The rain became more pronounced, although the glass dampened its sound. Beads formed on the outside. She ran her fingertips across the uneven ridges, paralleling a drop of rain, counting the droplets like a rosary. With the new glass in place, there was no need to close the shutters. She would see about getting glass in the windows upstairs before buying new beds. Curtains would also be a nice touch—beautiful damask ones, but worsted wool would likely have to do—something besides the shutters to guard against the draft on cold nights. Both would have to wait until spring. She had too much on her plate at the moment, not to mention the weaver was with child again. This must be the fourth now. The vicar said it was everyone's responsibility to repopulate the earth—what was left of it. The weaver took that duty most seriously.

Rumors of another brutal winter were thrown about. While most people felt such things in their bones, she felt them in her gut like an ill omen. Heightened intuition had come with the stranger, an unspoken gift he had left her. Some came to her for advice, while there were those who thought she had a touch of the devil. Esther fell into that category. If there were any creature capable of sorcery, she believed it was Esther.

She must remove thoughts of Esther. Such contemplation was doing her no good. Nor was it doing Esther any good. She believed thoughts come to pass. Maybe all the evil thoughts in the world wove themselves together to form the Edge.

The glass was a gift from a patron, a musician who was *also* her lover. She took on lovers shortly after the stranger appeared. Her longing for him made her reach out for something more. Her husband, because of his condition, pushed her away. Having lovers for a short time made it bearable. They were rarely after any more than the physical. Experience taught her that the trick to any good relationship was to become bored long before they did. It avoided heartbreak. There was that word again—heart. She was avoiding a condition that some thought her incapable of.

For now, she was content to let her current lover see her through the long hard winter. Planning was one of her best virtues, a habit that made her a good businesswoman.

Unable to rise and go about her chores, she sat transfixed at the window, staring at the glistening cobblestone street. As the rain faded, the moonlight made its way through the clouds. A good many of the stones farther down the road had sunk into the ground, dangerous to both man and beast. Pools of water, ankle deep, had formed. She always kept the stones in front of her door in good condition. Her reputation for running a clean establishment in good repair was honorable, and her dealings had been fair. She bore no shame or felt any shortcomings in that regard.

The rain had cleared everyone from the street. Everyone except for herself slumbered away, lost in their dreams. They were dreaming of the earth as before, dreaming they didn't live near the Edge. Most had only known the Edge. They were born after it happened. Some, no doubt, suffered from nightmares. On most nights, she could hear the snores from upstairs, but the rain drowned them out tonight. Not even a dog barked, nor could a whinny be heard from any of the horses in the stables. The cows and chickens were mute as well, an oddity.

The bell echoed from the adjoining room, her cue to fetch her husband's dinner. Her moment of solitude was all too brief.

She slept in the same room because it was convenient. Her bed was small and compact in the corner near her son's. Long ago, she had quit sharing her husband's bed, an arrangement he preferred. They once had used the library as their bedroom. Now she drifted between the two. She would always sleep in the library if she could, but it would not be right. She was not a callous woman, as some said. Her husband needed her. If she were not by his side, there would be hell to pay the next day, if not from him, from her own guilt. It would be a black spot on her soul, darker than her adultery.

The bell sounded again. The ring pealed out longer and more

urgent. Besides his dinner, there would be a chamber pot to deal with. He should know she had to deal with the guests first. His dinner was always delayed on Saturdays. He should not complain, although she knew he would. The lateness of his dinner meant that business was good. She would tell him that come spring, she would hire a scullery maid. He would protest at first; then, he would give in, telling everyone he had conceived the idea on his own. It was the ritual they followed. She was sure he wouldn't mind a young wench tending to his chamber pot *or* any other needs that her presence might arouse in him.

It was time she had someone to deal with menial tasks. Only two months ago, she hired one more lad in addition to the three she had to help with the garden and livestock. Her business was flourishing, and so was her importance in the town.

She poked the fire, illuminating the shadows for an instant, causing a congregation of rodents in the far corner to disperse. She placed another log on top of the disintegrating oak logs and watched as the flames rose higher.

She removed a slab of pork she had gotten from the butcher this morning off the smoldering coals and placed it on the tin plate along with a chunk of crusty bread. She would soon have pigs. Last year, she added chickens to the one milk cow they already had. It was a good idea, one her husband claimed as his own once he found that it kept the overhead down and increased profits. If only her husband would see they were in this together, things would be more tolerable. It wasn't her fault she had a better business head on her shoulders than he. If only she could be free from his resentment and ridicule.

Soon their son would be old enough to take on more responsibility. At eleven, he already tended to the animals alongside the lads she hired. He was also developing a talent for gardening. She had to give his father credit for this attribute. The geraniums she tried to grow in the window box had turned out disastrous. Her son brought them back to life.

The hardship her husband's affliction brought on her son vexed her the most. He was handed too many duties too soon in life. While wringing a chicken's neck, he looked at her with pleading eyes before dropping it and violently throwing up. She had trouble enough doing it herself. She remembered when her husband had derived a devious pleasure in the task. He might still be able to do it, but he was letting his upper body strength slip away. He would argue that if they were paying good wages for the help, they should be the ones to do it. Yes, a scullery maid would do nicely.

She took a sip from the tin mug and puckered her lips in reaction to the bitter taste of the brew from the wooden barrel, strong enough to make her husband easier to deal with and assure he would sleep through the night. She held the tin plate of lukewarm meat and the mug of ale and lingered by the fire just a moment longer.

She surveyed her surroundings—the new glass and the added tables. Their location on the main road to the Edge had much to do with their success. But without all her hard work, the business would never have survived after her husband's accident. He had hardly stopped screaming in pain when the other innkeepers rushed in to buy her out. A woman could never handle all this, they had said. But she did, and she was praised. Their memories were fickle. They had forgotten the many years of sainthood, strength, and determination. People could turn in an instant—a wag of the tongue here and a wag of the tongue there. Esther was the biggest tongue wagger of all. She had initially indulged in pity but only for a short time. Tears were for the weak. They had no place in her life if she were to continue. Let people say what they may. It was of no concern to her.

She murmured, *"Today, my world is broken, but yesterday my world was also broken, and it will remain that way tomorrow. All who are living now were born into this broken world. Everyone makes it normal. Broken is normal. What else can one do? I say we because when I look closely at other people's lives, all I see are broken lives. I've concluded that I can't fix anyone else's life. I can only fix my own, but I wouldn't know where to begin. The only hope I see lies in the stranger."*

She touched the glass again with her finger through the mug's handle as if erasing her reflections and contemplations and hurried to her husband's bedside lest another ring of the bell should wake their son.

"Dora, what took you so long?" Her husband's voice, as usual when it concerned her, was harsh and berating.

3
_____

A loud clap of thunder jolted Isa out of her slumber. Teetering in a void between the dream state and reality, Isa watched as raindrops ran in a zigzag pattern down the antique windowpanes. *Who was Dora?*

Something so familiar. *Déjà vu*, her grandmother would call it. In the dream, Isa *was* Dora. While still in bed, she tried to collect her thoughts and commit them to memory before they faded. She pushed the covers back in a robotic movement and placed her bare feet on the uneven, cold wooden planks.

It took a moment for her to register her surroundings. She looked with sleepy eyes around the room while sitting on the edge of the narrow bed, a bed that wasn't her own. She had sold her bed and most of the furnishings of the small bungalow she had purchased after moving out of her and Nick's house to take up residence at an old inn nestled amid cafés and small shops in a quaint village in the heart of France. The picturesque view of farmland in the background reminded Isa of her grandmother's appliquéd quilts. As a child, she watched as her grandmother needled her way across the fabric so fast and with such dexterity that the blue veins in her hands merged into the blue material she

18

used for the sky. When Isa asked her grandmother where the scene was, her grandmother replied, "Why, the place of my birth, France." The seed for this trip had been planted early in Isa's brain.

The dream was so vivid, more like a vision. She told herself it resulted from the traveling and her different surroundings. She had just flown across the Atlantic and was in a foreign country, not to mention the cheap wine she guzzled down on the plane. More than cheap—it was free. A delayed reaction, perhaps. Better strange dreams than a pounding headache, she thought.

It was by accident that she found the inn, a random click on something someone had posted on Pinterest. Like a well-kept woman, the two-story structure that dated back to the 1600s bore its age well. Sky blue shutters, wide open against rounded stones that had melded into numerous layers of cement, lured her to the single-page website that only described the inn as old with a rich history. There was a phone number, email, and physical address. What the picture didn't convey were the odors, so many of them, the remains of the past. Smells evoked memories—maybe dreams as well. The hearth, now blocked off, had the lingering odor of smoke. The room smelled musty and old, the way she remembered her grandmother smelling during the last year of her life.

France was an intrusion of the senses, a collaboration of modern and old. Isa sniffed the aroma of freshly baked bread coming from the kitchen below, something impossible in a modern hotel. She imagined Madame Claire downstairs removing the croissants from the oven, the layers all buttery and flaky, so much so that the outer layer clung to your fingers. Pastries were everywhere, as were flowers, bright and colorful in contrast to the couples in monochrome attire donned straight from the mannequins in sophisticated fashion boutiques. They sat at small intimate tables for two, sipping wine. Two seemed to be the magic number in this country. Everything Isa had seen thus far in France wavered between the old and the new. It was as if the nation sat in the crevice of time itself.

She remained in bed in a daze, feeling like she had been in a Rip Van Winkle sleep. The edge? But she mustn't get up yet. Rising abruptly would surely cause her to forget everything. *She would surely forget everything?* Those were not her words. She didn't speak in that fashion. She was still speaking or thinking like the woman in the dream—the woman who spoke of some edge, a figure in some historical novel. She had to record it before she went to the bathroom, or toilet, as they called it here. Washing cold water over her face might wipe the dream away.

Isa reached for her glasses on the nightstand. Her journal was still in the suitcase across the room. Getting out of bed and rummaging through her luggage might also cause her to forget. She found some yellowed stationery and a pen in the drawer, along with a Protestant Bible in French. The nubby leather surface would have to serve as a makeshift writing desk. The pen, cheap like the wine, would also have to suffice.

A tinge of blasphemous guilt crept over her as she wrote. In her mind, she heard the words of her grandmother: "Never place anything on the Bible. It's holy." Isa's church days were short-lived. They ended with her grandmother's death. Maybe it was okay. The Bible was Protestant, not Catholic. Her grandmother was Catholic.

Isa dismissed the thoughts and continued to write. She had always prided herself in having perfect penmanship, but there was no time. She wrote rapidly, trying not to forget a single detail. The pen's spring kept coming undone, spraying ink over her fingers. What would Dora have used? A feather and inkwell? The time period of the dream was unclear.

She wrote in sync with the rhythm of the rain. As the rain slowed to a drizzle, so did her transcription. Having written on every square inch of the paper and unable to hold her bladder any longer, she had no choice but to stop. She got out of bed, slid into her Crocs, and made her way to the bathroom—*no, toilet*— she reminded herself. *They say toilet here.* Relief. Isa hung her gown on a coppery hook wedged so far into the wood that it must have been original to the inn. Water from the shower cascaded over her body, triggering the images of the rain in the dream.

Isa toweled dry and peered out the second-story window to see a rose garden and a woman under a black umbrella entering through the back entrance. It had to be Madame Claire, the inn's owner. Beyond the garden was a small pond enveloped in a layer of mist. There appeared to be someone else a distance back on the other side. Whoever it was disappeared. A trick of the fog, she told herself. Madame Claire's husband, Monsieur Albert, said a larger pond was on the grounds. She wanted to see it, but the day was so wet and gray.

The innkeepers told her of amazing cliffs not too far from the inn. One could look over and see beautiful vineyards, but there was the rain. It was only a drizzle, but still… She would have to save the walk and vineyards for another day. Too bad. Yet walking would give her more time to think about the dream, to analyze it. Who were the people in the dream, and why was she dreaming of them? She would look up dream meanings online. No, no, the dream was nothing. Best to forget it. The dream was just a fluke of her surroundings and this radical change in her life. Its effects would wear off soon enough after a walk out in the fresh air exploring the French countryside if the rain subsided. Her stomach growled.

ISA HAD ARRIVED AT THE INN ONLY YESTERDAY AFTER A NIGHT IN Paris. A tall, energetic, vibrant woman, who Isa surmised to be somewhere in her sixties, appeared at the front desk upon hearing the bell.

"Madame Archambeault?"

"Claire. Madame Claire, if you must. We do not put on airs around here," she said in perfect English.

"I have reservations. I'm Isabelle Muir. Please call me Isa."

"*Oui,* I have been expecting you," she said, startled, perusing Isa up and down while reaching for a pad to record her registration. "*Oui...*" Her voice trailed off when a man entered.

"This is my husband, Albert. Please call him Albert. As I said..."

"No airs," Isa finished and smiled.

At present, she was the only guest at the inn. That would soon change. There would be an influx of cyclists from all over Europe, some from the states. Would Josh be among them?

"You are fortunate to have booked in advance. Most of the bicyclists will be men, a lot your age, maybe even single." Madame Claire said with a wink.

Isa could only blush. Romance was not why she came to France, she told herself.

"Will they be noisy?" Isa asked.

"Oh no. After strenuous riding, they will fall asleep, dead to the world. They may be loud or playful in the morning before they ride off again, though."

Isa held no romantic fantasies about what might or might not transpire during this trip. She saw the bicyclists as only a hiccup to the serenity of the rural setting. Madame Claire said the bicyclists had booked all the rooms in most inns and hotels around this part of the countryside, but only for a night. Bicyclists moved along quickly. They would stop again on their return.

Madame Claire also said this inn was the oldest one, predating the next oldest in the area by at least a century. To Isa's surprise, the oldest inn in this part of France came equipped with Wi-Fi.

Isa had researched inns for months before stumbling across the picture of this one. There was something oddly familiar about it even though she had never been to France. Perhaps it was the scenes from her grandmother's quilts. Had it not been for the low price, she might have looked further. She thought it was a misprint, but Madame Claire, in her email, informed her it *was* correct.

Madame Claire gave her a quick tour of the garden in the back and said, "You must have number eleven. It overlooks the garden and small fishpond."

"It is *destin*." Those were the words Madame Claire said as she gestured for Monsieur Albert to take up her bags. *Destin.* So many French words were similar to their American counterparts. Maybe it *was* her destiny. Maybe Madame Claire was a clairvoyant. Maybe Isa's name had also been *destin*. She had been named after her great-grandmother, who came from France.

Other than the lack of a bathtub in her room, the inn had everything Isa wanted. The countryside was a splendor to behold. It was far enough from the big-city bustle of Paris yet close enough by train. Everyone seemed nice. People in the village smiled and said *bonjour* as she passed. She might already have made friends in Madame Claire and Monsieur Albert. They might be curious why an unattached woman opted to stay in a countryside inn and not in Paris. But the French didn't question the way Americans did.

THE AROMA OF COFFEE AND HOT CROISSANTS GREW STRONGER. Prompted by hunger, she dressed quickly. The smell became more pronounced with each step of her sandals onto the worn, heavy oak planks of the stairway. She imagined all sorts—from peasant country folk to sophisticated gentry in powdered wigs— having once climbed these steps.

Fresh roses and pink tablecloths adorned the tables in the

common room. Their fragrance intermingled with oven-baked pastries and espresso.

Isa stood at the bottom of the stairs, peering over the empty tables before choosing the one next to the massive fireplace. *"Bonjour! Comment vas-tu? Café?"*

She had studied some basic French after finalizing her travel plans. *"Bonjour! Je vais bien. Oui, café,"* she replied. The slight smile on Madam Claire's face told her that her pronunciation was terrible but still decipherable. Luckily, the innkeepers spoke English. Most French did, but they preferred not to use it. Why should they make an exception for her? She was on their turf.

Madame Claire placed a small basket of croissants on her table with one hand and, with her other, poured the steaming brew into the waiting china cup. While doing so, she gave Isa the same mystified look she had given her at check-in, minus the gasp of surprise. A bit disconcerting, but Isa attributed the inspection as something French and shrugged it off. Madame Claire stopped her ogle only long enough to ensure she didn't overfill Isa's cup. Then she moved with an efficient elegance away from her table, disappearing into the kitchen. The coffee, the croissants, the table setting, and the very air here exuded a different kind of pleasure, bordering on the sensual and sultry.

China cups and saucers were a refreshing change from the paper cups at American coffee shops, not that she couldn't have opted for a mug. She either forgot to ask, or a long line made her feel like she was wasting precious time. Time—its passage seemed to be regulated differently in France. And not that the coffee shops back home were not out to please, but it was a rushed pleasure that got lost amid busy yuppies that never looked up from their smartphones or computers. She had been one of them, except her nose was buried in a book or her electronic reader, both of which Nick abhorred. An utter waste of time, he had said. She disagreed, but she vowed to live her life in earnest while in France, not fantasize about it from the pages of a book.

But what if she did occasionally opt for a book? Nick and, better yet, his sarcastic remarks were no longer in the picture.

Isa glanced at the newspaper one table over. Words she didn't understand. Greek to her. She smiled. No, it was French. Maybe that would change. She was regretting she hadn't studied French in school. Maybe she could yet learn. This vacation or life-finding mission—she hadn't yet decided what to call it—was still young. Experience had taught her that a lot could change in three months. Three months was what she allotted herself for this self-discovery adventure of hers.

Why did people use the idiom *it is Greek to me*? Why that language? She remembered it came from Shakespeare which brought to mind the Shakespeare and Company Bookshop, which was high on her must-see list while in France. Did Shakespeare think of it? Was Shakespeare even a man? She recently heard one theory that Shakespeare was actually a woman. Probably some poor schmuck couldn't understand Greek and said with a puzzled look on his face, "It's Greek to me." But as in most cases, an opportunist or one of higher intellect such as William or Willimina Shakespeare used the phrase as his or her own. Those things happened every day. She was sure it was no different from the dawn of man. How could someone so famous be so unknown? But wasn't that true with most ancient figures of note? Even about Jesus, there was so much speculation and controversy. No one ever knew the absolute truth when it came to historical figures. Both had lived so long ago, and time had a way of burying the past. She still had a lot to explore about her own self. She hardly knew her own story.

In college, she thought she had it all figured out. That was a laugh. Now, at thirty-three, she was diving into a deep well of discovery. Thinking about this made finding out about the inn's history more intriguing.

Monsieur Albert came through the door, holding it open long enough to shake the rain from his umbrella before placing it in the umbrella stand. There were several black umbrellas for guests, which she appreciated since she hadn't thought to pack one.

"*Bonjour*, Mademoiselle! Not to worry, the rain will cease by noon," Albert said, his rustiness in not using English that often showing. With no other guests for the moment, Isa had both Claire and Albert to herself. Both had already won her heart, but something about Albert was endearing. He possessed a quirkiness. One moment he could be gruff, and the next, he was the gentlest of souls. Isa practiced her biggest smile and said *bonjour* back as she had already learned that it was rude not to greet people you had dealings with in France.

"Monsieur Albert, I was wondering if you had time to tell me about the inn's history?"

He poured himself a cup of espresso and pulled up a chair. "We only purchased the inn last year and spent the winter updating the plumbing. The rooms are smaller, but now everyone has access to a private toilet. That wasn't so before. The last innkeeper died, and his wife was too tired and old to keep up with it. They had a son, but he had no interest in running the inn. Her son studied film in Paris and is living there now. So we got it, at how you say, a steal?"

"Do you know anything about the inn other than that?" Isa asked.

"I know it's old and still needs more work. This coming winter, we will make more updates. Maybe after your stay here, you can give us some suggestions. Like what would Americans want? But then we will need more customers. Being off the beaten path, it is hard."

"I find the inn charming the way it is. I like old places rich with history, but if I think of anything while I'm here, I will let you know. Do you know anything about the original family that owned the inn?"

"The Girards have always run the inn. The inn dates at least to the 1600s. The original owners were a couple like Claire and me, except they had a child, and we don't. What happens to the inn after us, God only knows."

Albert nodded toward the fireplace. "That is the original hearth. Over the years, there were updates, a more modern kitchen, and some adjustments to the rooms, but a lot is still as it was. I'm sure it operated as a pub on the ground floor. Most inns back then did. The story goes that the man couldn't walk, and the wife took over running the inn. I hope I don't lose the use of my legs. I love my bicycle." Albert laughed. "The son inherited it after that. That is all I know for sure. Anything else is only speculation. There have been many generations between. My wife and I moved here from Paris to have a quieter life. It was always our dream to run a small country inn. Some say the original couple haunts it, but I have seen no evidence. Maybe if we say it is haunted on the website, more people would come, but then, all buildings in France are old and have ghosts." He laughed again.

"Are there any Girards still around?"

"*Oui*, there is Madame Girard, the last one to own the inn before us. She has a house in the village. She is usually here during the summer but spends her winters in Paris with her son."

"Do you think I could see her?"

"Why do you want to see her? Such an odd woman."

"I think finding out more about the inn would be interesting, but if you don't think she would see me…"

"Oh, *oui*, she would see you. *Oui*, I'm sure. Don't let me scare you off. I will write her phone number down for you, or Claire could phone her. How do you say she is grumpy about the fact we got the inn for a steal, never letting me live it down? She is older than Claire and me but still has all her faculties. You might find her strange. I know I do."

"Oh?" Isa questioned. "Do you think she will mind talking to me?"

"*Oui*, the woman loves to talk," he snickered. "Too much, in my opinion. Her house is within walking distance."

"Merci."

As Albert predicted, the rain stopped, and by noon, the sun was out. Claire had called Madame Girard, and an appointment was set up for the next day. Isa visited the local wine and cheese shop, picked up a bag lunch, and headed for the cliffs everyone recommended. She spent the rest of the day reflecting on the beauty of the countryside, browsing shops, and having a late dinner of fruit and a salad at one of the cafés before returning and retiring to bed.

4

"You could do lots worse, Dora. An eligible bachelor and a judge's son no less," her mother said.

"A feminine boy if ever there was one," her father retorted, rolling his eyes as he looked up from tinkering with one of his latest inventions.

"Full of charm," her mother countered while handing Dora the vegetables she was to chop for the night's stew.

"Clumsy and awkward if you ask me." Dora smirked, pushing the onions to the side of the cutting board, saving them for last since they always brought tears to her eyes.

"If only you would take some initiative," her mother coaxed.

Dora admitted to being lazy in love. Since the Edge, panic and a sense of dread permeated the air—the possibility of *no* tomorrow. There were two attitudes: live while you can or what was the purpose?

"Time is a precious commodity. It isn't for wasting," her mother said. "Find a proper husband while you can."

Dora's mother had cast her eye on Adrien as decent and respectable. Dora supposed Adrien was satisfactory. She also thought if there was a charming prince who might come along and sweep her off her feet, life might be a different story. She looked young for her age. Her flat chest, which did her no favors, was one reason. She wasn't prince material. Besides, most princes met a gruesome fate when the Edge came about.

While Dora's mother spent a good deal of time fretting, her father, a congenial sort, stayed busy either inventing or fixing things. A lot of things broke with the Edge. Her father was good with his hands. "Don't worry, Dora. There is plenty of time to find a man," her father said.

No man could ever live up to her father. However, Adrien *was* the intellectual sort. She liked intelligence, in particular, what went with it—books. Adrien's father, being a judge, had one whole wall shelved in books in an upstairs room which was kept locked most of the time. And although Adrien was handsome in a farsighted way, the actual moment of attraction came when he dangled his father's key to the library in front of her and said seductively through crooked teeth, "My parents will be away well into the night."

The library was where they first made love, if you could call it that. His mouth took a downward turn upon seeing the slight lumps that could hardly classify as a bosom, but the disappointment on his face erupted into a smile when she insisted on lighting up the room with candles. "A brave woman, indeed," he exclaimed while ripping off his clothes.

He did not even suspect it was because she loved the room— the books in the room, that is. Dora positioned her head toward the bookcase. With each thrust, she read the titles, one by one. Being thoroughly engrossed in his uncoordinated, awkward shoves into her body, Adrien paid little heed to her lips silently forming the words on the books' spines. She lay on her back, head tilted, reading as many titles as possible, averting her mind from the painful stabs.

THE WEDDING WAS A BIG AFFAIR, SPARING NO EXPENSE WITH plenty of wine passed around. Someone of the judge's stature could not have it any other way.

Adrien's parents suffered a tragic death. Witnesses claimed the horse pulling their carriage was spooked. It turned over, and the judge and his wife were crushed almost beyond recognition when the rumors made their rounds. Fortunately, they lived long enough to see the birth of their grandson, who came eight months after the wedding. An early birth, they declared. Even though Dora's first time was awkward, it was fruitful. There were plenty of snide looks when Jean was born. He was such a plump- and rosy-cheeked baby. He was named for the judge to help allay any speculation or bad feelings. Adrien and Dora assured both families it was all above board. It *was* if you considered Dora did not realize she was pregnant until after the wedding.

There was gossip that Adrien had half brothers and sisters. The judge apparently had more hobbies than reading, Dora thought, but since illegitimacy had no claims in the courts, Adrien inherited the house and all it entailed, including the books.

What was to become an inn started as a home, one in which Dora planned on living in marital bliss, at least marital contentment, with as many children as she could produce. However, two things changed that.

First was the pilgrimage to the Edge, although calling it a pilgrimage was a bit of a stretch with it being so close. Some would say what happened was the curse of the Edge. Dora was pragmatic about such matters. "Pure superstition," she said. "I slipped. All there is to it." To call it a slip was oversimplifying matters. It was a rather nasty fall down the side of a cliff. If she had been standing just a few feet to her left when she fell, it would have meant certain death.

After the fall, things weren't right with her midsection. Call it her exalted sense of intuition or the fact that intimacy with Adrien was still painful after childbirth. The midwife poked and prodded. "Your baby-making days are over, dear." The midwife said the fall made Dora's womb wander around, but Dora looked up the proper term in one of the judge's books. She found the word uterus. A deep depression ensued. Jean's laughter echoing through the large house eventually pulled her out of her melancholy.

"The three of us will never use all these rooms. Sometimes I can hear an echo when I speak. We should start an inn," Adrien said one day while eyeing the house from the front and scratching his chin. Adrien missed the liveliness the house had once possessed with the comings and goings of the many people who knew the judge. "Yes, we must make better use of such a big house. That old oak will have to go," he said as he strolled around the house's exterior, Dora following behind him, carrying Jean.

"But Adrien, it gives just the right amount of shade to the library," Dora protested.

"No, what we need is plenty of sunshine. How else will we attract lodgers? And no need to hire anyone. I will do it myself."

"But Adrien…"

"Shush now," he commanded

AFTER THE ACCIDENT, ADRIEN WASN'T KEEN ON VISITORS. THE physician said it could have been worse. He told them of cases where a fall from something as small as a horse left people with no feeling in their bodies from the neck down. Adrien's body was dead from his waist down. He still had his life, although, behind his back, many said it might have been better had he died.

To Dora's relief, on some days, he was content to sit in his special chair with wheels, the one made by Dora's father, and talk to the guests as they came and went. But as time wore on, he made less and less effort to bother. Dora placed sheepskin on his bed, hoping the lanolin might prevent bedsores.

Adrien's accident was about the time Dora's innocence faded. There was the physical innocence, but more importantly, her mental and emotional innocence abruptly stopped.

Adrien wanted to close the inn after the accident, but Dora, even with her husband's special needs and a young child at her breast, maintained she could handle it. "I am young and strong," she insisted. "I will have no more babies. When Jean grows older, he can take on some responsibility, and my mother and father will help."

Although reluctant at first when Adrien brought up running an inn, Dora had grown accustomed to the stream and diversity of people who came through the door. Meeting new people was like opening a book for the first time. Each time patrons returned, it was like reading a new chapter. There were always those with undesirable character, but it was easy enough to send them on their way to one of the lesser-known inns. Near the Edge, their small village had an abundance of inns and shops. The one bright spot was a lack of poverty in their area. There may have been apathy but not poverty.

Dora's breasts not only swelled with nursing Jean, but they stayed that way, making her more desirable to Adrien, not that Adrien, in his condition, could or would do anything about it. Men now stared in her direction. Fortunately, Adrien was not the jealous type. That came later. Dora was not the unfaithful type. That also came later.

Most people blamed the Edge for life's predicaments. The Edge could do good things. It could do bad things. Everyone had different opinions on it. Dora had no particular view about it until the stranger enlightened her. She had made plenty of trips to the Edge with it being so close. Many made a pilgrimage once a year. Some went every two years, five years, or seven years.

Each had their reason for going and for the number of times they went. Some only ever went once in their lifetime. Few never went at all, thinking it evil.

Jean was a healthy baby. So many children born during the time of the Edge weren't. She thought of Esther, who had two children, neither of whom was blessed with good health. Esther had taken them both to the Edge for a cure, to no avail. There had been anecdotes of miraculous healings after pilgrimages. When it did not happen for Esther, she sided with the scientific community regarding the Edge. Dora thought Esther knew little about science. No one did. The earth on that fateful day swallowed scientists and princes alike. When the scientists and learned men went, most of the luxuries of life all but vanished. Lots of things became rare, one being books.

Those who were alive when it happened had grown old. Telling the story gave them a reason to live. There was not a conversation still to this day where it didn't come up. If it was not spoken outright, it was insinuated in some fashion. The world changed with the Great Event, at least in Dora's part of the world. At first, it was the Great Event. Some still referred to it as that. Later, it was simply the Edge.

Everyone said the night sky lit up brighter than daylight. That is when it happened, at night, at least from Dora's part of the world. A thunderous roar erupted, stirring people from their beds, women grabbing children, all helpless and all watching as something from the sky headed straight for them. The thunderous sound woke those who were asleep. The earth shook as sinner and saint alike bowed to the ground, begging for forgiveness. Others faced their doom with wide unflinching eyes. Many said it was the beginning of the end of time, but time, despite all the predictions, had a peculiar way of going on.

Churches called for everyone to repent. Pews overflowed daily, not only on Sundays. Scientists, the ones left, as most of them had been on the wrong side of the earth when it happened, pronounced it as a normal phenomenon. Normal? The clergy said it was a sign. As soon as the smoldering of all that was burning died down and the ash settled, the pilgrimages began.

The reasons for a pilgrimage were as diverse as there were people. Some went out of curiosity. The scientists who were left went to study what had happened. Some fancied an outing, a diversion that made all circumstances of life look small. There were those who went for both superstitious and religious reasons. Differing fields of thought grew up around the object that came from the sky and took a chunk of the earth away with it. It came in the twinkling of an eye. Had they known it was coming, would the scientists, learned scholars, and students of the universities situated where the destruction lay have fled? One faction thought the people on that chunk of land had their own village now, somewhere out in space. Some thought them the chosen ones. Others thought them condemned. A few thought the ones *left behind* were the chosen ones. Dora didn't feel chosen. The rumors grew. The ideas and speculations about the Edge were as numerous as the roaches that managed not only to survive but thrive.

Dora saw it as nothing but a huge hole, both physically and metaphorically. Huge was an understatement since no one could see the other side. She wondered if the people on the other side called it the Edge and if they were also making pilgrimages. She watched as both the sick and healthy, reaching out for some good fortune in their life, trekked past their inn. Their own good fortune had come in that the inn was on the main road toward the Edge. Since the event, seventeen other inns had sprouted up in the vicinity, but theirs was the landmark inn on the direct route.

With the Edge came a division in life—before the Edge and after the Edge. The before was becoming a blur.

5

*S*unshine streaming through the paper-thin lace curtains welcomed Isa to the new day. She stretched and grabbed her mobile phone by the side of the bed. Nine-thirty. She had overslept because of the dreams. Her appointment with Madame Girard was at noon. But before even thinking of showering and dressing, she grabbed her journal, which she had placed on her nightstand along with the new pen Madame Claire had given her before retiring.

Why was she having these dreams? Dreams could be the answers to questions, but sometimes they were just an unloading of events, thoughts, or things that happened the previous day, like a computer clearing its cache. Isa reconciled that she was dumping her cache—staying at an old inn and dreaming of it, inventing this miraculous story about its past during her slumber.

Monsieur Albert said the first innkeeper couldn't walk. In her dream, Adrien was a paraplegic. That hit too close to home. But where did the names Adrien, Dora, Esther, and Jean come from? She knew no one having those names. And what was this edge thing? That part of the dream was fuzzy, even though it was a mainstay in both dreams. Who was this stranger in the first dream? Why no name? And why was he only in the first dream? Dreams didn't have to make sense, but these dreams were like a soap opera playing out. Would they continue? Isa once read that if the head of the bed faced east, which hers did, vivid dreams would come. Since she planned on staying for a while, she could ask Albert if she might move the bed. But then, there was that part of her that didn't want the dreams to end. A part of her wanted them to continue, while another part of her wanted to be dead to the world, the way Madame Claire described the sleep of the cyclists.

After visiting Madame Girard, she would look up dreams and their meanings. Possibly this could all boil down to an overactive imagination. It was this place. It was the uncertainty of this whole wild pilgrimage. Pilgrimage? Why would she refer to this trip as a pilgrimage—like in the dreams? What was she doing? Or was it merely her insecurities, the little girl in her who had listened to her elders about the craziness of her wild notions, something her parents might say—something they certainly said when she told them that she had quit her job, and also when she told them of her plans to travel to France. In her heart of hearts, she did the right thing by coming here. She mustn't let doubt creep in.

She finished writing in her journal and stepped into the shower. As the hot water cascaded over her body, her thoughts returned to the present day. Some inns she had looked at shared a bathroom. She could only imagine having to share a bathroom with male bicyclists, not that they would all be male. They would filter in both today and tomorrow. Would Josh be among them? Get Josh out of your mind; this trip was not about Josh, she told herself. It was doubtful she would even cross paths with them, except maybe for morning croissants in the main room. But then she doubted if croissants were their thing, too unhealthy. She imagined them as more steel-cut oatmeal and fruit people.

While toweling her hair dry, she opened the doors to the wardrobe and scrutinized the selection of clothes she had brought. Since Monsieur Albert asked for her opinion, she would suggest an actual closet. She pulled her dress with the flowers, her best dress, from its hanger. Light and airy, it seemed the most appropriate for her visit with Madame Girard. She would stop along the way for a gift—chocolates, a tradition with Europeans. Isa had devoured every travel guide and internet video of other people's trips to Europe she could before coming.

The appointment with Madame Girard was at lunchtime. The French were notorious for their multi-course meals, even at midday. She hadn't given the meeting time much thought. She didn't expect Madame Girard to go to any trouble and should have thought to say something to Albert. Perhaps a cola without ice with a slice of lemon or a hot cup of tea. Tea would be lovely and more than enough. She wasn't much into soft drinks, contrary to what the French might think was a typical American taste preference. And she abhorred sodas without ice, another European habit. Growing up in Kentucky, Isa was a born and bred Southerner at heart, although she never could get into sweet tea. More than likely, Madame Girard would serve wine. Wine in France was the sweet iced tea of the South. But then again, maybe she would serve nothing or politely turn her away. What if Madame Girard didn't want to share her family history with a stranger? Maybe there was something to hide. All families had something to hide.

Monsieur Albert said she was old, but he didn't say how old. What did old mean in France? Since arriving, she had only seen fit, healthy-looking people, no matter their age, walking, bicycling, or sitting leisurely at outdoor cafés sipping wine. Europeans seemed to maintain vigor and alertness well into old age, something rare in America. Back home, people seemed old in their fifties and sixties, obese and riddled with disease, traversing on motorized scooters after disembarking from vehicles bearing handicapped tags, and the number of handicapped parking spaces took up as many as three rows. She had seen nothing like that here. The French knew something Americans didn't. Possibly it was the wine. Isa recently read that one glass of wine was equal to one hour of exercise, one of those facts Nick would say was utter nonsense.

Would there be an old people smell? Highly doubtful. The memory of the smell of her grandmother during the last year of her life persisted with Isa. Here, the odors didn't cling to the people so much but to the ghosts of the country's rich history. Her grandmother always talked about returning to France for a visit. She never did. And now Isa was fulfilling her grandmother's dream.

Isa remembered a party at McDonald's when she was in second grade. She walked past a table filled with senior citizens drinking coffee and talking about the good old days. Condemned to have a superhero olfactory sense, the first thing Isa noticed was the smell. It was like the smell of belly button, something she remembered her mother saying upon discovering Isa had neglected to wash that area. A belly button, at least a young one, could be cleaned, but old people smell was a different matter. It was as if no amount of Arm and Hammer or white vinegar could get it out of their clothes. If anyone else ever noticed this smell, they never mentioned it, and Isa was both too polite and too shy to say anything.

The odor was no longer there when Isa stood over her grandmother's coffin. The funeral home must have had a process to exterminate it. Or it flew off when the soul left the body, moving on to the next old person in line for the grim reaper. Regardless of the pleasant aroma of the croissants, the oldness of the inn crept through. It was as if Dora and Adrien still roamed the halls.

On one of those trips to her grandmother's house years before her death, Isa asked her about family history. She had her Bible. It had foldout pages in the center with lines and charts to record births, deaths, and family history. Isa was eleven. She had a new blue ballpoint pen and was eager to fill the pages in and practice her penmanship.

Grandmother's house was full of pictures of the past, people Isa didn't know, people that Isa thought her grandmother would be eager to tell her about. After all, they were Isa's people too. Grandmother was reluctant to give any information. Suspicious, she grilled Isa on the exact purpose of her questions, like Isa was a spy gathering information that might be used against her. Grandmother had been in France during World War II.

When Isa showed her grandmother her new Bible with the foldout center and explained she only wanted to preserve a piece of her past, her grandmother opened up more. Still, Isa only got minimal information. Grandmother told no funny or dramatic stories like Isa had hoped, something that would make her ancestors seem real. They were just names and dates written in beautiful penmanship on beautiful foldout parchment. Isa contented herself with that. She read the words—mere male and female silhouettes on the page. Dull, lifeless. Upon death, they went to their eternal homes with negligible life reviews. Isa imagined the baffled angels at the receiving line. "This is it?" they must have asked. Nor were there any ghosts or hangers-on in her family.

Perhaps her grandmother didn't think her sincere in her desire to learn the family history or thought she was too young for its closeted secrets. Maybe her grandmother was right in calling it a phase, something her grandmother referred to as one of Isa's projects. "Why this sudden interest in the family history?" she asked. She had to say Grandmother was right about her in that regard. Isa gravitated with an intense interest in something for a period to the point of obsession and then forgot about it, going on to something else. Maybe that is why both her marriage and her job as a librarian at the school ended. She lost interest and wanted to move on to something new. If she ever should meet her true soul mate, she should warn him. Maybe she should wear a sign against her flat chest or get a T-shirt printed up: I TIRE OF PEOPLE AND THINGS EASILY. EXCEPT FOR BOOKS. I NEVER TIRE OF GOOD BOOKS.

It wasn't until Isa finished middle school that her grand-mother sat her down and told her how she remembered life in France. Her grandmother's people weren't dull at all. Shortly after, Grandmother became sick, and within a year, she died.

AFTER ISA HAD WOLFED DOWN HER CROISSANT AND TEA IN THE hasty manner of Americans, not at all in the slow, relaxed way of the French, Monsieur Albert opened the door and accompanied her outside. "Such a nice day," he said, looking up at the sky and taking a deep breath to capture its essence. "Why so eager to see a crotchety old lady on such a nice day as this?" he asked with a slight grunt while handing her a piece of paper with the address and pointing her in the proper direction, saving her from having to answer what she thought all along was a rhetorical question.

The route was straightforward, only a little over a mile just on the other side of the village. Isa guessed Madame Girard wanted to be a respectable distance from the inn that had been her life, perhaps to give the owners privacy. Maybe she was afraid they might want to renege on the deal. Managing an inn had to be hard work. Owning a house was hard work. She wondered if Nick had kept the house.

Isa had only owned the bungalow in Lexington for a year after her divorce. It was not for her. Like everything else, taking pride in her own home was a short-lived obsession. It was good luck she could sell the house, pay the mortgage and make a decent enough profit to travel. She sold almost everything she had owned. She stored what she didn't bring on this trip in her parents' attic. Isa's parents had begged and pleaded with her not to do this, exclaiming how insane it was. Her parents, still in shock, were urging her to reconsider as she kissed them bye at the airport. Isa was, too, although she tried to hide it. It was as if some unknown entity had taken control of her mind, sold her worldly possessions, and boarded a plane to travel to a complete question mark.

ISA LOOKED AT THE ADDRESS ON THE PAPER AND STOPPED. SHE stood before a stone dwelling with the ubiquitous red tile roof that dotted the village's skyline. A garden of flowers swaying in the gentle breeze, their rich hues and sweet aromas an open invitation to the butterflies and bees fluttering and buzzing amid their petals, spanned the short distance between Madame Girard's house and the wrought-iron fence that ran parallel to the cobblestone roadway. Her eyes stopped on the red geraniums adorning the window box. She remembered geraniums being in one of the dreams. She checked the battery charge on her phone and opened the translation app, unsure if she would need it, but just in case. Monsieur Albert made no mention if she spoke English, and Isa forgot to ask. She opened the gate and clicked it back into place, making her way up the narrow path, the flowers on the material of her dress almost fondling the natural blooms. Isa climbed two steps, banged the knocker on the blue door once, and stepped back down. The door creaked open slowly.

Isa's eyes rose upward past dirt-stained clogs, bare freckled legs, beige capris with bulging pockets, a sleeveless white shirt exposing well-tanned muscular arms, and halted at a warm, friendly face sporting a gray bob. She was a fine athletic figure of a woman, not what she imagined at all. Nor did she appear as ancient as Monsieur Albert made her out to be. If she was, she concealed her age well. She wore no spectacles and sported no hearing aid. A beagle hound with sad eyes and droopy ears stood obediently at her feet. Isa heard no bones popping as the woman bent down to remove the beagle's leash and raised back up again in one rapid movement. "We were out for a walk just before you knocked."

"Madame Girard, my name is Isabella. But everyone calls me Isa. I believe Madame Claire told you I was coming?" Isa said, trying not to sound nervous as she handed her host the box of chocolates.

There was a definite pause as Madame Girard scanned Isa up and down before resting her eyes squarely on Isa's face. Madame Girard's expression reminded Isa of the same look on Madame Claire's face when Isa first arrived at the inn. After what seemed like a good half minute of appraisal, Madame Girard said in perfect English with not a touch of a French accent, "You remind me of her." Not *bonjour*, not hello, not come in. She was not French at all but British. She had married a Frenchman, she later explained.

"I remind you of who?" Isa asked while being motioned inside.

"Why, the first innkeeper!" she exclaimed. "Yes, the resemblance is remarkable."

Isa was sure Madame Girard saw the astonishment registered on her face. The first innkeeper ran the inn over three hundred years ago. There were no photographs of that period.

"Do you have a painting or drawing? Monsieur Albert didn't mention this when I asked him about the inn."

"No, dear, there is no likeness of her," she said, examining the puzzled look on Isa's face while looking pleased she had put it there.

Okay, so Monsieur Albert had warned her. Madame Girard was daft. That would explain it. In the states, Isa might have first thought dementia, but since she was British, the first term that came to mind was daft. Quick to follow was loony as in *Looney Tunes*.

Although billboards with neon lighting saying enter at your

43

own risk went off in Isa's head, she followed Madame Girard down the hallway, spying vases of fresh-cut flowers peeking from every room. They entered a screened-in porch which also doubled as a greenhouse. The garden view from the back surpassed the one in the front, if that were even possible. The scent of flowers was everywhere. No old people smell—only the aroma of lavender, mint, lemon balm, and roses. Madame Girard's skin was tan and taut, and the rosiness of her cheeks matched the blooms of her flowers. Embedded dirt under her nails bore witness she spent most of her time outdoors.

"I hope you don't mind. The day is too pretty. We must enjoy nature. That is one of the things I always hated about the inn business, inside way too much."

Her dog whimpered. "Now hush, Gromit, we are entertaining."

"Gromit! As in *Wallace and Gromit*?"

"Why yes."

"I love that show."

Madame Girard laughed. It was the first time Isa had heard her laugh. Isa's posture loosened.

"Being indoors—one of the things you hated? Was there more?" Isa asked.

"Paperwork. Couldn't stand the paperwork. I enjoyed talking to the people well enough. I still miss that. But the flowers, they are my best friends after Gromit here." She bent down and petted the dog on the head. "Not much time for flowers when you are running an inn. And not much time for a dog. Oh, I had more time for flowers when my husband was alive. He took care of most of the inn business."

"Your flowers are beautiful." Isa looked around at the different varieties. "You definitely have a green thumb."

A proud smile spread across Madame Girard's face. "Gardening is my passion." She pulled out a white wicker chair and bade Isa sit at the matching table, which already had a pot of tea with two cups and a tray holding a loaf of lemon pound cake along with plates and forks. She poured two cups of tea and sliced two pieces of cake. "Sweets are my third hobby—pastries and biscuits. Well, what do you expect? I *am* English. My husband loved wine." She laughed to the point of a snort. "Well, what Frenchman doesn't? It all tastes the same to me. Oh, I can tell the difference between a white, rose, or red. That's about it. Now tea, I could tell you the kind by aroma alone, same with flowers."

"That's amazing."

"Not really, dear. It boils down to your preference in life. Learning comes easily in matters you care about. And who knows? Maybe we were here before. We bring back what we loved in other lives when we're born to this life."

"Madame Girard, you said I reminded you of the first innkeeper, yet you said there is no painting or drawing of her? I don't understand."

"Oh, no, no, not of her. There *is* a small drawing of her son. I imagine he looked like his father, though. Can't see much resemblance between his mother and him."

"Forgive me for asking, but how on earth could you think I look like her?"

"Oh, I've seen her plenty of times. And it has nothing to do with the earthly realm, dear." She let out a deep-throated laugh.

Thoughts of Madame Girard being delusional flooded through Isa's mind while she did her best not to show any facial expression. Isa conjectured that Madame Girard's appearance of excellent health was exterior only. Isa formulated excuses in her mind to take her leave as she sipped on the herbal tea, a rose hibiscus, which was lukewarm now. Isa thought she would make some small talk, drink the rest of her tea, and eat her cake. She *had* to finish the cake. It was utterly delicious. She would say her goodbyes, insisting she not keep her from her gardening on such a beautiful day.

Madame Girard spoke a little about her son in Paris. Isa asked if she had any grandchildren. "A boy and a girl," she said, smiling. She seemed sane enough while talking about her son and grandchildren.

After swallowing the last bite of cake, Isa pushed her plate and teacup aside. "Madame Girard, I do so appreciate your time. I won't keep you any longer. I'm sure you have things to do. So I will say *au revoir* now."

"My dear, I thought you came here to learn about the first innkeeper, Dorcel?"

"Dorcel?" Goosebumps spread over Isa's arms, which didn't escape Madame Girard's keen eye to Isa's chagrin. There was also a slight sense of panic in the pit of Isa's stomach. She placed her hand on her midsection to dissuade the cake from regurgitating. Dorcel? Dora? Could this be just a coincidence? Did Madame Girard have some kind of second sight?

Isa wanted to get up from the chair, but her resistance dissolved with the mention of a name similar to the one in her dream. She questioned what she was doing here—here, not necessarily meaning Madame Girard's home or the inn, but in France in general. A feeling of homesickness, an apt companion to nausea, swept over her. The sudden urge to call her parents was strong. In triumph, they would say I told you so and gladly offer to pay for her return plane ticket home. Or maybe Isa could run back to Nick, but that wasn't possible. Even if it were, the thought scared her more than being in the presence of a deranged woman in a foreign country, plus the rumor was Nick had moved on with his life much quicker than she had. Isa took a deep breath and told herself to calm down.

Isa felt a warm touch on her arm. It was her host's hand. The touch somehow reassured her. Unlike their appearance, her hands were soft.

"My dear, are you cold on such a warm day?" For someone supposedly half-baked, not much escaped Madame Girard. Isa reasoned she had to be harmless. Gromit looked content enough, and dogs were the first to notice if anything was spooky or amiss.

"No, no, I'm okay. Dorcel, you say?" While Madame Girard was acutely aware of Isa's nervousness, she sensed her host picked up on Isa's reaction to the name.

"Yes, Dorcel Girard was her name, and Adrien Paul Girard was his," she said, looking at Isa while raising an eyebrow. "I have it all here in this book of family history. My husband's family history that is." She pointed to a thick leather portfolio at the edge of the table.

Isa knew she must have turned white. The slight breeze blowing through the screened-in porch provided some comfort, as did the sounds of laughter from children playing in the yard next door. She thought of her kindergarten reading group that came to the library on Wednesdays. Isa tried to turn the thoughts of children into a smile but failed miserably.

Madame Girard paused and then said, "Let me heat more water for tea. You look pale. You look like you could use another hot drink. And perhaps you will take another slice of cake. A smidgeon of sugar might do you good. Maybe a pinch of brandy with your tea?"

"No, no brandy." Isa had to keep her wits and thought of her grandmother. She was constantly plying Isa with sweets. Sweets or a University of Kentucky victory solved anything in her grandmother's house, and a hot cup of tea solved everything in Britain or soap operas. Isa guessed the French's remedy was wine.

"I get so few visitors," Madame Girard said while looking down at her dog. "Isn't that right, Gromit?" The dog lifted his head a centimeter from the floor to acknowledge his name. Isa tried not to let the last remark disturb her and only looked at the satisfied look on Gromit's face. She wanted to think it was satisfaction and not exhaustion from the walk. Isa had never owned a dog and didn't know how to judge.

"Yes, I think more tea would be nice," Isa said, attempting to hide a shaky voice while the *Twilight Zone* theme song was going off in her head. One part of Isa wanted to leave, yet her inquisitive nature kept her glued to the seat.

While Madame Girard left to boil more water for the tea, Isa carefully opened the fragile yellowed pages within the leather enclosure, the one part of her hoping for dull and boring, the curiously intrigued part of her hoping for some answers to her dreams or visions. After this new revelation, Isa reinterpreted her dreams as a vision. Isa turned the worn, delicate pages. There were names and dates, all in French. What did she expect? Answers spelled out in English?

She came to a picture of a young man. It appeared to be a photocopy of the original, a charcoal drawing, the son Madame Girard spoke of. She examined the rather detailed drawing. If what Madame Girard said was true, that she looked like Dora, then she was right. The son bore no resemblance to his mother. Where was the original drawing, she wondered?

The whistle of the teapot brought Isa out of her deep concentration. In a few moments, Madame Girard returned with a fresh pot of tea, an Earl Grey tag hanging over the side, standard issue for the English and Captain Picard.

"I thought maybe a little pick-me-up, some caffeine this time around," Madame Girard said as she handed Isa the cup.

Wanting to end the suspense once and for all and the madness going on in her head, Isa asked, "Madame Girard, you said I reminded you of her. How could you know something like that if there is no painting or drawing of her?"

"Why, her ghost, dear. I've seen her ghost more times than I care to count. She was quite a fixture at the inn."

6

*B*e careful what you wish for: those words rang in Isa's ears as she departed Madame Girard's cottage. Was it a wish, fate, or *destin*, as Claire had pronounced it? It had to be a little of everything, pieces of a jigsaw puzzle coming together, a series of events, each a stepping stone to the next. The car accident had been the starting point, the moment of reflection that caused her to question her life. Afterward, a string of coincidences propelled her forward—serendipitous moments where all the angles coincided to bring her halfway across the world where she was chasing her future, by some odd turn of events, through the past.

A seemingly mundane memory occurred to her. Once while sitting beside a pool, concentric circles in the water caught her eye, mesmerizing her. An insect propelled its hair-thin legs, spinning in a circular motion. In contrast to the creature's size, the ripple effect spanned almost the entire pool surface. Why had it ventured into the water? Why had she ventured out of her comfort zone to a distant land where the language and customs were strange? Where life was exotic and unusual? The moment of doubt took a back seat to the voice spurring her on all along.

She would grow, learn, live her life beyond the pages of a book and see the splendor of France her grandmother remembered as a child. She had accepted Nick's dare to live her life outside the confines of printed pages even though he hadn't expected her to respond to his challenge so boldly.

She spied a nearby pool net and offered a life preserver to the creature in the pool. Would someone be so kind to her? Did she need a life preserver? Had she, like the insect, bitten off more than she could chew?

A MYRIAD OF THOUGHTS FLOODED ISA'S MIND AS SHE LEFT Madame Girard's cottage. She tried to collect them all while she strolled and shopped in the tiny village at a leisurely pace, avoiding returning to the inn. She wondered how the landscape might have looked when Dorcel or Dora inhabited it. It would stand to reason that Dora was what she went by. After all, she went by Isa, not Isabella. Maybe later, she might tell Madame Girard about the dreams, that is, if she even saw her again.

Isa's uneasiness hadn't escaped her host. After mentioning the ghost, Madame Girard talked about England and recommended places Isa should see in Paris. She spoke more about her son and grandchildren. She even took Isa to her backyard and elaborated on her wide variety of flowers. They both stood at the fence while Madame Girard talked to the neighbor children in French. Before leaving, Isa concluded Madame Girard to be okay, not so daft after all. Plenty of people have claimed to have seen ghosts—even Josh.

Josh was the guy she dated before Nick. Dating was wishful thinking on her part. More accurately, they hung out. And usually, it was in groups. Sometimes when they were alone, he told her things.

Since his family was military, he traveled a lot and had

phenomenal stories. Once, he told Isa he saw a ghost, not exactly a ghost, but the shoes of a spirit. Who makes up a story like that? He was twelve or thirteen and living in an apartment in Raleigh, North Carolina. He said one of the adjacent apartments had trouble keeping tenants. Rumor had it a murder had been committed there. In his apartment, he saw an old-fashioned pair of shoes sitting on the stairs, ones pilgrims might wear—those of a small boy. His hand went right through them when he reached down to inspect them further. As he did so, they vanished. He said Raleigh was full of ghosts. Why wouldn't there be ghosts there? It was, after all, one of the oldest settlements in the US.

Isa reasoned there were a lot of strange things out there. She had read about plenty, but reading about them and experiencing them was different. Maybe Madame Girard *had* seen Dora's ghost. And perhaps Isa, too afraid to have such experiences herself, gravitated to the people who did.

She had met Josh in college at the University of Kentucky Student Center. They bumped into each other, literally. He backed into her causing her drink to spill. Apologetically, he invited her to join some friends he was hooking up with at Good Foods Co-op, a place he said he met with friends often, where he offered to buy her another drink. She was a sophomore, and he a junior. It was near Halloween at one of those get-togethers that the talk turned to ghosts.

Denise, one of the girls in the group, was loud and brassy and rubbed Isa the wrong way. She had picked up a book on ghosts by a local author. There was talk about taking flashlights and exploring the haunted places around town on Halloween night. It never happened. Instead, they gorged on candy and cheap wine.

Like Isa, Josh was shy. A kiss here or there, always with closed lips and always by some weird circumstance or seemingly accidental, like the way he had bumped into her at the student center. The one time she knew Josh's passion had been aroused was the one night in his dorm room. His hand traveled upward, under her sweater, almost to the point of cupping her breast. He quickly moved his hand away when his roommate, Nick, walked in.

Everything went back to how it had been between them—friends hanging out together. It was only out of desperation she had cried on Nick's shoulder. He had made it easy for her, seeking her out at lunch one day, practically coaxing Isa into bemoaning her problems to him, even though that night in the dorm room was the first time she had ever encountered Nick.

Josh didn't call, text, or email—nothing. When Isa suggested to Nick maybe she should be the one to do so, he advised against it.

"Does he talk about me?"

Nick hesitated. "Guys don't do that."

"Do you think you might casually mention me and see what he says?"

"Gosh, Isa. We're not in first grade. Forget him."

Easier said than done. By Christmas break, Josh had moved out of Nick's dorm room. Next semester, she went to Good Foods Co-op more than she cared to admit, hoping to run into him but instead grew fat on lattes to compensate for the disappointment.

Before she knew it, her friendship with Nick, revolving around some symbiotic fixation with Josh, subtly materialized into relationship status. Big mistake. Nick was almost Josh's opposite in every way.

She lost her virginity to Nick. After graduation and one late menstrual period, they announced their engagement. There was speculation over such a rushed preparation, but speculation was all it amounted to since Isa's period finally came. Nick's first reaction was to go to a bar and celebrate, not to discuss calling off the wedding. Both of their parents were already too much into the planning. They had already made the guest list, ordered invitations, and secured the church.

With all of the hoopla, Isa felt like a porcelain doll unable to speak, a Geisha girl in white for everyone else's pleasure. She wanted to protest, but things had already gone too far, and Geisha girls didn't complain. In robotic progression, she forged ahead, swept along in her parents' and future in-laws' exuberance.

Isa secured three bridesmaids: her roommate, the cousin she hardly knew who lived in California, and her sister-in-law, Nick's brother's wife. Isa's gown was a strapless empire waist dress, a strategy at the time to hide the baby bump that might be showing.

If Isa could label the experience of planning the wedding, it would be like an anchor in murky water pulling her under. Almost every decision she made was voted down by Nick's mother, who insisted on contributing toward the wedding, which by her reasoning assured her a say so in every matter, down to the lettering on the invitations.

"Isa, don't be so selfish. Mom always wanted a daughter, and she wants to help," was Nick's response.

"What about *my* mother?"

"She helped you pick your dress, didn't she?"

A week before the wedding, Isa's cousin in California backed out because she was starting a new job. Nick suggested several people, one of which was Denise. "What?" Isa exclaimed. "Why on earth would you suggest Denise? Denise isn't even on the guest list."

"Okay, don't get so hostile. I thought you two hung out together in college," Nick said, taking a step backward.

"I never hung out with Denise. Don't you remember me saying I didn't like her?"

"Oh yeah, right."

With only two bridesmaids, the wedding was still a big affair, everything Nick's mother ever wanted. Isa's mother tolerated Susan, Nick's mom, but loved Nick, who knew how to charm when needed, and if her mom had had her way, she would have gone along on the honeymoon. They went to Las Vegas, not Isa's decision but a surprise gift from Nick's parents. They both aimed to please—their parents, that is. Pleasing each other was a different matter. Isa would have preferred something more serene like the ocean, the mountains, or the inn she was in now.

The honeymoon was not the only surprise Nick's parents bestowed on them. A house came next. Nick's parents were borderline wealthy. Isa had to give them some credit. They showed restraint. The house was a modest split level. Their lives were being planned before their eyes.

Nick's parents running his life didn't bother him at all. If anything, it was convenient, an excuse to never have to grow up. It was the primary source of contention between them and what most of their fights were about at first. Isa wanted more independence, not from Nick but from his parents. She missed her parents. Shortly after the wedding, Isa's father was transferred to Texas, and she and Nick were in Lexington, living down the street from her in-laws. Isa saw her parents, at the most, once a year. Nick insisted on holidays with his family, arguing flying was expensive. Even though his parents had money, he and Isa didn't have it to spare, he asserted. She counter-argued that her family had offered to pay for the tickets. He retorted that it would be a strain on them to do so. Isa always gave in.

During the last year of Isa's marriage, she began walking in the arboretum. The jogging path was in clear view of Nick's parents' house when the trees were barren of leaves. She averted her eyes in the opposite direction whenever she came upon her in-laws' two-story colonial. It wasn't long until the walk turned into running. Pounding the path of the park helped to clear her head. When she wasn't running, she was sitting under a tree, absorbed in a book, an escape from her world into someone else's world. Not that her world was bad, but rather a world devoid of love and emotion, and most of all, excitement.

Isa often wondered what had happened to Josh. She heard his family had moved again and that he had transferred to a different college. Nick feigned ignorance on his disappearance, which Isa thought odd, seeing they had been roommates.

Whereas Nick and Isa rarely talked, Josh and Isa had talked about almost everything under the sun. They had even talked about joining the Peace Corps when they graduated. When she married Nick, she felt for the longest time that she had sealed her world shut, which might not have been so bad if the world she sealed herself up in hadn't been so broken.

After college, Nick went to work for his dad. That was the plan, majoring in business in preparation for eventually running the family business. Isa continued another year in school, getting her master's in library science. She loved both libraries and children, which made taking a position as a librarian at one of the elementary schools ideal. She would have liked to think it was on her own merit, but she knew Nick's father had talked to someone on the school board, the main reason she didn't give herself the option of returning after her three-month pilgrimage, the term she was giving it now. When back in the states, she would look for work somewhere in Texas near her parents.

She loved being a librarian. It was the one thing in her life going right, yet something deep down inside Isa was bubbling up to the surface—something compelling her to change everything about her life. She realized the physical act of running symbolized her desire to run from her current situation.

She ran in the evenings while Nick was working late. That happened more frequently. There were plenty of nights she ate alone. She read a lot of travel books. She watched internet videos, watching other people travel. She discovered Rick Steves.

Nick had no desire to travel. Everything he wanted was in Lexington. Between the fights, on the rare occasions they talked civilly, they discussed selling the house and buying a bigger one.

Having a family was a one-sided conversation. Nick's older brother had two children, another convenience for Nick. His parents didn't pressure them to provide grandchildren since they already had them. Having children was Isa's only motivation for moving to a larger house. For Nick, it was about prestige and following the American dream. No, she meant his parents' dream. Everything in their marriage was about pleasing Nick's parents.

One night after eating alone and reading the same paragraph over and over, she discarded her book and opened her laptop. The first time she googled Josh—nothing. Had he disappeared off the face of the earth? She panicked. She looked under obituaries. To her relief, nothing. She didn't think to erase the history.

How many times had she thought about Josh while out running? It was more than thinking. It was fantasizing. There was nothing sexual in the fantasies. She didn't think women fantasized that way. At least she didn't. There were a lot of what-ifs. What if she had not listened to Nick and called or texted Josh? What if Josh had taken her into his arms and kissed her, pressing against her enough to feel his desire? He would tell her he loved her. Okay, there was a little bit of sex, well, a lot of sex involved in that particular fantasy. What if they both had gone off after college and had joined the Peace Corps? What would their kids look like? She was committing adultery in her mind, if not in her heart. Her failure of a marriage with Nick was making it convenient to forget her hurt with Josh.

THREE YEARS AGO, SHE AND NICK FINALLY WENT THEIR separate ways on her thirtieth birthday. It took one small U-Haul attached to the back of her Toyota Camry to remove all her belongings from the house that Nick's parents gave them. She wanted to keep it simple. There was no he said, she said, this is mine, this is yours. She even left the rings behind. It was the lack of fight left in her that tortured Nick the most.

As she was pulling out of the driveway, he ran out, not to beg her to come back or say they could work it out, nothing of that nature. He placed his hands on the top of the car with a grip like Iron Man. Isa stopped the vehicle and rolled down the window lest she break his wrists or run over his feet. With mocking in his voice, he said, "He ended up marrying Denise, the girl you didn't like, the one you always called the drama queen." Her heart sank. Nick's mouth broke into a devilish smile as he released the car.

After eight years of marriage, she would like to say she at least knew Nick a little, but she didn't. Nor did he know her. It was cohabitation—roommates who had five-minute sex once a week in the beginning. She knew it was a mistake. She thought he did too. But they kept up the ruse, pretending to do normal couple things together—couple things being his family gatherings.

THE CAR ACCIDENT HAD BEEN THE TURNING POINT. ONE Saturday night, a year before the divorce, they went out for dinner. It was one of the rare times that Isa's parents were visiting. While waiting for the light to change and getting ready to pull into the restaurant, an auto plowed into their backside. Isa's father sat up front with Nick, and Isa and her mom sat in the back. Isa took the brunt of the impact. The seat belt locked, but her neck hurled forward. Intense pain ensued.

An ambulance came. Every movement of the stretcher felt laborious. The nerves in her neck were on fire. The paramedics gave her a paper bag to breathe into. She was hyperventilating. Everything became fuzzy. If they gave her something, she didn't remember. She went in and out of consciousness, and during the times she was aware, she felt as if she were encased in a bubble. The world around her was a blur. A doctor stood over the stretcher she was on. Or was it a bed? It had to be the emergency room. Nick was by her side. A brace was on her neck. She didn't remember how it got there. Why was the doctor working on her legs? It was her neck that was the problem. "Can you feel that? What about now?"

"Feel what?" she responded. The doctor had been pricking her legs for some time with something.

"Do you feel any sensation in your legs?" he asked. His voice was mechanical, but his face showed alarm.

"They feel numb like they're asleep."

Isa never worried about illness or injury. She was young and a runner, in the best of health, physically, that was. Emotionally might be a different story.

The doctor heaved a heavy sigh and sat for a moment, planning his words carefully. Isa kept drifting in and out of proximity with the world, seeing only a fraction of what was happening around her. Nick's head was cupped in his hands while the doctor spoke. When the doctor walked away, Nick looked at her, red-faced with tears pouring down his cheeks. She had never seen him cry, not even at his grandmother's funeral.

When she opened her eyes again, she saw Nick and her parents huddled in a corner, looking over at her, talking in whispers, but she heard the word paraplegic before her mother broke into tears. More white coats appeared—orderlies. She was wheeled away for X-rays. Later, Isa didn't remember being X-rayed. She must have drifted off again, but afterward, she found herself alone in a room.

Paralyzed from the waist down were the words she heard. It was one of those moments when her entire past flashed before her. Before she had pushed the past away, she fantasized about a different life but always fell back into the same old rut. Now, it appeared a different life was being decided for her.

It wasn't just *her* world that had changed. Nick's had too. She had run five miles at the Arboretum the morning before the accident. It would be her last.

What about her career? Could she maneuver in a wheelchair through rows of books? She wouldn't be able to reach the top shelves. Why was she thinking this? Reaching bookshelves would be the least of her worries. One instant had changed everything.

Isa had seen the lady who had rear-ended them out in the hall with her husband. He was comforting her. What about an apology? She at least deserved that. She never saw the woman's face clearly. Nor did she register the doctor's face. Everything that was happening to her was happening internally. What happened around her seemed like a dream. She kept fading in and out. Her life with Nick kept replaying in her mind.

This would serve him right if he had to take care of her for the rest of their lives. He could no longer work late. Or maybe he could. His parents had money. They would just hire a nurse for her if needed. Worse, they might shove her into a home of some type. Nick would, after a respectable period, file for a divorce. She would move in with her parents. No, that would be too much of a burden for them. She could learn to live with her disability. She was strong. People manage all the time. What about all of her dreams? What about traveling? She was only twenty-nine, or *almost* twenty-nine. Her birthday was two weeks away.

Isa stared up at the white ceiling. Scenes of her life played out before her. The plastered fake smiles on both her and Nick at their wedding. His fraternity buddies, her few friends, more like acquaintances than friends. Isa had never made any close friends. The closest she had to friends were the teachers in her school. She didn't confide in any of them, nor they in her. Nick, on the other hand, seemed to have plenty. Ned, one of his fraternity buddies, was Nick's best man. They drank beer together after work. As far as Isa could tell, that was the extent of it. Did Nick confide in him? Did Nick talk about Isa and how unhappy he was with his life? She didn't think so.

Nick compartmentalized his life. There was work. There was his family, his parents, his brother, and his brother's family. There was his social life, hanging out with Ned and the other guys. And there was her. Isa was the most minor section of the pie chart. Her parents had paid a fortune for their wedding—almost a fortune. Susan insisted on contributing. For what? It all boiled down to a trap of a marriage for both of them. And now, this. How could it get any worse?

Practice gratitude. Be thankful. That is what she read in all of her self-help books, the ones Nick made fun of. She had been grateful for her health. Now she didn't even have that. Was this the cosmic two-by-four hitting her in the head? Or the neck? Most of her body lay there with no feeling. All the feeling was going on inside of her head.

She wanted children of her own, not children borrowed from other parents during the daytime for nine months out of the year. Could she even have children now? All the fights she and Nick had. Regret, shame, nothing good was entering Isa's mind. Her grandmother and the family tree, all the lives lived in standby mode. She had been in standby mode for the longest time.

Anger pervaded her whole being. The anger turned into determination. The determination turned into prayer—a prayer more like a demand to the universe, to God. This wouldn't happen. She thought of Superman and how, in the movie, he had flown around the planet and turned time backward to save Lois Lane. She didn't have Superman. Josh wasn't Superman. Why was she thinking of Josh at a time like this? Josh didn't even care enough to stand up for her. Neither did Nick, for that matter. She only had herself. No, she had God. Wasn't a part of her God? All those self-help books interpreted Christ's message like that. You become what you think. Had she thought herself into this situation?

Something from within her cried out, not verbally, but the sound sent vibrations throughout her body, even to her legs. It was primal. She remembered the Bible verse, which said that one could move mountains with the faith of a mustard seed. Somehow she knew she was at the crossroads of her life. What was it going to be? It was her decision. All those verses she had learned poured into her mind. *Seek, and ye shall find. Ask, and it shall be given.* She wasn't asking; she was demanding. *Ye are gods.* She would walk. She would travel with or without Nick. Maybe she would even have children with or without Nick. Maybe their lives together would change. If not, she would change on her own without him.

The doctor came in. He removed the brace from Isa's neck. He told her it wasn't as bad as they had thought. He said her neck was fragile. It would be over if she ever had a significant jar in that area again. Isa knew beyond a shadow of a doubt it was the prayer. She had been given a reprieve. They gave her prescriptions for pain. Nick rolled her out of the hospital in a wheelchair.

The crisis was over. As far as their marriage was concerned, things went back to normal, the same as before. Emotional issues were swept under the rug, as always. She didn't walk out of Nick's life. Not yet. It took a year to recover fully. Her neck remained weak. Sometimes she would feel pins and needles in her legs. She tried to run again, but the jarring caused relapses of pain in her neck. She listened to positive affirmations while taking the summer to recuperate. When school started, she began walking, feeling lucky to be doing so, embracing each step with gratitude.

Nick and Isa never talked about the accident. It was as if it had never happened. Nor did either of their parents. Sometimes the teachers she worked with would notice her head drooping in the teacher's lounge and ask her how she was doing. In silence, Isa used one of the affirmations and said out loud with a smile,

"I'm doing great." In reality, it took every bit of determination to hold herself together.

Then one day, her weekly phone conversation with her mother took an unusual turn. Her mom asked her if she was happy. This was not like her mother. "Is everything all right with you and Dad? Are you both okay healthwise?"

"No, Isa, don't worry. We're fine. We've been talking. You know you could move to Texas."

"What do you mean?"

"We know you aren't happy in your marriage. We see it in your face when we do see you and when we talk on that thing called Skype. We hear it in your voice. You know you've been given a second chance since the accident. You should do something about it. You're still young." There was a pause. "You know, Isa, I've never spent a penny of what your grandmother left me. I've been saving it for you."

The conversation was surreal, something she never expected to hear from her parents.

"Are you sure you and Dad are okay?"

"Yes, Isa, we're fine."

"I thought you liked Nick."

"Maybe we never really knew him."

～～～

AFTER ANOTHER YEAR AND SEVERAL BIG BLOWOUT FIGHTS, ISA packed her suitcases, sat at the kitchen table, and wrote the note. Isa didn't move to Texas. She put a down payment, part of her grandmother's money, on a small bungalow close to the school. A fixer-upper. It would give her something to do. More so, it would give her dad, a hobbyist handyman, something to do during his vacation.

She could walk to work. She was doing much better physically. But mentally and emotionally, she wasn't in much better shape than before. She was kidding herself that she had made changes. She was still living a lie. She was the divorced librarian giving her daytime to her job and traveling vicariously via Google Earth and other people's internet vacation videos at night. In reality, she had exchanged one claustrophobic situation for another.

Sometimes she still resorted to putting Josh's name in the search bar. On one occasion, two things came up. He was an assistant professor of geology at Atlanta. She looked up his university and found a picture of him. He had grown more handsome. In another entry, he was a bicyclist who would be traveling across France during the summer. She wondered if Denise was traveling with him. Were there children? What part of France?

Isa put the bungalow up for sale. She gave her notice at work. A young girl fresh out of college was waiting to take her job and house. Location was everything to the young woman. She didn't even try to negotiate the price down. Maybe it was all those positive affirmations on Isa's part. Still, Isa felt a tinge of guilt as she handed over the keys to the house and car. She would need neither after the purchase of a one-way ticket to Europe. She had only planned on spending the summer in Europe but felt she had to walk away from everything to make a fresh start. Her parents insisted on paying her cell phone bills. It was her lifeline should she need one. Her dad shrugged it off, saying, "How could we sleep at night? God forbid our daughter should be abducted into some sex trade ring or accidentally get involved in drug smuggling." One of Isa's dad's favorite movies was *The French Connection.*

NOW SHE FOUND HERSELF IN AN INN STATIONED ALONG THE bicycle route that Josh could or might not be participating in.

What on earth was she doing? And if that weren't enough, she was having dreams about an innkeeper named Dora married to a man named Adrien, who was in an accident and lost the use of his legs. Then she finds out these people in her dream were real. If she were back home, she would see a therapist, but she was in a strange country where strange things were happening. There had been no miracle for Adrien, but there had been for her.

ISA WALKED IN AND OUT OF SHOPS OVER PAVED AND REPAVED cobblestone. Her feet ached. The feeling of aching feet comforted her. Life could have turned out differently. While she walked, she reasoned away any subconscious motives that may have led her to book an inn on the bicycle route. No, it was just a coincidence. Josh was a dream in the past. Finding him here would be like finding the proverbial needle in a haystack. Isa kept walking, trying to erase all thoughts while she took in the landscape that reminded her so much of her grandmother's appliquéd quilts.

While deep in thought, the uneven solidness of the stones changed to a spongy, wavy softness. Isa looked down at her sandals to find she was standing on an unkempt lawn amid ancient tombstones. Once when so absorbed in thought while running, she had looked around to find herself in an unfamiliar neighborhood. Josh had permeated her thoughts then too.

She looked up to see a church. She recognized the bell tower. It was the church that stood in the center of the village. She was in the churchyard, standing on the outskirts of the church's cemetery. It was maybe a half-mile distance on the other side of the inn. At least she had her bearings. The inn was a straight shot if she concentrated on where she was going on her way back. It would be getting dark soon.

Isa cut through the grass and the headstones to get to the

other side of the church where the road to the inn lay. On the other side, the name on one of the stones caught her eye—Adrien Paul Girard. The letters were faded but legible. In the fading sunlight, the dates were indecipherable. A French inscription was on the weathered, crumbling gravestone. The lettering had worn away in a lot of places. Trying to guess enough to put it into her translator app proved futile. Madame Girard would more than likely know what it said. But would Isa even see Madame Girard again? Standing before the grave seemed, as Madame Claire said, "*destin.*"

Isa relaxed into the moment, something she had tried to learn from all of the self-help books she had read. Now she was experiencing what that meant. Being here, at this moment, was her fate. Meeting the strange English woman who was transplanted to this country as she now was, was also her fate. Isa looked at the graves next to Adrien's, searching for the name Dorcel. It wasn't to be found. Maybe Adrien died first, and Dorcel remarried and was buried beside another husband. It was getting too dark to explore more. She would come back during the day, more prepared, even if it meant another visit to Madame Girard.

Today was check-in day for the cyclists. Feeling ragged and weary from the walk and all the revelations of her visit, Isa entered the inn through the back, but not before peeking into the common room, scanning the crowd. There were no familiar faces. She made her way up the narrow back stairwell and slid the key into the lock of room eleven. After undressing and lightly washing her dress and hanging it to dry, she stood in the shower, letting the water erase all thoughts from her mind. She got into bed, buried her head in the soft pillow, and waited for the dreams.

7

---

*T*he stranger said he knew her, or that he would know her, and that he *had* known her. He spoke using peculiar terms and in riddles. She did not know him. He was not someone she would likely forget. He called her by the name Dora with much tenderness and yet with authority. The pure sound of his voice was something one could trust. She didn't know where he came from. He never said, not directly. Nor did he give her his name. She wished she knew his name. Why hadn't she asked? It would be the name she would repeat in her mind and heart over and over again. She denied being in love. Their meeting was nothing like that. If anything, it was beyond that.

"The time has come," he said.

DORA COULD SAY HER INFIDELITY SPRANG FROM TWO DISTINCT things. One was the stranger. Based on that, one might say he was an evil influence, but he showed her there was something more to life. She refused to call that evil. The other was her husband, not that she didn't love Adrien. She did. It was the persistent complaining, anger, and sarcasm directed toward her. She couldn't say she wouldn't do the same if she were in his position. She had done her best to wait on him, attend to his every need, and give him every bit of encouragement she could muster. In the beginning, she was deemed a saint. Soon enough, saints, who were not true saints, fell from their pedestals. Dora's fall was short.

Other than lovers, she filled the void with books. There was so little time. Dora read in the late hours of the night after everyone was asleep. Sometimes she brought a book from the upstairs library and read by candlelight beside her husband's bed. She had searched through the judge's library for clues to what the stranger meant. She had even asked vague questions of the clergy, not wanting to arouse suspicion. There was suspicion enough, what with the Edge.

Adrien had nothing but time. When not complaining or wallowing in self-pity, he, too, read. Dora envied him in that regard. Asking her husband for his opinion would elicit questions she was ill-prepared to answer. They didn't have a trusting relationship. Dora didn't think it ever was so, not even preceding the accident. But maybe that was her trying to justify things. He resented the fact that he was dependent on her. He resented the fact that the business had grown under her management.

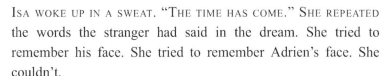

Isa woke up in a sweat. "The time has come." She repeated the words the stranger had said in the dream. She tried to remember his face. She tried to remember Adrien's face. She couldn't.

Grabbing her journal from the nightstand, Isa wrote about the new dream and transferred everything she had written the first day on the lone piece of paper onto her new journal's crisp white pages. The brown leather bore embossed letters on the front saying JOURNAL, the same word in both French and English. It was not old like the leather binder Madame Girard had handed her, but in time if it survived, its stressed and antiquated binding might entice some curious soul to read its pages.

Besides recording her dreams, she wrote about her visit with Madame Girard and her stay at the inn thus far. Isa wrote her general observations about the people and the countryside. Her grandmother's voice resonated inside her head, "How long will this journal fad last, Isa?"

"It's lasted for over a decade, Grammy," she said aloud.

Her grandmother's interruption or thoughtful teaching, whichever it was, made Isa vow to be faithful to this one obsession in her life. Since she couldn't discuss or didn't want to discuss what had happened with a therapist, she would do her best to reflect upon all that had happened in her journal, even if it meant writing about Josh. What better way to analyze and get her wild fantasy about him out of her system.

If she were still the librarian at the school, she might have the sixth-grade class experiment with journaling. The library was still in her blood. Maybe she was unwise to pick up and leave. No, fate brought her here. Isa wrote everything that popped into her mind, no matter how absurd or daft. *Daft, such an English word,* she wrote.

She wrote until the rich fragrance of freshly baked bread wafted up through the stairwell of the inn. She looked at her phone. Seven a.m. Along with the aroma of the croissants, male voices and laughter drifted upward. The cyclists—she had almost forgotten about them. There was still plenty of time to shower and get breakfast.

$\mathcal{T}$he common room was abuzz with cyclists. The only familiar faces were those of Claire and Albert. A surge of disappointment, then relief, trickled through Isa's body. What was she thinking? It was hard admitting to herself that she had even contemplated it. Impossible to believe that she flew across the Atlantic on a whim that she might run into and hook up with someone she somewhat dated in college twelve years ago—someone that may or may not be in this vast country of France. And he was married to Denise of all people. A marriage to Denise couldn't last. She hadn't seen a ghost as Madame Girard had, but she had created one—a fantasy man based on a brief relationship, if one could even call it a relationship. Was she that desperate? She had the gall to think Madame Girard daft.

"Mademoiselle Isa!" The voice startled her. Madam Claire stood beside her, gently brushing up against her arm. "Do you want tea, coffee, or espresso, perhaps?"

Isa smiled, happy to be back in the present. "*Bonjour*, sure, I mean *oui*, I will have some tea, Earl Grey if you have it." Isa preferred jasmine, but thinking of yesterday, Earl Grey rolled off her tongue.

Madame Claire smiled. "You saw Madame Girard. How did that go, if I may ask?"

Before Isa could answer, a group of cyclists looked their way and shouted something to Madame Claire in French.

"*Excusez-Moi*," Madame Claire said abruptly, moving toward the bicyclists' table.

Isa was glad for the interruption. She wasn't sure how to explain the visit to Madame Girard. Isa took a bite from one of the croissants in the basket on the table. With tons of butter folded into the flaky paper-thin layers, it tasted like a piece of heaven. What made them so spectacular here? Back home, she rarely gave them a second thought, seldom eating them unless chicken or tuna salad was wedged in the middle.

Isa thought of croissants as French even though she knew they originated in Austria, an odd fact she had picked up in a book. The French had a talent for croissants, the same with cheese, baguettes, and wine. Oh, and macaroons. As with croissants, she hadn't understood what all the fuss was about until coming here. She had them once at an art festival in the states, but there was no comparison. While croissants were the unsweetened version of heaven, macaroons were the sweetened version.

Everywhere there were display cases full of rich, elegant, decadent tarts, torts, eclairs, custards, petit fours, crème brûlée, her favorite, and macaroons in a full spectrum of colors as if they had jumped off Van Gogh's palette. Even McDonald's had them. She had snapped a picture of them in the display case along with Egg McMuffins. No one would believe her back home. The pastries at the plethora of *boulangeries* dotting the rues were works of art, possibly bordering on what could be found at the Louvre. She hadn't been to the Louvre yet. Of course, she would go. She could not come to France without visiting there. But one could also not visit France without experiencing the food, a whole culture unto itself.

She took another bite of the croissant, chewing slowly to enjoy its rich texture. Back at home, she gulped down her meals, a habit forced upon teachers, one that proved hard to break.

ON HER FIRST NIGHT AFTER ARRIVING IN FRANCE, SHE SAT IN A café in Paris. One of the servers, using mouth-to-hand gestures in slow motion, spoke in English, as it was apparent she was not French. "Eat slowly." He even dragged out the words in slow motion.

He didn't come back to ask how the meal was. Not a trace of crepe remained on her plate. Yet, the waiter made no appearance as if it would be rude to do so until her meal was fully digested. She looked around to see others in no hurry to leave, their dinners long gone, consuming second bottles of wine while they talked and laughed. A few were smoking cigarettes. She was a loner, out of place, trying to learn the customs, the food culture, and the unrushed manner of life.

She dropped her stiff posture, easing back into her chair, perusing the dessert tray thoroughly before picking one as well as ordering a second glass of wine to sip slowly while she people watched, sorting the tourists from the French—a rather juvenile game considering she was at a café along the Champs-Élysées, one of the most touristy places in Paris. A good portion of the crowd stood out as displaced as her. Tomorrow she would board the train for a more serene, secluded part of France, hoping the inn she had chosen was not a disappointment.

SHE TOOK ANOTHER BITE OF HER CROISSANT, EASING INTO IT LIKE a seductress in a French painting. She was not disappointed.

"So, Mademoiselle Isa, what are your plans today?"

She jumped and reached for her glasses on the table, not actually needing them since she was nearsighted. It was more of a knee-jerk reaction to hide the nakedness of her thoughts.

"How did your meeting with Madame Girard go?" It was Albert this time. The inn had returned to its serene atmosphere, with most of the cyclists moving outside.

"Oh, I don't know. I was thinking of a change of pace. I might catch the train and go up to Paris. I have only spent one night and day there thus far. I will have to take day trips to get it all in. What do you think?" Isa thought she needed to escape the peasant life for a while and see how the eighteen King Louises lived or how Monet or Manet lived. "I might visit some museums. See some Monet or Da Vinci?"

"Ah, the museums? Perhaps the Louvre or Orsay? Then on other trips into the city, the lesser ones."

"Which would you recommend?"

"Do you like the stuffy old painters with every stroke in place, or do you like the impressionists Monet, Cézanne, or Van Gogh? You mentioned Monet. That would be Orsay. Leonardo would be the Louvre. Everyone goes to see *The Mona Lisa*. It will not be what you expect. Did you know she was once stolen?"

"No, I didn't."

"*Oui*, around a hundred years ago, from the Louvre. Now it hangs on its own wall, roped off with four guards overseeing it, always surrounded by a multitude of tourists with cameras. It looks tiny on that one wall."

"Well, I'm a fan of the impressionists, notably Monet, but I will have to see *The Mona Lisa* while I'm here, even if it is small. But today, I'm leaning toward the impressionists."

"Then Orsay it is. But better you should go farther north and visit Giverny, Monet's home. The flowers this time of year will be magnificent." He put his thumb and index finger up to his lips and gave a smacking kiss, a typical French gesture, the same one the waiter used after placing the crème brûlée before Isa that first night on the Champs-Élysées.

"Then, Monsieur Albert, I will take your recommendation, and I thank you for it. I mean merci beaucoup."

He smiled. "And your meeting with Madame Girard?"

"It was interesting. It left me with many questions."

"Ah, I thought it might," he said with a wink.

"You sound like you know more about this inn's history than you let on."

"Hmmm, I might, but we will save that for another day. You have just enough time to catch the train. Should I have Claire pack a lunch? You will want to spend as much time as possible at Giverny."

"No, don't bother. I'll grab something on the train."

Isa climbed the squeaky floorboards to the second story and grabbed a few things for the trip, one being her guidebook. She would read up on Giverny on the train. It had been one of the internet videos she watched before coming. However, she found things looked different in real life, and as helpful as the videos had been, she felt comforted in finding Albert and Claire, who had stepped in as surrogate parents. She laughed, thinking of Madame Girard as the odd aunt.

There was so much to see, but she wanted to take it slow, as the waiter said. She had the summer. Maybe Claire and Albert would let her help out at the inn if she did ever return to France. They would need more customers if that were to come to pass. She laughed out loud. She could become their pastry chef and stay covered in flour all day, becoming the inn's new ghost—Dora's doppelgänger in more modern clothing. Could a spirit have a doppelgänger? Maybe she and Dora could hang out together and take shifts haunting the inn, a ploy that might bring customers to the inn.

Isa grabbed her backpack, ran down the stairs as fast as the worn planks would let her, and waved *au revoir* to Claire and Albert.

THE TRAIN WAS INCREDIBLE—AMAZING THE SECOND TIME around. At least this time, she boarded without a problem and was in her correct seat. Also, it was less crowded. Her first time was catching the train in Paris when she came to the inn. There was no vacant seat to be had. She had splurged on first-class tickets but sat most of the ride in second-class seats. After public transportation in the states, they seemed rather lavish to her. Maybe if the conductor had told her when scanning her ticket, but no, she guessed that was not the French way. Perhaps he thought it an intrusion, or maybe he thought *crazy American.*

If she hadn't ventured up to the café car and peeked beyond the divider to see what second class looked like—what she thought was second class but was actually first class—she would have never discovered she had been experiencing it firsthand.

After that discovery, the stress was on. She could see no vacant seats on the train whatsoever. So where on earth could her rightful seat be? Should she move? Her luggage would be in second-class. She didn't want to haul it down long aisles. Maybe she could leave it in second-class and go back for it when the train stopped. She asked a steward who sat on the bench with the luggage between cars if he could help her find her proper seat. He was more helpful but didn't have much more of a clue than she did. Possibly it was because he didn't speak a word of English. Having purchased her ticket online before coming, it was in English. She found the corresponding number in first class, but the seat was already taken. Isa learned later that besides not being in the right seat, she wasn't even in the right car. She resigned herself to finish the trip sitting in second-class, berating herself the whole way. When she disembarked, she walked back and forth, studying the train. Car numbers were in bold print along with the numbers **1** and **2**, signifying classes. If only she had looked. This time she felt prepared, at least more so. She thought she might write a book, *Exploring France for Dummies,* when she returned. It had probably already been written, but did the people who wrote these guidebooks take into consideration people like her?

Today's trip was going smoothly. Everyone was silent on the ride except for one couple sitting across from her and another group a few seats up. Of course, both groups were Americans. Their loud conversations competed with each other. Sinking into her seat, Isa tried to blend in as one of the natives. It helped that she wore standard French issue muted colors on this particular day. She was becoming European. She flattered herself. While she could have grabbed her headphones from her backpack, she opted for eavesdropping.

The couple was from Texas. Besides Dallas coming up more than once, the accent was a dead giveaway. They were older, a man and a woman, not married—traveling companions. Both spouses had died. At least, that was what Isa surmised. Trying to be discreet, she looked for wedding bands and saw none. The woman had done her research. Isa saw her pull out a Rick Steves' guidebook.

The couple sat facing each other with their tray out, sharing a bottle of Scotch, drinking it from paper cups they had procured from the café car. The woman got up to use the toilet. A whole half hour went by. Isa began to worry but saw her partner was unconcerned. He made no move to check on her. That was another thing that told Isa they were not married, not that she was a great expert on marriage. But she would like to think that even Nick, had she had remained in the bathroom for thirty minutes, would have been pounding on the door to see if everything was all right.

As for the other group, they were the ones that most caught Isa's attention. Three men and three women sat facing each other. Two of them comprised a couple. The woman repeatedly said, "How many times have I told you that?" Sometimes she followed it with, "Dear."

The man responded, "Now, honey," or "Yes, honey."

A lot of bragging was bantered back and forth. "Some poor jerk couldn't keep up," one of them said.

Were they mountain climbers? Hikers? No, Isa discovered more into the conversation they were cyclists—seasoned ones in their forties or perhaps fifties, well-tanned and muscular. They munched on snacks and wine. They reminded her of an older version of Ross, Rachael, Phoebe, Joey, Chandler, and Monica on *Friends*.

Was everyone here to bicycle except her? Finding one among thousands would be impossible. She needed to eradicate Josh from her mind.

The bicyclists became louder with each bottle of wine consumed. Today they were taking the day off from riding. They were casting their votes for the restaurant they would eat at after sightseeing, where they would likely consume more wine. Isa listened to the couple using terms of affection like dear, honey, and sugar even though their conversation didn't merit it. Nick had never so much as called her anything affectionate. Maybe their terms of endearment and joint enthusiasm for bicycling kept them together. The married couple looked to be the oldest in the group.

Finally, they arrived in Paris. Isa was at Gare Saint-Lazare, the train station Monet painted, although she saw little resemblance. She was sure the shopping mall you went through to leave the station was absent in his day, as were the pastry shops and the Starbucks. Isa noticed that Starbucks, unlike McDonald's, did not change its menu for the French. One thing led to another, the shops, the metro, the train stations, no in-between places. She had an hour before a different train would leave for Giverny. She stood at a table in the corner of a café having a cup of tea, watched people come and go, and imagined what it must have been like for Monet. Probably he knew everyone, and everyone knew him. After all, he would be the one sitting before an easel with a paintbrush in hand.

Two ladies from Michigan came up behind Isa. One tapped her shoulder and asked if they could follow her. Isa smiled. Had she actually pulled off the French look?

"I found my way through trial and error, ladies." They weren't shocked at all when she answered in English. They looked to be in their sixties—a very well-kept sixtyish—no doubt using their husband's charge cards to travel. But then Isa was using some of her grandmother's money.

"So what gave me away?"

"What?" The one named Jane asked. They had already made introductions.

"How did you know I was American?"

"We heard you order tea at the café counter. We were thinking Southern," said Carol.

Isa complimented them on their knowledge of American accents. "Kentucky," she said.

That was Carol's only contribution to the conversation. Jane did most of the talking. But when it came time to board, everyone went their separate ways. It was only a forty-five-minute trip to Giverny, but Isa looked back to see them both snoozing away. She imagined Josh being on this journey with her and being able to put her head on his shoulder. If only for a day, she wanted to erase Dora and Adrien from her mind. It would be nice to erase Josh as well.

The scenery en route to Giverny was not as fantastic as the scenery outside of Paris, a countryside filled with vineyards and manicured farmland. On this leg of the trip, there was a lot of graffiti she didn't understand written on stone walls, and upon leaving the city, she saw only a few cows of the white variety and a few sheep scattered about.

From the train, there was a bus that went to Giverny. There was also a walking trail. She wouldn't have as much time at Giverny as she would have liked if she took the route involving city walking and crossing a five-mile long bridge if her kilometer conversion were correct. She opted for the bus. She wanted to suck in as much of Monet as possible. There would be plenty of walking for the duration of the trip.

Giverny was a splendid piece of tranquility with water, color, and aromas that Isa could have resided in for the remainder of her days, that is, if you could have shoved the fanatic picture-taking tourists back onto the bus. But then, she was one of them. She sat on a bench, trying to imagine she was the only one there as the rest of them must have been doing. It wasn't as hard as one would think. The whole picturesque scene elicited a meditative repose among her fellow travelers.

Not only were the gardens for viewing, but the house Monet had once lived and painted was open to tourists. The colors from his garden leaked onto the walls. Isa could have learned French cooking in that kitchen. Bright yellows and blues made the sun and sky blush. Monet's studio looked as though he had only stepped away for a brief time, perhaps to sit in his rowboat among the water lilies. Reproductions of his paintings lined the main room's walls. Isa overheard one tourist who thought they were real. She might have expected that from one of her students but not from an older man in his forties—American, of course.

She ran into the Michigan ladies again on the arched bridge over the lily pond. A lone boat waited for Monet at the water's edge. Jane graciously took Isa's picture standing on the bridge overlooking the boat. Carol suggested she might use it for her

Facebook photo. Isa caught the last bus back, taking what she hoped would not be her final look at Giverny as she boarded.

There would be no time for the Orsay. There was so much to see, but she had the summer to see it in. Then she would have to plan her life and find a job. She didn't want to think of that now. She rode the last train back to the inn. It was dark and the dinner hour for most. On her walk from the train station back to the inn, she passed cafés with small round tables where couples sat side by side drinking wine. Their good physiques, quite evident even without the spandex, told her they were the newly arrived cyclists.

Weary from a crammed-full day, Isa trudged up the uneven steps, took a shower, and fell into the comforting softness of the narrow but cozy bed. The thin lace curtains revealed a brightly lit moon. Nothing could keep her from a sound slumber tonight. She blacked out before her head even hit the pillow.

9

*I*sa's deep slumber went well until sometime in the middle of the night. She woke with a start, bolting upright in bed. Someone was in the room. Isa made no sound and tried not to breathe as a rush of cold air brushed over her. Perhaps it was a cyclist who had forgotten his room number or drunk too much wine. But she had heard no knob turning, no door opening. Besides, her door was locked. She remembered checking it.

Isa sat as rigid as a corpse, holding her pillow in front of her chest as if it were a bulletproof vest. "Who's there?" she called out in a meek voice. But there was a deadly silence. If anyone had so much as turned in bed in an adjoining room, she could have heard it.

Moonlight shone through the window like a spotlight with a soft-focus filter. Isa took her eyes off the door and gazed around the room. Then she saw the intruder. Her gut told her immediately who it was, although she didn't want to believe it. The figure, a mere slip of a woman, stood bent over the fireplace. She wore a light brown long skirt with a white billowy blouse that hung loosely over her midriff. The sleeves of the blouse were rolled up to her elbows. Wisps of unkempt dark hair hung down the side of her face, the rest pinned up into a bun and tucked under a white, somewhat dingy ruffled cap, like the ones Isa remembered seeing at Colonial Williamsburg when she was small. Her shoes were leather, reminiscent of ballet slippers, cracked from wear and water.

She poked a non-existent fire in the hearth. Her poker disappeared through the grate that blocked the opening. The grate must have been placed there lest some romantic soul staying at the inn tried to build a fire in it and burn a piece of the village's history down. Isa sat frozen, watching the woman. Without warning, she turned to face Isa. She appeared startled. It was Isa's face staring back—her doppelgänger, indeed. The figure that looked so real dissolved in slow motion before Isa's unblinking eyes. The eyes, the last part of her body to fade away, were her own.

Isa sat frozen for what seemed like an hour. She didn't know if it was from fright, curiosity, or even hope that the woman might reappear. Isa thought about getting out her computer and Skyping with her parents. She could use their warm, comforting faces. But then, she might break down. It took everything she had to resist the urge. She told herself to be grown up. They would know what time it was here and only worry. They would want her on the next plane back home.

She had Skyped with them upon settling into the inn, showing them around, convincing them that everything was going well. They had looked relieved. She had only been sending short emails after that with the promise of longer ones. Her parents had finally begun to accept that their daughter needed this adventure. She did not want them to alter their opinion about her life-finding trek. It was sheer exhaustion and gravity that took over her body as she slumped downward, awkwardly going back to sleep, fighting it the way a child fights naptime.

Isa awoke in the same distorted position that her body had

fallen into. Exuberant masculine voices echoed upward. Isa heard the creak of the floorboards. Her nose whiffed in the smell of espresso and pastries. She looked over at the clock on the nightstand—almost nine.

By the time Isa made it down to the main room, Madame Claire was busy stacking chairs and moving tables to one side so she could sweep up. There was the exception of one lone table still intact in the corner. It was occupied by an auburn-haired, bearded, freckle-faced man. Although he was clad in jeans and a polo shirt, she recognized him as one of the bicyclists. Isa had seen him sitting at one of the cafés with his wife. She wasn't with him this morning. She thought he might be around her age, the wife with the same red hair and freckled complexion, maybe a tad younger. They say that couples start to look like each other after a while. Isa reasoned they must have been together since grade school.

He was nursing a large pot of tea. He put aside the French newspaper he had been staring intently at and, with an unmistakable Scottish accent, called out, "Might as well join me. It appears I have the only table in the house." He looked at her. Then he said, *"Vous aimez le thé?"*

"What?" Isa asked.

"Oh, American."

"Yes," Isa replied.

Still shaken from last night's experience, Isa walked over to his table. He looked harmless enough, and Madame Claire was only a few feet away. He politely pulled out a chair for her. She sat across from him without speaking. He yelled out something in French to Madame Claire.

"I asked her to bring out some more croissants and another teacup. Or do you prefer coffee? You may think it a bit strange, but I carry my tea with me. It's a Scottish breakfast blend unless you prefer something else?"

Isa nodded. "Tea's fine."

"You're not much of a talker, are you? Cat got your tongue?"

"Sorry. I guess I'm still trying to wake up. I didn't get much sleep last night."

"Are you sure? In another couple of hours, it will be noon." Without giving Isa time to reply, "Hmmm, well, I slept like a log. Being out on a bicycle all day will do that for you. Do you ride?"

"No, I just walk."

"Well, that's one way of getting around."

Madame Claire brought another teacup, and the red-haired man poured Isa a cup. It smelled strong. Isa took a sip. It tasted as strong as it smelled, also somewhat bitter, but it was just what she needed.

While she sipped, he pushed the newly arrived plate of croissants in her direction. "The last in the house, eat up. You look like you could use a little meat on your bones."

Thinking him rather brash and wondering if he was looking at her chest when he said that, Isa took a croissant from the basket. She was hungry and too tired and shaken over last night to be offended. She tried to come up with something for small talk, but nothing came. He had no trouble filling the void in the conversation. "We should have made introductions first. I'll start. Hi, my name is Daniel Stewart, and you are?"

She extended her hand, which he took inside his rather large one. "Hello, my name is Isa. Isa Muir."

"Isa, that's pretty. Short for?"

"Isabella."

"Oh, Spanish, meaning you are devoted to God."

With a mouth full of croissants, Isa struggled out with, "I never heard that before."

"Really? You didn't know what your name meant?" he asked with an incredulous look on his face.

"I never gave it much thought, only that I hated it growing up."

"No, you shouldn't hate a name like that. I like it." He began to sing, somewhat off-key, "You know what that say about Spain?"

"No, what?"

"That it's pretty. And because Daniel has been there, he knows."

Isa laughed, finally thinking of something to say, "Big Elton fan? No, you couldn't be because those aren't the exact lyrics."

"I was paraphrasing," he grinned. "And you laughed. You're real flesh and blood, not an automaton. Anyway, my grandmother is Spanish, and I *have* been there several times, every summer when I was young. Also, I do like Elton. You do, too, right? Everyone loves Elton ."

Isa quipped in disbelief and sarcasm, not because he was an Elton fan but because his grandmother just happened to be from Spain. "Yes, I do. I have even seen him in concert. My favorite song is *Your Song*. I think you are making every bit of this up!"

"No, I swear on your devotion to God that I am not," he said with the most distinct and pleasing Scottish accent. "Not *Rocket Man*? Because you looked like you were off in space somewhere when you descended the stairs. Well, Y*our Song* is everyone's favorite Elton song. Not mine, though."

"It's my favorite song, period. And I suppose your favorite is *Daniel*."

"Ah, brilliant deduction, Isa," he said with a twinkle in his eyes. Isa noticed their blueness. How could she not notice?

"As for my devotion to God, how do you know I'm not agnostic or atheist?"

"Are you?"

"No."

"Oh, well, good to know."

Isa drank some more tea and took another bite of the croissant. "Why aren't you out with the other bicyclists and your wife?" She felt like one of the schoolchildren asking ridiculous questions. She thought about asking him if he knew Ewan McGregor but let it pass.

"Well, Isa of America," he paused. "I am correct in assuming you are from America? I don't miss an accent, although I couldn't place the exact region or state as you say. Definitely not a New York accent. That is the only state I have been to in America. I'm not out today because I twisted my ankle yesterday. Just a wee bit, mind you, but still not in the greatest shape for constant peddling. So I'm taking a day of rest. And as for my wife, well, I haven't met her yet."

Isa's eyebrows raised. "Then, girlfriend?"

"No, no girlfriend either. Are you propositioning me? The quiet, serious ones always get straight to the point."

Isa coughed up some tea. He laughed. She saw him look over at Madame Claire and give her a wink. Definitely a flirt. She didn't know exactly how much of the conversation Madame Claire overheard, but she seemed rather intent on listening, sweeping the same spot meticulously over and over. Isa wiped her mouth and said, "I saw you at a café with a woman. You appeared to be married." She regretted saying it almost immediately. Was she coming off like an inquisitor from the Spanish Inquisition?

"Ahh, married in the womb, you might say." He paused. "We're twins."

"Oh, now I see the reason for the uncanny resemblance." Isa tried not to show any expression on her face lest he take it the wrong way as he seemed to jump to conclusions and state his opinion easily. Still, she couldn't resist. "She looked younger than you."

"Thirty-three minutes, to be exact, a fact our dear mum never lets us forget. Well, she never lets my sister forget it. I'm the favorite one for that reason. Jumped right out. But Kate, well, you know lasses, always have to wait on them. It was excruciating labor, not that I remember much about it. But that's how my mum tells it."

"What do you do in life? I mean, as a career when you are not bicycling across France? I'm guessing comedian."

"Accountant," he said with a blank face.

"Well, you couldn't make that up."

"Actually, Isa, I am—making it up, that is. A bit of fun, not that we are not already seriously meandering into humor. I'm a teacher, professor, to be exact. I teach mathematics, and my students adore me."

"I'm sure they do."

"Well, Isa, I take it you have no boyfriend since you are here alone. I see no engagement ring or wedding band. You're free. Correct me if I'm wrong. I deduce that I'm right. I did have an ancestor that worked at Scotland Yard, not that Scotland Yard has anything to do with Scotland other than getting its name from the Scottish king. But getting to the facts is in my blood. I'm free, too, at least for today. So why don't we share all this freedom we have today together? What do you say?"

Madame Claire chuckled from across the room.

Isa looked at the unblinking, piercing blue eyes of this man, awaiting her answer. If it hadn't been for the ghost in her room last night and lack of sleep, she would find all of this quite amusing and scary, but after the spirit, this was anything but scary. The Scottish stranger named Daniel sitting across from her had taken her mind off the ghost, if only for a brief moment. Maybe he could do it for the day. Isa sat like a deer in headlights. Was this a date? She had not dated anyone since the divorce. She was a grown woman. This man was so alluring. Everything inside her said to take a chance. Why had she come to France? The decision was based on a reboot of life. Still, she hesitated.

She looked imploringly to Madame Claire, the only mother figure she had at this point. Madame Claire waved her hand in the air, a sign of approval that said either off with you, or go for it, or maybe just get out so I can finish my cleaning. At any rate, Isa had Madame Claire's blessing. Not having any other plans and needing to get out in broad daylight where ghosts didn't exist, Isa said, "Sure, why not."

Isa pardoned herself for a moment to return to her room to get her backpack. She sprinted into her room and grabbed it from beneath the nightstand lest the ghost was still lurking. On her way out, she hesitated in the doorway, peering back into the room to reassure herself. All looked normal. Maybe the whole thing had been her imagination. The entire idea of a ghost had been planted in her mind by Madame Girard.

By the time she got back down the stairs, Daniel was waiting with a picnic basket supplied by Madame Claire. A baguette and bottle of wine poked through the cloth.

Madame Claire stood with her arms folded like a statuesque Cupid, congratulating herself on a mission accomplished. Isa said, *"Merci. Au revoir!"* Daniel said the same, much better than her, with something added in French that Isa couldn't quite make out but guessed was don't wait up. Isa was in a new country with a man she had only met less than an hour ago, yet somehow, she felt perfectly safe. What were her options? The apparition in her room or the solid chunk of a man standing beside her.

"Isa, Madame Claire tells me you arrived less than a week ago. Have you been to the southern coast yet?" Daniel said as they walked out the door.

"No, I haven't."

"Then you are in for a treat. Are you game?"

"Why not? I came here to explore France."

"We will need to make only one stop along the way."

"To tell your sister where you'll be?"

"No, to get some sunscreen. You may have noticed that I burn easily."

---

10

*J*t wasn't until Isa sat side by side on the train with a man she had only met less than an hour ago that it sunk in she was on an actual date. Something spontaneous, unplanned. It was both strange and exhilarating at the same time. Maybe *destin*, as Madame Claire put it. Possibly the apparition, Isa's twin, looking back at her from the fireplace, was trying to enlighten her on what was yet to come. She shouldn't read so much into it. Daniel was merely killing time, nursing a sore ankle. Still, it was momentous for Isa, her first outing with a man since Nick.

Dating had not been something she had thought about, or it was something she didn't *want* to think about. Back in the states, she had wrapped herself up in school activities on and off the clock. A librarian's work was never done, or at least that is what she told herself. Since she lived within walking distance of the school, it was easy to do. There were parent-teacher meetings, art shows, decorating for various school events, and dances. Isa volunteered for anything there was to volunteer for to fill the void. But that had been going on long before the divorce. Sure, her colleagues had occasionally tried to fix her up. She always managed to change the subject. When she handed in her resignation, saying she was buying a one-way ticket to Europe and selling her house and car, jaws dropped to the point of TMJ disorders. There must have been rumors she was not the meek librarian hiding behind the glasses and books they envisioned her to be. Some of them had even looked at her like she had some terminal disease and was living out the rest of her life satisfying the requirement for a final fling. In a way, they were right. It was the yearning to have any kind of involvement, something real before it was too late.

Isa was both cautioned and held in awe for making a bucket-list leap at such a young age. After the initial shock wore off, everyone offered suggestions, living vicariously through her daring.

The older staff said, "If I were young again, or maybe upon retirement?"

The younger staff admired her bravery and said, "I'm going to start saving now."

The middle-aged ones breathed a heavy sigh, "Just one more year, and my youngest will be through with college and maybe…"

The ones who had already been to Europe talked about their own experiences and gave her every helpful tip they could think of. The ones who hadn't been offered advice as well.

Isa had opened a can of worms and expected the school board to come down on her any day as she had possibly started a mass exit. While on break, teachers eyed their tablets and smartphones, looking up faraway and exotic places, everything from Caribbean cruises to China. All the commotion caused by her announcement wore down after a week.

Isa expected a small send-off at work with cake, punch, and coffee in the teacher's lounge, along with the usual student cards and drawings. What she didn't expect was the magnitude of the event. After a few days of silence on the subject, the unexpected happened. An intercom announcement asked everyone to come to the gym the last hour before school let out for the summer.

The only thing missing from the unexpected gala event was Champagne or French wine. Of course, alcoholic beverages weren't allowed on school premises. Grape juice in clear plastic cups sufficed. Isa praised her students' ingenuity. They decorated the gym in French decor. Unbeknownst to her, teachers, parents, and students were all in on it. Even some of the parents were there. She got the usual homemade cards from students. But instead of individual departing gifts, a collection had been taken up. They presented her with a cash bundle totaling $347, a hefty sum for teachers.

At that point, any thoughts of abandoning the intended trip, which at times Isa thought to be such a foolish, stupid endeavor, were dismissed. How could she not forge full steam ahead after such a send-off? It was either do or die or else hide her face in shame. A tear-stained face brushed against each student as she hugged each goodbye. It was *It's a Wonderful Life* in reverse. She was free to travel, no husband to tie her down, no savings and loan calling her back, and sadly, no children at her apron string. After France, Isa would think of children. Possibly a husband first, but it was a new day and age.

Now she found herself sitting next to this wild and wonderful Scotsman, someone she picked up at an inn this mid-morning. Or rather, to be completely honest, he had picked *her* up and rescued her from a ghost, although he didn't have a clue. During her first week in France, she had met a couple of delightful innkeepers, a strange English lady, a ghost, and a Scotsman, not to mention the sites she had taken in. And now she was on her way to the French Riviera.

"SO, ISABELLA, ISA, FOR SHORT, WHAT'S YOUR STORY?" DANIEL asked as he removed his shoes and rested his feet in the empty seat in front of them. They sat in one of those groups of seats facing each other, the kind the cyclists had sat in on her previous train ride. Isa assumed it was to rest his twisted ankle. "I hope you don't mind if I spread out a bit. If my feet smell, tell me." He laughed. It was a deep masculine chuckle.

"No, not at all. Does your ankle hurt?"

"Not too bad. If I had biked today, though, it would have started acting up. Better safe than sorry. We have two hours on the train, and I'm all ears to hear about your life. What brought you to France?"

"There is not so much to tell."

"Oh, come on, Isa. I knew this was going to take a bit of prodding. I deduced this morning that getting words from you would be like breaking a monk's vow of silence."

"Well, okay. For starters, I'm a teacher like you. Well, not a teacher but a librarian at an elementary school, or was, until I decided to travel for a while."

He lit up and exclaimed, "I knew it! I had you pegged for a teacher and an elementary one at that. No, no, hold back your applause. It was elementary, my dear Watson. Do you mind if I call you Watson? I think we make quite a team."

"Do you have a serious bone in your body?" She couldn't help but think of Ron Weasley, an older Ron Weasley with a beard. That, of course, would make her Hermione Granger.

"Well, you know what they say. Opposites attract."

"Okay, I will grant you maybe I'm a bit on the serious side, and you're, well…"

"No, Isa," he said, laughing. "There are times I can be deadly serious. I'm just trying to get you to meet me in the middle somewhere. I will admit I'm using the same tactics with you that I use on my students. They come into my class thinking mathematics will be boring—the first-year students who have to take at least one math class. So I always start by trying to lighten it up a bit."

"Oh, I see. So give me an example. I am interested in your teaching techniques. I may want to emulate them someday."

"Let's go back to the beginning when I first taught. I started out teaching history at a high school. They needed a teacher, and history was my minor. You've heard that Scotland's castles are full of ghosts?"

"What does teaching history have to do with ghosts?" she asked, blasé, trying not to show any alarm at the mention of ghosts.

"I like to tell it from the ghost's perspective. At the beginning of the class, they are laughing at my antics, those that aren't scared. You might be surprised at how easy it is to scare six-foot teenage boys. Somewhere in the middle, I have their wide-eyed attention. By the end of the semester, they have some history under their kilts. It came at them from a different perspective, something they won't forget. By the end of the year, I have won the favorite teacher award, yet again, for another year. Your turn."

"My turn?"

"Are you a good teacher? A good librarian?"

"I would like to think I was. I was dedicated, maybe too much. I gave everything I had to the students, to the entire school, for that matter."

"Yes, somehow, I thought you might. And when you go back to it, you will be an even greater teacher."

"I'm not so sure I'm going back to it."

"You will. I feel it in my ankle."

"You mean in your bones, don't you? I think that could be a touch of arthritis developing."

"No, no, I'm not that old."

"I know you are only thirty-three minutes older than your sister. How old is that in years?"

"I'm thirty. I won't ask how old you are since asking a woman her age is impolite."

"I'm older, thirty-three. Does it bother you to be with an older woman?"

"Thirty-three is hardly old. But it is good to know that I'm in mature hands. Experience counts," he said with a grin and a wink.

"Don't bet on me being experienced."

He changed positions when the conductor came down the aisle to check tickets. Isa took the interruption to return to her serious mode. "Daniel, since you were talking about ghosts, do you believe in ghosts?"

"There are as many ghosts in Scotland as bagpipes and kilts."

"Does that mean you believe in them?"

"I suppose as much as any Scottish person does. So that would be a definite yes, or maybe a semidefinite yes since I haven't seen one myself."

"Would you like to see one?"

"I don't know. I think I would, but an actual encounter might take some flippancy out of my teaching." There was a pause. "Why, Isa, do you know where one is?"

"I don't know. Never mind. We can change the subject."

"Hmm, it's obvious you're hiding something. Remember, you can't fool Sherlock Holmes."

"Okay, well, this is going to sound silly."

"That is how all ghost recounting starts," he interjected.

"What?"

"This is going to sound silly or preposterous or something of that nature. That's how all people start a ghost story. I assure you it won't sound silly. I've heard plenty of ghost stories in my day."

"Okay, last night, and now last night seems so long ago, but last night something happened," Isa stuttered.

"Oh, so when we met," he raised his wrist to look at his

watch, "approximately two hours, ten minutes ago, I was not meeting the usual vibrant, enthusiastic Isa, which I assume you are. I was meeting the Isa, who was a bit thrown off by something that went bump in the night. Yes, that would explain your far-off manner."

"Yes, you could say that, although I don't know how usually vibrant and enthusiastic I am."

"I think you are, at least for your elementary school students."

She thought a moment. A smile came to her face. "Yes, you're right. I had never thought of it before, but I was. I was always enthusiastic around my students."

Daniel smiled a knowing smile as he repositioned his ankle.

"Are you sure your ankle isn't bothering you?" she asked.

"No, it's fine, really. The seats are a bit cramped, but nothing like airline seats. I'm a happy camper. Not to worry. Please go on with what happened."

With that, Isa related the events of the ghost's appearance in her room to him. She followed with her meeting with Madame Girard and her account of the spirit. She left out the dreams. Too much to bring up on a first date.

The freckled skin around his blue eyes crinkled a bit, and he looked at her earnestly. "You do have incredible eyes."

"What?"

"You said the ghost had your eyes. That means that you both have beautiful eyes. Eyes are always the same."

"The same?"

"Yes, from soul to soul."

Isa remembered what the stranger in her dream had said—the part about the eyes never changing. She must remember to write that in her journal. It was hard to remember every little detail, but bits and pieces came back with different things triggering the memories.

"Isa, we must solve this mystery," Daniel said resolutely. "If there is anything I like, it is a ghost, history, and mystery all rolled into one." He took her hand, and it felt so natural.

THEY HAD ENTERED THE LAST PHASE OF THEIR TRAIN RIDE, coming upon the coast of southern France. It was astounding to see how much the azure sea outside the train window matched Daniel's eyes.

"There will be a few stops, one right after the other until we reach Nice. How about that bread and wine? It may be too early in America, but hey, you're in France. And in Scotland, it's never too early."

He moved into an upright position, and they pulled out their trays. Isa thought of the couple who drank Scotch from the paper cups. It was then she finally noticed he was over six feet tall. He towered over her five foot three inches. She usually didn't think of herself as short, considering most of her days were spent hovering over elementary students. She imagined him in a kilt with hairy, freckled, sunburned legs.

They toasted to a beautiful day of sightseeing and solving the ghost mystery.

a perfect day greeted Daniel and Isa as they departed the train. Eager tourists skidded between them, one bumping Isa. Out of chivalry, a sense of protection, or perhaps attraction, Daniel took Isa's hand. Much larger than her own, it was a mixture of soft and rough. Even though the crowd from the train had made their way past them, Daniel continued to hold her hand as they skimmed through narrow jigsaw streets until they reached the walkway above the sea. Swimmers and sunbathers crowded the thin strip of pebbly beach. Isa did a double take, noticing a couple of the women were topless. She averted her eyes. If Daniel noticed at all, he didn't appear interested.

"Do you want to go in?"

"I didn't bring a suit."

"You don't need one. Didn't anyone tell you about Europe before you came?"

Isa looked over at the two topless women sunning on the beach. They looked to be in their fifties. Isa raised her eyebrows and felt her face flush simultaneously, wondering if she might be so daring before leaving Europe.

"Kidding," he laughed. "We'll dip our toes in. How about it?"

"Okay, I'm for that."

Still holding her hand, they walked down steps to the beach area and a little way out on the round rocks.

"It isn't what you expected, the beach?"

"No, we have sand back home."

"Yes, it's the same in Scotland."

"It's so narrow," Isa said. They had maneuvered the sunbathers, who were almost packed on top of each other, like two people trespassing through a minefield. Every type of body imaginable, from burnt sienna and leathered skin to smoothly oiled young flesh in thongs with bra straps cast off on their towels, adorned the cramped rocky shoreline.

Upon reaching the edge where gentle waves washed in, Isa, with her free hand, discarded her backpack and reached down to take off her sandals.

"You might not be able to walk barefoot. You have to build up callouses for the beaches here," he said.

She leaned on him as she placed a foot into the water. She sensed his approval.

"It's beautiful. So clear. I love the shades of green and blue. And barely any waves."

"That's the Mediterranean Sea," he said with a smile. "Just a wee bit of wave. Nothing like the fierce tide crashing against the rocks in Scotland."

Daniel rolled up his pants, exposing the same legs Isa had imagined, minus the sunburn. They entered the water, sinking calf-deep, only a foot from the edge, into the rocks. The golf-ball-size rocks were like quicksand.

"We will try to experience as much as possible, this being your first time here."

Isa wasn't sure if there was a hidden meaning but replied, "The water is crystal clear."

"Crystal clear—that could be a metaphor. Maybe everything will become crystal clear about the ghost. Maybe, even life. France has a way of doing that, don't you think? Why I love coming here," he said, laughing.

She looked into his blue eyes, also crystal clear. "Or maybe just accept life the way it comes to you. Americans seem always to be fighting against it. I see the opposite in France."

He smiled. "Things are already clearing up, I see." He continued his discourse on beaches the way a teacher might. "All beaches are different, Isa. In Scotland, rocks and cliffs are prevalent. The water is often murky and rough, a perfect habitat for ghosts. Maybe why there are so many there. I want to take you to Old Town," he said.

With that, he reached for her waist and steered her out of the water. They meandered away from the beach through narrow cobblestone alleyways, sweeping through the crowd. Isa counted at least six different languages being spoken. It was the height of the tourist season, yet with Daniel, she didn't feel like a tourist but a VIP on a private tour. They walked at a leisurely pace in and out of specialty shops. Of particular interest was a toyshop. Daniel examined each toy with fascination. Isa couldn't help but think he was either a kid at heart, or that his biological clock was ticking louder than her own, or both.

They examined olive oils, leather jackets, scented soaps, chocolates, cheeses, and perfumes.

"Are you hungry?" Daniel asked with his free hand on his stomach.

"I'm starved." It was nearing the end of lunchtime for France, just before the restaurants stopped serving before the wine break.

They found an empty table, an almost unachievable task, amid the crowd and sat down for some wine and pizza.

"I feel like the works. Do you want dessert? I feel like something sweet. We can have tea and dessert after the meal."

The waitress came out to take their order. Daniel picked a wine, and Isa chose a pizza. The table was barely big enough to hold both.

"Only one pizza. Impossible!" the waitress exclaimed in English. The word impossible echoed like a church bell.

Isa wanted to say all things are possible. After all, she was, sitting with this seemingly marvelous man in a country she never had until a year ago imagined herself being in. Instead, she blurted out, "But we plan on ordering desserts as well," Isa said.

The waitress, not wavering in her position, again said, "Impossible!"

Daniel abruptly got up from the table while the waitress stood there. "Come on, Isa. I know somewhere else. Better."

"What was wrong with her?" Isa asked when they got out of earshot.

"Who knows? Maybe she's going through a bad breakup or something. Don't let her ruin our day. I know this place will be to your liking, but we must hurry before they close for lunch." He held tightly onto her hand, pulling her along as they practically ran out of Old Town.

"Your ankle," Isa exclaimed.

"It's okay, really," he said.

After about a good half mile, they stood before a small seedy-looking place. The sign above the door said LE SPEAK EASY. It was something one might see in New Orleans, where the outside wasn't much, but the food on the inside was out of this world. Isa had been to New Orleans once on a family vacation during one summer college break and had always wanted to go back.

"I hope you don't mind vegan," Daniel said to Isa as an older lady greeted them at the door. The lady was American.

"We are getting ready to close," she said.

Maybe it was seeing their agony, or perhaps it was Daniel's

pensive blue eyes, but she rolled her own eyes a bit and said, "Oh, okay. Come in."

They sat at a table in the back. The woman placed a wooden bowl filled with black olives on the table and disappeared behind a curtain that separated the dining area from the kitchen. She returned with a plate of food, placing it in front of the lone man that sat at another table. Isa counted eleven possible spots—all crowded together. Was it a coincidence? The number eleven seemed to be coming up a lot. Her room number back at the inn was eleven.

The hostess returned to their table and explained that she usually only took reservations and only cooked accordingly.

"Well, bring out what you have left," Daniel said with a smile and twinkle in his eyes. Isa surmised Daniel's blue eyes could get him about anything he wanted. It was obvious he knew it and used it to his advantage.

While the owner was back in the kitchen, Daniel told Isa about coming here before with some of his vegan cycling buddies. He explained that the food was primarily organic, all of it vegan and macrobiotic. Being a Scot, he was used to a lot of meat, but he reiterated that they were there for the experience. And he thought Isa might like a touch of home, seeing the owner was originally American, a transplanted Californian.

The woman came back out, bringing freshly squeezed carrot juice which they drank heartily. The woman once again disappeared into the kitchen. While Daniel and Isa waited, Daniel talked about Kate, his twin sister, who was a psychologist.

The woman reappeared, bringing two plates out with something resembling a quiche. She informed them it was a potato leek pie. On the side was a salad with sliced avocados. She explained the accouterments on the table. Daniel opted for the nutritional yeast, which would give it a cheesy taste, perhaps to make up for the loss of the pizza. The woman was charming and talked to them during the meal as Daniel and Isa were now the only customers left. She had come to Nice during the seventies as a young woman. She spoke fluent French but talked in her native language with them. Isa wondered if she might also become fluent after forty years of living here. The woman was a staunch vegan and animal activist. She was helpful and inspirational, perhaps hoping to convert a Scotsman away from his haggis.

When she came for their plates, she said, "I have banana ice cream if you are interested in dessert."

"I love bananas," Daniel responded.

It tasted like the custard Isa's grandmother used to make.

The lady locked the door behind them. Daniel looked at Isa, "I have never felt so healthy." They both laughed.

"I never thought to ask you if you might be vegan or vegetarian," he said.

"I've had brief bouts being a vegetarian when I ran. Never lasted very long. But if I could eat like that every day, I think I could do it."

"You didn't tell me you ran."

"That was several years ago, and besides, we only met this morning."

"It seems like a lifetime ago, doesn't it?"

"I don't know exactly how to take that, but yes, it does," she said smiling.

"I meant it in a good way. There is something else you must see while we are in Nice."

They walked back toward the coast and on the walkway until they came to the base of the Castle. He directed her attention to the waterfall up above them. "You know, Isa, we also have what we call Castle Hill in Edinburgh and an Old Town as well."

Daniel told her a little about the history of the Castle. "It had been a fort that was now in crumbles. They recently unearthed a church or monastery, and an archeological dig is underway."

Bypassing the elevator, they climbed the mountainous steps,

stopping at intervals so as not to tax Daniel's ankle too much. They reached the waterfall they had seen from down below. It was incredible. Isa was glad she had grabbed her backpack, which housed her camera. Since the trip began, she thought they had already taken hundreds of pictures, including videos. She had let Daniel do most of the honors. He also took a lot of his own with his cell phone. Daniel was big on selfies. After a while, they resorted to asking perfect strangers to take pictures of them, which Daniel wasn't shy about. Since photography wasn't the forte of either of them, half of the photographs would have to be dumped due to blurriness. Most pictures involved general horsing around, which Daniel was also big on, despite a lame ankle.

Daniel kept coaxing Isa near the edge, but she refused to get too close. "What's wrong? Are you scared of heights?"

"Yes, I am."

"Why?"

"I don't know why. I always have been, even as a little girl."

He took her into his arms. "Don't worry. I won't let you fall."

A shiver went through her body. No man had ever said anything like that to her, not even Nick. For a moment, she thought she might still be asleep at the inn, dreaming Daniel the way she had dreamed Dora.

"Come on," he said, looking down at her, releasing her waist, and taking her hand again. They trudged more steps. She should have been tired, but she felt so light.

At the top, they passed the roped-off area where a crew of what looked like professors and students were sifting through dirt at the site where the church would have been. They watched for a while. Then Daniel hurriedly dragged her away, "I know a great place away from the tourists. We can sit in the grass, gaze at the sea, and watch the boats."

Daniel led her to a grassy spot at the highest point. Isa leaned back against Daniel's chest while they feasted their eyes on the harbor and sea. However, they were more enthralled with each other than the view. Daniel asked, "Did you notice the guy with the beard looking at you?"

"No, I guess I was more interested in whether or not they were finding anything. I wasn't looking at anyone in particular," she said.

"He couldn't keep his eyes off you. But then, I don't blame him."

"Hmmm, I didn't notice."

"I hope my jealousy isn't showing," he said.

She laughed him off and relaxed further into his arms. His protection and the touch of jealousy merged into a relaxed feeling throughout her whole body, something one might feel while still lying on the table following a massage. Isa looked out over the calm waters and reflected on the last days of school, and all the comments and well wishes bestowed on her that day. They must have been prayers answered. At that moment, there was no doubt left in her mind about coming here, even with the ghost, maybe even because of the ghost, but primarily because of this strange guy, whoever he was, even if all she got with him was this one day.

They watched as the natural light faded and the city lights and streetlights came on. The sea was no longer azure blue but a well of vast darkness faintly lit by the full moon. They sat into the wee hours of the morning, talking like they had known each other for all of their lives.

"It is so..." At that moment, Daniel bent over and kissed her. "beautiful," she finished.

The sun was only thinking about peeking through when they made their descent. Time had been lost on them. Daniel wrapped one arm around her as they made their way down until they reached the elevator, which, this time, they boarded.

They crossed through Messana Square, captivated by the seven statues sitting in meditative poses atop poles. In the remaining darkness, they still bore their neon colors from the being's cores, sequentially emanating light against the indigo sky.

"They look as if they are conveying the secrets of the universe to each other while watching over this centuries-old harbor town," she said.

Daniel explained that they were indeed in conversation, hence the name *Conversation à Nice.*

"They look like Buddhas," Isa said.

"Many people say so."

"I think they are Buddhas watching over all who come to Nice. I feel their presence watching over me, watching over us."

"You may be right, Isa. I certainly feel watched over at this moment." He squeezed her tight against his body.

The rising sun brought the vendors setting up their wares in Old Town.

"Today, it will be antiques. Tomorrow, flowers." They walked through the almost vacant streets while the city was stretching and yawning, only waking up. They found an open-air café where the servers were unstacking tables and placing them along the walkway. One of the servers beckoned them to come in and motioned Daniel and Isa to one of the tables he had just finished setting up. A plate of croissants, obviously for the employees, sat on the table next to them. The waiter asked in French what they might like. Daniel responded in French. Isa said one of the few French words she knew, "Croissants." The waiter quickly grabbed the already filled plate and sat it before them.

"I love this country," she said.

Daniel laughed. "That's not how they do it in America, I take it."

"Hardly."

The waiter returned with a large pot of tea and some butter and jams.

"Are you sleepy? We didn't sleep at all," he said.

"No, surprisingly, I'm not. You?"

"No, not now, but we can save sleep for the train."

"Do you think Madame Claire will think anything because we didn't return?" she asked.

He looked at her smiling and burst into a hearty laugh. "No, this is France. And we are adults."

The city had started to stir as he drank the last of his tea and said, "We'll check out the vendors, but there is one thing I want to do first if that is okay?"

"What?"

He put some Euros on the table. "You'll see. Come with me." They stopped in front of a sign that read COIFFURE. "I meant to get this beard shaved off before summer but never got around to it. Might as well get it done professionally, along with a trim, don't you think?"

"Your hair and beard *are* a bit scraggly. I just thought it was your normal look."

"No, you'll see my normal look in about an hour."

Isa sat in a lounge area, sipping more tea while studying the history of Nice on her phone and occasionally eyeing the shirt-less man, who was getting a shampoo, through the opening of the salon area. Things were *indeed* different in France.

Daniel appeared in the waiting room looking like a new man, groomed to the hilt, unfortunately with a white outline dotted with freckles where the beard had once been. The same tender skin circled the back of his neck.

"Do you like the new me?"

"It will take me a bit to adjust," she replied.

They made their way through the vendors. Isa swirled around, holding an off-white Victorian-era dress against her body. "What do you think?"

Daniel responded by taking a video with his cell phone. "If you were on a Scottish beach under the moonlight with wild waves and rocks in the background, you might pass as a ghost— a beautiful ghost."

Daniel got the brilliant idea that they might make a small movie. He haggled the seller down on the price of the dress and presented it to her. Daniel was full of surprises. It was not until later that it dawned on Isa that he might have been asking her to come to Scotland. She dismissed it as silly—a fantasy. He was only living in the moment. Tomorrow he would probably ride out of her life on his bicycle.

Daniel picked up toy vehicles at one booth, examining them as a child might. Carved *Tintin* characters caught Isa's eye. She bought an old book, of course in French, for what reason she didn't know. It was only a couple of Euros. It felt good in her hands. After examining it further, she placed it in her backpack, along with the two others, *Pride and Prejudice* and *Somewhere in Time,* she had not bothered to remove since coming to France.

An elderly man at the adjacent booth greeted them, "*Bonjour.*" He directed them in under his canopy. A display of antique canes caught Daniel's interest.

"What do you think?" Daniel asked, picking one up.

Isa's heart jumped, seeing him resting on the ebony lacquered walking stick that bore a blue sapphire that matched his eyes. Daniel and the crowd melted into a haze as Isa's mind traveled back to her dream of the stranger. The resemblance hit her like that cosmic two-by-four she had experienced at the time of the accident. Daniel was not only the man in the dream but was now in the flesh. It was, as he said, crystal clear. Isa felt herself emerging back into the light from the tunnel she had momentarily disappeared into upon hearing her name. The voice became louder. It was Daniel. "Isa, Isa? Are you okay?"

She tried to smile. "Yes, I'm fine."

"You don't look fine. You look pale." He put his hands on her shoulders and looked into her eyes as if searching for signs of disease.

"No, really, I'm good," she stuttered. "I think the no sleep thing is just hitting me."

"You had me worried. I will ask the price. It will help support my ankle. I'm sorry to be so broken."

"What was that last thing you said?"

"I'm sorry to be so broken. I mean my ankle. I hate feeling broken on such a glorious day out with you. I don't want a twisted ankle to get in the way. The cane will undoubtedly help. Don't you think?"

She tried to put the dream out of her mind. "Yes, it will. You should get it. And it is a glorious day."

"I'm glad." He winked. His blue eyes sparkled. "Just let me settle up with this gentleman, and we'll find a place away from the hubbub if that's possible. Okay?"

"Okay," Isa responded.

They walked back along the ocean one last time and sat on some rocks against the shoreline. A small boy stood by a pool of water on the shore. Isa saw Daniel staring at him in a retrospective manner. She almost said a penny for your thoughts, but let it pass. The boy's shadow reflected in the water in the backdrop of the morning sunlight. The reflection struck her as something familiar. It came to her, another crystal-clear moment. Dora was a shadow of her former self. Isa said nothing to Daniel about her revelation. She didn't even know how it was possible. Intuitively, she perceived it.

They spent most of the day exploring Nice, only making their way back to the train station in time to catch the last train leaving. They slept, Isa's body curled into his, his head resting on hers.

12

When she and Daniel returned to the inn, Claire and Albert only glanced their way with a nod and bonjour. Albert's absorption in his newspaper and Claire's unconcerned look as she carried a basket of laundry to another room implied everything was normal. The mundane still went on in the background while fate made its forward strides.

Daniel gave her a lingering kiss and smiled before departing the doorway of room number eleven. With her back to the door, she took a deep breath and listened to his footsteps as they faded down the hallway. Nothing was said about tomorrow. She would always have the memory even if nothing more happened, or so she told herself.

It was late, and she should have been exhausted, but she lay in bed with the last two days' events on her mind—two days that seemed more like one long day that went by incredibly fast. She had met a man who was easy to talk to and be with. And then there was the dream, possibly a precognition of this man, to come into her life, not someone from the past. Everything thus far about this trip had been like stepping into a parallel universe. She remembered talking to Josh about their possible existence, about how some scientists were concluding parallel universes were real.

Eventually, the thoughts of all of the bizarre things that had happened to her since arriving in France, in particular meeting Daniel, ceased; her eyes closed, and sleep took over.

When Isa *did* wake, she remembered no dreams. Sunlight was coming through the window. To her delight, she had slept like a log. Better yet, there were no ghosts during the night; if there were, they didn't disturb her sleep. "Thank you, Dora," she said out loud.

Not even bothering to look at the time, she hopped into the shower, washed and towel dried her hair. She took extra care in applying her make-up, not that she wore much. She donned her floral dress, the one she had worn to see Madame Girard. Checking herself in the mirror, she hesitated before putting on her glasses. Could she get by without them? The fact that she wore glasses didn't seem to faze Daniel. Would he like her better without them? Contact lenses had always been out for her. The thought of something foreign touching her pupils was one of her fears, like heights. She wavered a bit before placing them in the case in her backpack.

She felt like a teenager. Would he be waiting for her downstairs? There was no guarantee. She kept telling herself it was okay if a day and a half were all she was to have with him, but who was she kidding? She would be heartbroken if he checked out without at least saying goodbye. Maybe this kind of thing happened all the time in France. If *one* Daniel were to come along, then another one might. Once again, who was she kidding? Daniel was unique. Then she thought about the stranger in the dream and how he had not returned to Dora.

She had never before connected with a man like she had with him, not Josh and definitely not Nick. Quit stalling, she told herself as she stood in front of the mirror. She slipped on her sandals and almost ran down the dented stairwell, smelling the allure of the pastries as she did.

The common room was empty—no Daniel, no Claire, no Albert. She looked at her phone. It was only nine. She could smell the croissants in the kitchen. She wondered if she should knock on the kitchen door, but she heard no sounds. Could Daniel still be sleeping?

Ten minutes passed before a cheerful Madame Claire entered. "Isa, you're up. Sorry, I was out back in the garden. What will it be this morning? Coffee, tea?"

"Either is fine."

"I see. Like most Americans, you are not addicted to your coffee."

"No, I'm just an occasional coffee drinker."

"A moment," she said.

Claire returned with a tray holding a teapot, teacup, and saucer, along with a selection of teabags and a basket of croissants. "Your young man left his box of teabags behind. I put a couple on the tray for you."

"Left them behind?" Isa felt her jaw drop.

"*Oui.*" A worried and sympathetic expression covered Madame Claire's face. "He left to catch the first train out this morning. It left at 5:30 a.m. You didn't know?"

All Isa could do was stare down at the one tea bag that stood apart, the one in which the tea leaves were in a translucent pyramid-shaped pouch. If only someone could read them for her.

"Madame Claire, I'm sorry. I don't think I'm so hungry this morning." Isa got up, doing her best to put on a brave face as she made her way to the staircase. As soon as her back was turned and her sandal had touched the first step, she felt the wetness running down her cheeks. She sensed Madame Claire's pitying stare on her backside as she ascended the stairs.

She jiggled the key in her shaky hand, finally getting the door to open after several attempts. She entered, closing it behind her, and stood there. The emotions had been so different last night when she stood in the same spot after Daniel had kissed her goodnight. She tried to think logically, reminding herself she wouldn't do this. What was the line from *Casablanca*? "We will always have Paris." One day, when she was old and gray, she would tell whoever was listening, "I met a man. We had Nice." Then she would show the pictures as proof.

Everything about this trip, thus far, had been so unusual and splendid at the same time. Was it all downhill from here?

She eyed her journal on the table. She sat on the edge of the bed and wrote, releasing her emotions through the pen. No one would ever read it. But then again, maybe when she was an old woman, she would pick it up, read it, and laugh, taking only the good memories into her heart. With that thought, she closed the journal, put it back on her nightstand, got up, and brushed the creases from her dress. She went into the toilet and reapplied her makeup before grabbing her backpack, from which she retrieved her glasses, before bounding down the stairs to catch the next train to Paris. While visiting Orsay, she would forget about ghosts, Daniel, the inn, and her past, if only for a day. She would explore the artists from 1848 to 1914, a time period absent of Dora and Adrien or her and Daniel.

WITH HER FOREHEAD BENT AGAINST THE TRAIN WINDOW, SHE watched the countryside glide past like fresh dabs of paint on a canvas. The whole landscape resembled an impressionistic painting with ever-changing brushstrokes.

It was one o'clock by the time she made it to Musée d'Orsay. She was determined not to starve herself because of love. Love? Was she in love? No, she couldn't fall in love in a matter of two days. She hardly knew Daniel. Her stomach growled. "Stomach, you win over love," she whispered. Taking only a fanny pack out, she surrendered her backpack at the museum entrance and walked upstairs to the café.

She stopped at the clock, mesmerized by it. Time. Most things were controlled by it, worldly things, that is. She looked out over the Seine and at the architecture, the scene photographs didn't do justice to, before turning the corner to the café.

"Jasmine tea, please," Isa said to the young waiter.

"American," he stated. "I am saving up money to travel there."

"Aw," Isa said, "I sold everything I owned to travel *here*."

His eyes grew big. "I hope you love it then."

"What is not to love?" she asked.

"And where in America, if I may request? I hope you don't mind. I am practicing my English."

"I am thrilled you are practicing your English. Say ask instead of request. But your English is good."

He smiled.

"I'm glad your menu has English subtitles. My French is practically nonexistent. I will take the quiche and salad. I'm from Kentucky."

"*Oui*, whiskey, horses, and fried chicken."

"You have certainly done your homework."

He smiled. "I am Pierre." If you need anything, let me know.

Isa watched as he chatted up a table of young girls after putting her order in. She had already studied the history of the museum. No need to bury herself in a brochure or her phone. She knew the museum had been the site of a former palace. There were so many palaces in France. How many did royalty need? Obviously, too many since a rebellion ensued. It was turned into a hotel and train station, thus the famous clock. The trains would have to run on time after all. There were ramps and lifts for luggage, elevators for passengers, and sixteen underground rail tracks. But the rails were too short when faster, longer trains came along. It was about to be torn down in the seventies but was saved to house France's nineteenth-century painters.

Pierre returned with her tea and entree. "Might I recommend the chocolate cake if you have room for dessert later? You must save room because it is superb."

"Actually, Pierre, I could use some chocolate today."

Isa lingered on the balcony, snapping shots of the Seine and watching as couples took selfies against the backdrop before making her way through the museum, doing her best to take every aspect in.

On the train back to the inn, the thought occurred to her that she should write a book about her French experiences. Who said a librarian couldn't write a book? Anonymous, perhaps a pen name?

It would start about her thirty-six-hour affair with Daniel—not platonic, but about how Daniel had turned her into a brazen woman, the way the stranger turned Dora into one. Okay, hardly brazen. Maybe if she had been, Daniel might not have departed so abruptly. By the end of the summer, though, she would truly learn how to be French. She would never be allowed to sit foot again in an American school system.

IT WAS LATE WHEN ISA RETURNED TO THE INN. SHE ENTERED THE common room, seeing Madame Claire in her robe. "Mademoiselle Isa, I waited for you." She handed Isa a note addressed to her. "When I cleaned your room, I found it under the rug against the door slot. I hope what it says will make you happy again."

Isa opened the note and read.

Isa,

I got a call in the middle of the night from my parents. My grandfather had a heart attack and is intensive care. Both Kate and I got the first train out. As much as I wanted to tell you in person why I had to leave so suddenly, I didn't want to wake you. I don't know what will happen with my grandfather. My mum said we should come right away in case we need to say our goodbyes. I will return to the inn as soon as I can. Please, please do not check out before I get there.

xoxo,
Daniel

She closed it and took both of Madame Claire's hands into her own. "*Merci,* Madame Claire. *Oui,* it makes me both happy and sad. Daniel had to leave because his grandfather had a heart attack. He said he would return as soon as possible."

"*Oui,* it is sad about his grandfather. But I knew he was not the kind of man who would just up and leave without saying goodbye. He and his sister have been coming here for years."

"Thank you for waiting up to give me this. It was kind of you. I can sleep well now. Good night, Madame Claire."

"Good night, child."

13

A week passed. It was on a Sunday when Isa, upon entering the common room, beheld Daniel's broad smile.

"Your grandfather?" she asked, taking his outstretched hand.

"He's out of the woods, at least for now. Moved in with our parents. I would have been back sooner, but there were a lot of arrangements to make."

He pulled out the chair for her, leaning over and kissing her on the cheek. He looked over at his sister. "Isa, this is my sister, Kate."

"Kate, hi. I'm glad to meet you." Isa extended her hand.

"Likewise. Daniel told me about the outing you had. I'm impressed by a woman who could make him shave off that awful beard. Our mother was even more amazed when she saw him," Kate said.

Daniel gave Isa a wink.

"Oh, it was not my idea."

"Well, whatever possessed him to do so, our family is grateful."

"You slept in. We have been waiting for you. In ten more minutes, I was going to knock on your door. No, burst it down."

Claire appeared at their table. *"Bonjour,* Mademoiselle Isa! Your usual?"

"Bonjour! Oui s'il vous plait," Isa said like a schoolgirl reciting French before a teacher. Claire disappeared back into the kitchen.

"Daniel has also told me about your ghostly encounter," Kate said. Isa saw Albert glancing over the top of his newspaper upon hearing this comment. He leaned in a little closer but said nothing.

"This has more than piqued my professional interest," Kate added.

"Professional? Daniel told me you were a psychologist. Are psychologists interested in ghosts?"

"The paranormal interests me. As a psychologist, I try to find natural explanations for otherworldly sightings. In many cases, there are perfectly rational reasons a person feels they've seen a ghost. It is the cases I can't explain that intrigue me."

"Kate is not your normal Scot," Daniel said, laughing.

"Do you think my situation can be explained?"

"Most can," Kate said. She took a sip of tea. Isa noticed she drank her brother's brand.

"I do hope you're right."

"I hope you don't mind that I shared this with Kate," Daniel said. "I probably should have asked you first."

"No, that's okay. You said you wanted to help. And twins share everything, don't they?"

"No, Isa, not everything," Daniel said most firmly.

Kate rolled her eyes, and Albert tried to conceal a laugh behind his newspaper. Claire entered the room, setting out a fresh pot of steaming tea, a teacup, and another plate of croissants.

After Claire entered the kitchen, Isa asked, "So, Kate, do you believe I may have actually seen a ghost?"

"Isa, I don't believe or disbelieve. The only way to get to the bottom of this is to remain impartial. You can understand that, can't you?"

"Yes," Isa said with some hesitation, glancing over at Daniel as she said it.

"The thing is," Isa continued, "that right now I almost want to forget it and pretend it never happened." Isa heard a slight murmur from Albert. Isa knew it wasn't from something he read in the paper. She doubted he was even reading the newspaper.

Daniel, being his usual outgoing self, said, "Okay, Albert. Quit hiding behind the paper. Pull up a chair and tell us what you know."

Isa had to admit she was attracted to Daniel's boldness. There was also his sense of humor, wavy chestnut-red hair, and blue eyes. She had to rule out his legs on the attraction bit. She usually didn't go for extroverts, but he had his extroversion under control. Some people were over-the-top. She immediately thought of Denise, which led to a thought of Josh—only a brief one.

Albert remained where he was but laid down his newspaper. He looked at the three of them most solemnly, *"Poursuivre ce,* how do you say?"

Claire peaked around the corner. "Pursue it." Albert raised his newspaper once again after saying his piece.

Daniel looked at Isa and Kate. "Well, there you have it. We must investigate."

"What do you want to pursue?" Claire asked.

"More history of the inn, dear," Albert said, glancing over his newspaper.

Both Isa and Claire gave Albert a puzzled look. He waved it off as Claire returned to the kitchen. "Let's not say anything just yet. My wife has always been obsessed with the ghost. Hard evidence is what we need," he said in a whisper.

"Isa, you will do this, won't you?" Kate asked. "Please don't be insulted in any way by what I said. There always has to be a skeptic in these situations."

"Ah, I see a paper in this. Isn't that what you are thinking, Kate?" Daniel said.

"Who knows?" she said. "Would you mind if I wrote something and submitted it to a peer-reviewed journal, Isa?"

"I guess not. You wouldn't use my real name, would you?"

"No, I wouldn't have to."

"I guess it would be okay," Isa said.

Daniel nudged Isa. "Don't worry. She is not as skeptical as she lets on. All Scots believe in ghosts at heart." Kate gave her brother a disapproving look which he shrugged off.

Even though Isa felt a bit coerced, now, more than ever, she wanted to proceed. A whole support group was rallying behind her.

"I concede to your wishes. I'm outnumbered, it seems. But I don't want to be a guinea pig."

"Of course not!" Kate said. "It will all be aboveboard."

"Don't believe her, Isa. Kate may want to put you in a cage for a while and watch you run mazes, but don't worry, I will be your most ardent protector," Daniel said.

Albert put down his newspaper and pulled his chair over to their table. "How do we begin?"

"Oh, now you want in on this?" Daniel laughed.

"It could mean more business."

So everyone had an angle, Isa thought. Kate wanted to be published in a journal, Albert wanted to attract business to the inn via a ghost, Isa wanted some understanding of what was happening, and Daniel, well, maybe he wanted to be a part of her life—she hoped.

"I think the first thing we must do is to gain another audience with Madame Girard," Kate said.

"You want to see Madame Girard again?" Claire asked, coming from the kitchen. "I will give her a call. Albert, get my bike for Isa. She is the only one without one."

"Isa, you look different?" Daniel paused. "You're not wearing your glasses. Won't you need them? You look beautiful with or without them."

14

$\mathscr{T}$he presence of Albert, Kate, and Daniel on the second visit made all the difference in giving Isa's nerves a boost when she knocked on Madame Girard's door. While Isa thought their congregation of four might appear frightful, only Gromit looked a little ruffled at their appearance.

"I have been expecting you," Madame Girard said as she opened the door wide, revealing the aroma of freshly baked pastries and strong coffee.

Albert introduced Kate and Daniel. Madame Girard quickly glanced over them, asking if Earl Grey would be okay. "Albert, I also made espresso. I know it is your favorite."

She bade them all have seats and asked Albert how the inn business was going. Albert spoke in French, *"Bien Erma, le business serait meilleur si un fantôme, en particulier, n'effayait pas les gens."*

Although Isa didn't understand what was said, she picked up on the fact that Albert and Madame Girard were on more familiar terms than she had initially thought; she knew his drink preference.

Daniel whispered the translation into Isa's ear, "He said business would be better if a particular ghost didn't scare people away."

Madam Girard responded abruptly, "Oh, poppycock, Albert. I told you about the ghost before you purchased the inn. And you thought it was just that: poppycock."

Albert grunted, and Madame Girard went off to the kitchen to get what she had prepared. Isa offered to help, but Madame Girard wouldn't hear of it. "You're guests."

In her wake, Albert mumbled, "Disconcerting woman if ever there was one."

What was going on between those two? Madame Girard was the perfect hostess.

She returned with small cakes, tea, and the espresso for Albert, all resting on a large platter that Daniel quickly relieved her of, setting it on the table. Gromit had gotten accustomed to the group and lay peacefully at Madame Girard's feet. His ears only perked up when Madame Girard said, "Now about the ghost."

Everyone drew in closer, anticipating Madame Girard would solve the mystery once and for all. Then life would resume its ordinary routine for everyone but Isa. Life would never be normal again. How could it be after experiencing this country and the man sitting next to her? She could never go back to ordinary.

"There were many incidents at the inn before you took it over, Albert," Madame Girard began.

"And you could have told me," he said.

The ghost, or Madame Girard's failure to warn Albert fully about the spirit, was a contention between them, but Isa sensed it went deeper.

"I did, Albert, and what did you do? You laughed it off and said nonsense," she countered back with one of those I told you so glares. Albert did his usual grunt.

"Please, go on with the story," Kate said.

"Well, before areas of the inn were made into proper rooms, there was a large room upstairs. It was a library. Room number eleven now," she said.

"That's the room I'm in," Isa said excitedly.

"Yes, I think that would stand to reason, dear. Well, that was said to be Dorcel's favorite room. She would lock herself up there for hours during her last days."

"Do you know why?" Daniel asked.

"As I said, it used to be a library," Madame Girard said as if the answer were obvious. "She loved to read, and that room had the best view of the garden. The bookshelves were still there when my husband and I took over the inn. We tore them out to make the room bigger for guests with large families. But when we did, we found something." She paused. Madame Girard had a flair for storytelling, and part of Isa was hoping that was all it was, but with the mention of the library and it being in her dream, she thought not.

"Okay, Erma, enough with the suspense. What did you find?" retorted Albert.

She gave him a condescending look before continuing, "Here, Albert, have some more espresso, not that you need any more caffeine." She poured. He ignored. She went on after her dramatic pause and leaned in closer the way someone relating a ghost story around a campfire might. "We found letters."

"Letters?" Kate asked.

"Yes, letters, correspondence she didn't know where to send, or for that matter, didn't even know who to send them to. You also might call it a diary or journal of sorts." The thought of Dora keeping a journal sent shivers up Isa's spine. She reached for Daniel's hand.

"Were they to a man, a woman, a relative?" Kate asked.

"Oh, most assuredly a man."

"What were they about?" Daniel asked.

"They were about her broken world, her philosophy, her

questions about life, and people she met at the inn and what they were like. There was this one woman in particular that she didn't get along with at all." Madame Girard looked over at Albert. "She poured out all her hostility toward her in the letters as if whomever she intended to send them to could fix it. She casually mentioned affairs she had had, like they meant nothing to her. She also wrote about her husband, Adrien, and his accident."

"Esther," Isa whispered under her breath.

"Isa, did you say something?" Daniel asked.

"I'm sorry. It's just the woman she didn't like, her name was Esther, or I think it was," Isa said.

"It was," Madam Girard exclaimed.

"How could you know that?" Kate asked. It was apparent her skepticism had been somewhat dented.

"I just know." Instead of backing away, which might be a typical response, Daniel squeezed Isa's hand tighter.

"And she talked about her son, Jean," Madame Girard continued.

Isa felt Daniel's hand tense. At this point, Daniel and Kate gave each other a look, not a look Isa could classify, just a glance, something she surmised happened often among twins.

"You have these letters?" Isa asked, knowing they would be in French, but she had excellent translators at her disposal, people who were as interested in what the letters said as she was.

"No, I'm afraid not. They were in an old binder, the title of which had completely worn away, and most of the pages were missing. The letters were barely legible but still readable. I had set them aside, meaning to copy them, but they and the binder must have gotten lost in the move. You know how moving can be. I was heartbroken over it when I realized they were missing. You know, one of those things you intend to do, but we were so busy with the move. What I regret is that I didn't read them all. I had a few set aside in a separate pile. Even they disappeared. Anyway, I thought it most strange that both piles went missing."

"You said she was having affairs. Do you think this was a lover that she was writing to?" Kate asked.

"I think this man was more than a lover. I think he was the love of her life. It was much more than physical."

"But she didn't mention his name in the letters?" Daniel asked.

"She didn't know his name."

After being silent for a while, Albert asked, "How could she be in love and not even know his name?"

"Albert, there is a lot you don't know about women and affairs of the heart." Albert rolled his eyes. Isa thought the strife between Madame Girard and Albert was mutual.

"Do you know where Adrien and Dorcel are buried?" Daniel asked.

"Adrien and Jean are buried in the cemetery of the old church in the center of town, but the headstones have worn down. Oh, you can still make out the names. However, if you didn't know who you were looking for, you wouldn't know it was their graves. Jean is buried along with his wife and his descendants. Adrien's grave is off a bit, buried alongside his parents."

"I saw his grave. I accidentally found myself walking on the church property. I didn't see Dora's. I mean Dorcel's."

"Oh, you won't find a grave for her."

"Why not?" Isa asked.

"Well, if she did indeed jump off the cliffs, which was the story handed down, it would be ruled a suicide. Suicides are not buried on church grounds. Since the inn has remained in the same family all these years, there may have been some doubt. King Louis XIV of France issued a criminal ordinance in 1670. It stated a person who had committed suicide was to be dragged through the streets facedown and then hung up to show, after which the body would have been thrown on the garbage heap. All of the person's property was confiscated. Perhaps the son had the body whisked away and buried in secret. I'm sure Jean must have buried her somewhere, but the actual site was never recorded. We will never know."

They looked at each other in surprise. Madame Girard sat with a satisfied look on her face, rather pleased in having captivated her audience.

"More tea and cake, anyone?" she asked as if she had just recited lines in a play, and now it was the curtain call. Isa remembered Madame Girard's son was in the theater. The talent must have come from his mother. However, that fact did not cause Isa to doubt the story. There were the letters, although hardly proof since they were no more. No one seemed to doubt Madame Girard. Perhaps her story was exaggerated, as was everything in the theater. But there were her dreams, the dreams that only she knew about. There was a part of Isa that wanted to tell everyone at this point, but she didn't know how to proceed. This whole thing was becoming too bizarre. It would have been too cumbersome to add her dreams into the mix at this point, but she wanted to explain how she knew about Esther to Daniel. That would mean telling him about the dreams. If she told him, would he run away?

Madame Girard brought out the book that she had previously let Isa peruse. Daniel and Kate looked it over, abruptly stopping with Jean's picture. Daniel's eyes were transfixed to the sketch, as were Kate's, but Kate's eyes were moving back and forth from the image to Daniel. Kate was studying Daniel's reaction to the picture more than anything else. His captivation with the photocopy told Isa that something was amiss, an understatement, considering all that had transpired thus far.

Everyone said their goodbyes and *au revoirs*. Each thanked Madame Girard profusely, all except Albert. To their shock, Albert robotically kissed both cheeks of Madame Girard, an entirely normal French custom but somehow unexpected between the two of them, and said in a surprisingly cordial manner, "Claire said when you have the time away from your flowers, Erma, won't you please honor your sister-in-law with a visit?"

"Albert, you know I'm not much for coming back to the inn. Tell her she needs to break away from it now and then. We need to catch up in person, not over the phone."

"Oui, je suis d'accord," Albert said.

Daniel whispered in Isa's ear. "He agrees."

Kate, Daniel, and Isa looked at each other, somewhat stunned, but at this point, they had become used to surprises.

They stopped by the cemetery. Isa led them right to Adrien's grave. Madame Girard was right. All found it rather odd that Adrien's gravesite was shorter than most, not much bigger than one would find the grave of an infant. They added the fact to their list of mysteries.

As they were walking away, they saw an old priest walking from the other end of the cemetery.

"Monsignor Durand, *bonjour*," Albert said.

Isa thought if possessed, she may need his services but said nothing. They got on their bicycles and headed back toward the inn.

THAT NIGHT KATE, DANIEL, AND ISA ATE WITH CLAIRE AND Albert in the kitchen. After all that had happened, they had a common bond and acted more like an extended family than people who had only met weeks ago. So much had happened in such a short period. Isa had imagined nothing like this when planning her trip.

Albert uncorked the wine and poured. "Claire, your sister-in-law requests the honor of a visit."

"Albert, no one knows better than her how busy this place keeps me. Why can't she come here?"

Busy? To Isa's knowledge, she, Daniel, and Kate were the only ones staying at the inn. Was she referring to her garden work or the baking, perhaps?

"You know she won't set foot in this place anymore. For the same reason you won't leave," Albert huffed.

Isa wanted to know what Albert meant but feared she might be intruding to ask.

Daniel held no such qualms. "What would that reason be?"

"Erma, even though she would never admit it, is interested in the ghost, but at the same time fears it, while Claire is afraid if she were to leave, she might miss an opportunity of seeing it," Albert said.

Daniel reached for Isa's hand under the table and gave her a look that said it was okay. She looked at Albert, who gave her a nod.

"I've seen the ghost."

They stopped eating, their forks mid-air, all eyes on Isa, especially Claire's.

"It was on the first night the cyclists came. I heard something in my room. At first, I thought it might be one of the cyclists coming into my room by mistake, but my door was locked. I saw a woman dressed in old garments poking the fire. Of course, there was no fire. It was where the fire would have been. Her poker went right through the now closed-up grate. She turned and looked at me. She appeared to be as scared at seeing me as I was at seeing her. Then her figure evaporated into the air.

"I must have sat upright in bed for an hour, afraid to go to sleep. All was so quiet—like you said, Madame Claire." Isa looked at Claire. "All the bicyclists were sound asleep, dead to the world."

"You saw her face?" Claire asked.

"Yes, and she looked like me."

"I knew it."

"I now know why you stared at me like you did when I arrived."

Claire's smile was one of both relief and affirmation.

Daniel's grip on Isa's hand remained firm while using his other hand to raise his wine glass. "Here's to solving our mystery."

"To solving the mystery," was repeated by all as they clanked glasses.

"When I saw Dora—that is what I call her—I was scared at first. I had never seen a ghost before. I can't say for certain, but I think if I were to see her again, I wouldn't be so frightened. I don't understand Madame Girard's fear of her. She doesn't seem the type to be frightened of anything," Isa said.

"No, she isn't," Claire said, looking over at Albert as if he had opened more cans of worms today with a visit to his sister-in-law than those of the paranormal nature. "She has just left the inn behind, and as you probably gathered today, she and my husband have this antagonism toward each other. Have them in a room together for only fifteen minutes, and they are snapping at each other. It's just their nature. I was the most surprised today when he offered to take you there. They had an unhappy marriage in a past life and can't let it go. Oh, and I had my suspicions it must be something more than the history of this inn. Or maybe it's jealousy," she said, laughing. "Jealousy that Erma married my brother this time around instead of him. Albert and Erma were lovers when I met him."

Daniel, Kate, and Isa looked at each other in surprise.

"Claire, sometimes you are just as bad as Erma," Albert said. "Don't you know it was all over with Erma when I met you?" Albert leaned over and kissed his wife.

Daniel winked at Isa.

"You believe in past lives?" Kate asked.

"As much as I believe in ghosts. Go talk to the priest at the church," Claire said with a knowing look as if a confession or talk would solve everything.

"Why?" they chorused.

"If you want to shed some light on your mystery, just do it," she said.

"We saw the priest today from a distance. Monsignor Durand," Isa said.

"No," Claire said. "Not Monsignor Durand. There is a younger one. Father Foley is who you want to talk to—him and only him. No, you mustn't talk to Monsignor Durand about such matters."

Daniel, Kate, and Isa looked at each other as if they were given their next clue in what seemed like a Nancy Drew or Hardy Boys mystery. Satisfied, they finished their dinner with no more talk of ghosts.

15

_I_t was a long dinner, even by French standards. Leaving the ghost behind, Daniel and Isa talked about their excursion to Nice. Kate spoke about her practice and a young man she met during her bicycling jaunt. They were planning that he should come up to Scotland for some cycling. Daniel, a typical brother, twin or not, was prying her with questions about her love interest. Isa listened to the conversation, feeling at home. Dora's ghost had bonded the five of them.

Dishes were washed and counters wiped down. Kate, along with Albert and Claire, retired for the night. Daniel and Isa walked out to the garden and sat on a bench, where they kissed like teenagers. Coming up for air, he said, "I thought that dinner was never going to end."

The passion almost took Isa's mind off of the day's events. At the same time, it brought her back to what had transpired. "Daniel, I need to tell you something, and after I do, you may not want to kiss me again or even see me again. You may totally write me off. And Kate may have me committed to a psych ward."

Undisturbed by her announcement, he said, "Kate doesn't do

that. It's not her job. She might recommend you to someone else. She never handles straitjackets herself." He remained straight-faced for a minute, then broke out laughing.

"Daniel, you are not at all taking me seriously."

"Yes, Isa, I am. I don't think you could say anything that would make me want to stop kissing you, or more for that matter."

Isa blushed. If Daniel blushed, his complexion hid it. But somehow, she thought Daniel had quit blushing at around ten years of age.

"I take you very seriously. In fact, I'm getting quite serious about you."

"Daniel, I feel the same." She paused. "But let me tell you this, and if you don't get up and walk away, then maybe we can explore this relationship we've started."

"I promise you I won't walk away but shoot. That's Scottish for continue with your story."

"I think the phrase came from America, but here goes." She stuttered, not knowing where to start. "Do you believe in dreams?"

"Believe in them? Like my dream of us further exploring this relationship? Yes, definitely. Or, as in the fantasies I experience during sleep, things I usually can't remember? Yes, to that too."

"Since I've been at the inn, I had three incredible dreams before I saw the ghost."

"I'm listening?"

"They were about everything that Madame Girard told us and more. But I didn't know about the suicide."

"Isa, are you saying that you saw this stuff in your dreams—some type of clairvoyance?"

"No, more like it was me as Dora experiencing them."

"Dora? Yes, you said that's what you called her earlier."

"Dorcel may be her proper name."

Isa proceeded to tell Daniel what she had remembered in her dreams.

Daniel became somber, and his face turned ashen.

"What's wrong?"

"Nothing. Really. Continue," he said.

"Are you sure?" she asked.

"Yes, please?"

"Well, part of the dream was like something from a science fiction show. Or maybe the dream was metaphoric. Something catastrophic happened in Dora's world. Like a chunk had fallen away. Or maybe there was a big hole or something like that. Whatever had happened, it had happened in previous generations, or I think it did. I'm not sure. Whatever it was, it had futuristic overtones. I don't know what to make of it. I can't remember that part clearly. I just know this thing about an edge kept coming up. It's all so confusing."

"Dreams are like that. They jump around. It may not even be literal, only symbolic. That's where Kate might come in. She could help."

Isa nodded and continued as she had to get it all out before he walked away. "And the lady who Dora didn't like, her name was Esther. I remember that part of the dream, specifically."

"Yes, you said the name Esther at Madame Girard's."

"I also knew about the affairs. Madame Girard was right. Dora didn't love the men. It was more of a comfort thing. Sometimes it was a means to an end. The men helped her in various ways with the inn's running."

"Are you saying she was a prostitute?"

"No, I don't see it that way, but then I was experiencing myself as her. She didn't want to cheat on Adrien. She didn't even have affairs at first. Adrien grew to resent her. He was bedridden most of the time. Besides having a young child, she had to be Adrien's nurse and run the inn. She had a real business head. She did everything well, too well. I got the impression he

THE INNKEEPER ON THE EDGE OF PARIS

was bitter about his condition and jealous at the same time. It drove him to criticism and sarcasm." Isa paused. "In general, he was an ass to her. Or maybe I'm overanalyzing. Adding to the parts of the dream I remember."

"Well, Isa, you have to feel somewhat sorry for him."

"Don't get me wrong, Daniel, I do, and she did as well."

"You sound like you are one and the same."

"I don't know. It seemed that way." She paused. "And Daniel?"

"Yes?"

"Do you think I might be possessed?"

He laughed and kissed her forehead, "No, I don't think you are possessed."

"Maybe that is why Madame Claire wanted us to talk to the priest. She didn't say it, but maybe she thinks I am. I mean, how could I know all this stuff? Why did I dream it, and why did I see the ghost?"

"I don't know, but as you can see, I'm still here. I'm not running away from you. We will get to the bottom of this. The explanation may not even be logical, but you are not possessed. But you *have* possessed me."

"Hmm, yes, you're still here, but what about her looking like me? When she turned to look at me, she had my face, my eyes."

"It means you both have the most beautiful eyes in the world. I could lose myself in your eyes."

Upon hearing that, she wanted to leave all the ghost stuff and the mystery behind and climb into bed with Daniel. She knew he felt it too. He took her hand. He moved his stare from her to the ground, making her doubt what she had just thought.

"See, you *are* thinking of walking away."

"No, Isa, not at all. "He sighed and looked away from the ground back into her eyes. "A moment ago, you asked me what was wrong. You see, something happened at Madame Girard's for me too. It's as if whatever this thing is, it's consuming both you and me."

"It was the picture, wasn't it?"

"How did you know?"

"I don't think the look on your face and Kate's escaped anyone. I saw how you lingered over the picture and how you and Kate looked at each other afterward."

"There was a reason for that. You see," he said with a bit of hesitation. "Granted, it is only a sketch and an old one, but he looks just like my Ian. Kate saw it too."

"Your Ian?"

"Yes, Isa, I have a son, and as surprising as it may seem, his name is Ian, the Scottish version of John. And Jean is the French version. Now we'll see who walks away."

She laughed.

"Why are you laughing?"

"I'm laughing because I'm relieved that I'm not the only one this thing, whatever it is, is happening to. And I'm laughing because if you think about it, this whole thing is incredible, like something out of a Stephen King novel."

With that, Daniel started laughing hysterically. They both did. He pulled her up from the bench, and they twirled around in each other's arms until they could laugh no more.

She stopped mid-twirl. "Maybe I shouldn't be laughing. You have a son? You told me you weren't married."

"No, not married."

"Divorced?"

"No, out of wedlock, but he is a big part of my life."

"I would be disappointed if it weren't so," she said.

After he had kissed her again, she said, "There is more since we are baring our souls."

"What more could there be?"

"Brace yourself." Isa continued, "I *was* married. His name was, well still is, Nick."

"Was—I'm glad. I feel sorry for Nick. If he let you go, he must be a loser. Please tell me he is not a paraplegic."

"No, not at all. A bit of a couch potato and a bar hopper, well, a lot of a bar hopper, but not paraplegic."

"How fresh is this breakup? Is that why you came to France?"

"Divorced for three years now and no children. Nick didn't want them. I did. And I think I came to France to find you."

He smiled.

"Have you ever been married? I mean to someone other than Ian's mom?"

"No, Isa. I'm not married. Never have been. We have joint custody."

"So, how did Ian come into the picture? Not that I'm naïve and think you must be married to have a child."

"He came into the picture by me being young and foolish and not using contraception."

"Oh, I see." Isa was silent for a moment.

"Do you want to see a picture of him?"

"Yes, of course, I do."

"Do you want to see a picture of Nick?"

"I guess if you want to show me."

"I was kidding. Seriously, do you think I carry a picture of my ex around? I think some of your humor is rubbing off on me."

He grinned. Daniel got out his wallet and removed a small picture. "This is him in his football uniform. He loves football. I believe you Americans refer to it as soccer."

"I can see some of you in him."

"Yes, the red hair, but he looks like his mother in the face."

"How old is he?"

"He'll be eleven this Saturday."

"And his mother?"

"How old is she?"

"No, silly. What is your relationship with her?"

"Our relationship is good. We were both young when it happened. Getting married was not an option. It would have been a mistake. I see her when I pick Ian up for visitation. And we both go to parent-teacher conferences together. Besides soccer, he loves history. Takes that after me, of course. Math is a different story. Stephanie, his mother, is married now. She helps her husband in his accounting firm. Ian has a great stepfather. Gets along fine with him too."

"And you and Ian?"

"We hit it off well. Ian's a smart, well-adjusted lad. But I guess I'm prejudiced. I have him all summer since I'm off, except for the two weeks I make the bicycle trip. I'm hoping one day Ian will join me. I'll be leaving for his birthday soon."

"So this, what would normally be your cycling vacation, you're spending with me?"

There was an awkward silence before Daniel spit out, "Would you like to go to Scotland? That is, to meet Ian and go to his party?"

"Hmm, I don't know."

"Does it bother you that I have a son? Or am I rushing things?" Daniel asked a bit dejectedly.

"No, not at all. It's just, well, there is so much, isn't there? The next thing might astonish you or scare you. I don't know which."

"And the next thing is?" Daniel asked.

"I know the man who Dora was writing to."

"You know his name?"

"No, I don't know his name, but he is you."

"Me!" Daniel gasped.

"You still don't think I'm posses…?"

"No!" he said most adamantly before she could even finish the sentence.

"He looked like you in the dream. I didn't see it at first. But he had a cane. Then, in Nice, you bought a cane that looked like the one in my dream. I saw the two of you standing there—interchangeable."

Daniel started laughing again, outrageously.

Isa slapped his shoulder in frustration, "Do you think I'm making this up?"

He grabbed both of her hands in his, "No, Isa, No, but I am beginning to believe that we might all be in your dream, or maybe you are in mine. If you are in mine, and if it means I would be without you, I don't want to wake up."

He hugged her and looked into her eyes, "You promise there is no more."

"No, nothing of any significance that I can think of."

"Isa, I hope you don't think, but…"

"My room?"

"I was hoping you would say that. Mine is a mess."

While holding hands and walking up the staircase, Daniel said, "You haven't given me your answer about Scotland?"

"I'll let you know in the morning," she said.

"Oh, then I had better be good." He laughed.

16

*A*fter one more time making love, Daniel donned his pants, carrying his shirt and shoes back to his room to take a shower. Isa listened as he crept barefoot on the creaky floorboards.

By the time Isa made it down the stairs, dressed in khaki capris and a tight blue top, the color of Daniel's eyes, the pot of tea and croissants were on their usual table.

"Enfin," came the voice of Madame Claire from the kitchen doorway.

"Bonjour," Albert said with a wink, raising his head above his newspaper.

"Bonjour," Isa responded.

"What did Claire say?"

"Enfin? It means finally. I don't think she is referring to your late arrival. You two know these walls are paper thin, don't you?" Kate said.

Albert lowered his newspaper long enough to say, "I will put isolation on the list of improvements."

"Isolation?" Isa asked.

"Insulation," Daniel said as he came bounding down the stairs. "Is the tea on?" he asked in an exuberant voice.

"You're late for the tea party, aren't you?" Kate said with a smirk.

"Oh, I don't know. What time is it?" He looked at his watch. "Ten-thirty? Did I sleep that late?"

"Oh, sleep was involved?" his sister said with a smile.

"Isa's going back to Scotland with me, Kate. She will be there for Ian's birthday party."

Kate smiled. "Honestly, I thought that might be a given, considering how things have progressed between the two of you."

"Will there be kilts involved at this party?" Isa asked.

Daniel laughed. "You will never see me in a kilt. Haven't got the legs for it."

Kate snickered.

"Your legs aren't that bad," Isa said with a cringe on her lips. "You wear cycling tights, after all."

"I only wear the tights out of necessity. But I draw the line there."

"Isa, believe me, you don't want to see him in a kilt. He stopped wearing shorts in grade school, not of his own accord. There was a family intervention asking him not to."

"So, Kate, why aren't you with the bicyclists?" Isa asked.

"It's lonely without Daniel." She laughed. "No, I never do the complete tour. I have to get back to my practice and the university."

"So, what is the plan today?" Kate asked. "Should we go see the priest that Claire suggested?"

"The ghost is why you really cut the tour short. Fess up," Daniel said. "Why you returned with me. To write that paper."

Madame Claire popped her head out of the kitchen doorway. "I already called the priest to tell him you might be coming by. Make sure you ask for Pare Foley. Monsignor Durand wouldn't understand nor approve of such matters. Pare Foley is, how do you say, much more open-minded."

"Merci, Claire, we will do that," Daniel replied.

"I feel like I have put everyone's life on hold with this nonsense," Isa said, directing her statement toward Kate.

"Don't feel that way, Isa," Daniel said. "It's an adventure, a mystery, a piece of history, and a psychological drama we all want to solve. Isn't that right, Kate?"

"I think you left out the most important element, Daniel," Kate said with a grin.

"And that would be?" he asked.

Eying both of them, Kate said, "I see the blush of love."

Isa's hue changed. Daniel didn't miss a beat and responded, "I did mention psychological drama, did I not?"

Kate smirked.

"Kate, speaking of love, I would like to know about this man you met," Isa said.

"Touché, Isa!" Daniel exclaimed, expressing his approval at her quick wit. "Yes, Kate, do tell," he said, following Isa's lead.

Isa noticed that Daniel's thoughts and hers often harmonized, something Isa was beginning to feel as both a comfort and a luxury. Nick and she shared no such intricacies in their relationship. The whole life with Nick was fading from her mind, off in the distance somewhere in that parallel universe. Josh was fading from her mind as well. What had she ever been thinking? But then those desires led her here to Daniel. Except for her students and parents, that life was slipping into the background. This new life with Daniel and Dora's life, if what she was experiencing concerning Dora was real, was now at the forefront.

Kate turned a bright red. She and her brother were different in that respect. Kate was more private than her brother. Maybe that was why she was not yet married. But then thirty wasn't an old maid. She had put her career first—a smart move Isa could now appreciate. Maybe if she had made the same choice, fate would have brought Daniel and her together sooner.

Kate explained she had met Marc when several groups of bicyclists had stopped for a pizza break at a café. Marc was from Paris, a medical intern.

"Isa, won't you stay at my apartment while you're in Scotland?"

"I don't know," she stuttered, looking at Daniel.

"It's just my relationship with Marc is hardly as far along as yours is. It would get me off the hook. I would feel more comfortable if Marc stayed with Daniel at his cottage." She looked at Isa pleadingly.

"I guess. If Daniel doesn't mind."

This was the first time that Isa heard that Daniel had a cottage. The idea of a Scottish cottage appealed greatly to her, the way Pemberley appealed to Elizabeth in *Pride and Prejudice.*

"Well, I do mind, but I also feel the need to protect my younger sister."

Kate smiled.

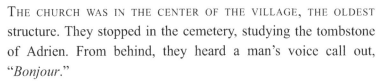

THE CHURCH WAS IN THE CENTER OF THE VILLAGE, THE OLDEST structure. They stopped in the cemetery, studying the tombstone of Adrien. From behind, they heard a man's voice call out, "*Bonjour.*"

In unison, they turned to look and saw a young black priest. If Isa had to guess, he was somewhere around their age.

"Pare Foley?" Daniel asked.

"At your service."

Isa couldn't quite place his accent. It was not French. They introduced themselves and told him that Madame Claire had advised them to see him.

"Pare Foley, I can't quite place your accent," Isa said.

"A bit of Creole. I'm a visiting priest from New Orleans."

He explained how the French Catholic churches had recruited priests from other countries to help revitalize what he termed a dying church. The average age of a priest in France was seventy-seven, and the congregations were not much younger. It was all part of a bigger plan to get young people back into the fold. Like himself, most of the new priests were more accepting of new ideas. Isa recalled how old she thought Monsignor Durand looked.

"Pare Foley, it is so nice to meet you," Isa said. "But honestly, I'm not sure why we are here, only that we came because Madame Claire recommended we should come."

"Ah, *oui*, she did call me yesterday explaining some of the situation."

"Father, she told you of the ghost then?" Daniel said.

"Yes, and more."

All three stood awkwardly, not knowing what to do next. Even Kate, always the professional, stumbled around for their next course of action.

The Father, accustomed to comforting people, smiled and explained, "Madame Claire and I have become great friends. We have had many religious debates, mind you. Friendly ones. We have also discovered that we have many beliefs in common, some of which the Catholic Church would not sanction. Yet a lot of priests, younger priests such as myself, are embracing what one might call more open-minded ideas about the paths to God."

"And your take on ghosts?" Daniel asked.

"I come from New Orleans. I grew up with ghosts. Also, reincarnation." This was the first time this term had come up. Isa's whole thought process had been along the lines of possession, not reincarnation.

"Reincarnation?" Isa questioned. She knew this to be beyond Kate's pragmatic views, but it had to be better than possession.

"It's possible from what Madame Claire was telling me. Had none of you thought of it?"

"Father, as a trained psychologist, I don't think in those terms," Kate said, affirming Isa's thoughts.

"My dear, as a priest of the Roman Catholic Church, neither do I, at least not on the record. Still, let's say studying such things is a hobby of mine. After all, most of the world believes in reincarnation. There has been some compelling evidence for it. I prefer not to close my mind on such matters."

Daniel listened intently while staring at the grave.

"Father, I was not raised to believe in it, but I think somewhere in my core, I thought it might be the case when I saw the ghost of Dorcel," Isa said. "But my conscious mind dismissed it."

"Isa, is this something you would like to explore?" the Father asked.

"That is why we are here. But how do you explore something like this?" Kate asked.

"Kate, I am surprised that you, being a psychologist, have not suggested hypnosis," he said.

"I *had* thought about it to get at the root of her dreams. Isa, I hope you don't mind. Daniel only mentioned that you had some dreams, not what they were about and that I might help."

"I don't mind. I'll do anything. Well, almost anything, to find out what is going on," she said.

"Father, I know about past life regression, but most in my profession, like the Roman Catholic Church, don't sanction it," Kate added.

"Yes, I expected as much. But if you are game, more importantly, Isa, if you're game, I would like to regress you."

She looked at Daniel. His look told her he was with Isa in whatever she decided to do. She looked back at the Father. "If it gets us closer to the truth. What do I need to do?"

"I would need to do some preparation, and it would be best

to do it when the Monsignor is away. He will be dining with some parishioners tonight. Can you come back at dinnertime? Perhaps take an early or late dinner? Isa, please keep yours light if you decide to eat beforehand and dress comfortably, something loose."

They agreed to come back at seven.

"Father, why is Adrien's grave so short?" Daniel asked, changing the subject.

"I would suppose his legs might have been amputated. There would have been no need for a longer casket."

"These other graves," Isa said, "must be those of his parents."

"Yes, I believe they might be," the priest said.

"Bourgmestre?" Isa asked.

"It means mayor. He must have been the village's mayor," Father Foley said.

"Oh, not a judge."

"I suppose the two probably went hand in hand."

They said their goodbyes. As they turned to walk away, he said, "Please come in through the side door. That is my private office."

ather Foley's cramped office was lit only by white altar candles. Yet it was illuminated enough to see that two of the four walls consisted of built-in bookcases. There were leather-bound volumes, some with ragged spines along with newer hardbacks and paperbacks, the overflow wedged wherever there were spaces to be had. And still, stacks spilled out onto his desk. Amid all the book chaos, which Isa found delightful, the sounds of gentle falling water emanated from the lit-up computer screen on Father Foley's desk.

Two fold-up chairs sat next to an overstuffed recliner with an afghan thrown over it. Isa imagined Father Foley reading there into the wee hours of the morning.

After a few pleasantries, he directed Isa to the recliner. Daniel took the chair nearest Isa.

"Are we ready?" Father Foley asked.

With apprehension, Isa looked to Daniel, who nodded, and then back to Father Foley. "I'm as ready as I'll ever be, I guess."

"It's important to be comfortable. We don't want any distractions. You might want to remove your sandals. I see you are wearing loose clothing." Isa had changed into her sleeveless white shift dress after showering. "You could become cold during the session. Please use the afghan if you do."

Isa felt a quick clasp of Daniel's hand, his way of asking her if she was sure about this. Isa nodded her approval to proceed. With that, he released her hand, and Isa snuggled into the leather upholstery, throwing the afghan over her feet.

Father Foley asked that Daniel and Kate be as quiet as possible. Maybe in other circumstances, he might have asked them to leave, but Isa sensed that he knew she needed them there. Isa had no idea what the precedent was in such cases.

"Isa, before we start, do I have your permission to record this?"

Isa looked over at Daniel and Kate. Kate nodded yes, and in return, Isa nodded in agreement. Recording such sessions, she thought, must be standard practice for psychologists. With that, he leaned forward and inserted a disk into his computer. He hit some keys and said, "Everything is set when you're ready."

Father Foley sat back in his chair. "Isa, I want you to know that before we start, if at any time during the trance or regression you feel uncomfortable and wish to come out of it, all you have to do is give me a signal. We will say that if you feel uncomfortable, you will raise your right hand from the arm of the chair. Is that agreeable?"

Isa nodded.

"You're in no danger. If it goes well, it will be like watching a movie. Just go with what you see."

After a bit of wiggling around on Isa's part, he asked again if she was comfortable.

"I'm fine." She gave a weak smile.

"Okay, then we are ready to begin."

"Isa, I want you to take a very slow deep breath. Now hold it. Now let it go. Slowly. Please continue to do this. You may make yourself as comfortable as possible while continuing to do this. As you continue to take deep breaths, I want you to release any tension you may have, beginning with your feet. Feel all the tension being released in your feet. Continue breathing."

Father Foley continued in this manner, working his way up Isa's body. He continuously told Isa to be aware of her breathing while giving her instructions to relax various parts of her body. He said at any time that if she needed to scratch her nose or something similar, feel free to do so. Isa almost laughed and panicked at the same time. What if she needed to fart? Something Daniel might say.

After concentrating on expelling extraneous thoughts from her mind, Isa did manage to relax almost to the point of drifting off to sleep with the help of Father Foley's soothing voice. The thought of drooling entered her mind. How ridiculous she was being. She was resisting. Once again, she concentrated and settled into the sound of Father Foley's voice. Almost at the point of forgetting Daniel and Kate were in the room, the priest's voice became her lifeline to reality. Her body felt like a feather yet heavy at the same time, the weight of her body melting into the chair.

"You don't have to think. You don't have to listen. You don't have to do anything except just allow yourself to lie in that chair feeling warm, relaxed, and comfortable. Just become aware of the feeling of the chair against your back and your head." His voice took on a rhythm. "Let yourself go, deeper and deeper. That's right."

Isa could feel her body dissolving into nothingness. Only some strange part of her remained, the peaceful feeling she had always tried to reach through the meditation tapes she once listened to but never quite attained. The closest thing to it that she could think of was the runner's high that she had on occasion experienced, except with this, her body wasn't doing any work.

It was no longer Father Foley's voice but just a voice hovering in the air.

"Imagine a house situated in the middle of a beautiful

meadow. It's all you could imagine in the perfect house, the perfect cottage."

Cottage? How could he know what she needed to hear?

"It has a welcoming door and beautiful windows to let the light in. There are plenty of trees and all kinds of beautiful flowers. This house is so welcoming. There may even be children playing out in the yard."

Yes, she wanted children, at least two, maybe three.

"The house may be filled with happy people, people who are family, people who are friends. The house has seen many events, witnessed births, and experienced deaths."

Isa thought of her grandmother.

"People have come and gone. There have been weddings, christenings, and even funerals."

Don't think of Nick, she told herself. She concentrated. She saw herself in a white dress standing beside Daniel. He was in a kilt. She almost laughed. Should she laugh out loud? No, no, don't think of that. She commanded herself to let go of any thoughts.

"The house has been home to a lot of happiness and sadness, but it is predominately a happy house. Center on the children playing outside, running through the meadow, laughing and running. Inside the house, there's a staircase. The staircase can be wooden, carpeted, marble, or anything you want, whatever you love in a staircase. It has a handrail. You are upstairs. I want you to take hold of the handrail and descend the stairs. At the bottom of the staircase, you will find a door, and behind the door, there is something wonderful. I want you to begin to go down that staircase now. We will count the steps together."

Isa thought of the many steps she and Daniel climbed to the top of Castle Hill at Nice.

"So *ten*...going down the first step...and *nine*, down again...and *eight* ...more relaxed...and *seven*, more relaxed...and *six*, feeling completely relaxed...and *five*, deeper and deeper...*four,* each step is taking you deeper down...and *three,* deeper and deeper...and *two,* nearly there...and *one,* nearly at the bottom...and after one there's just *zero*...nothing...and in the center of that zero there is a warm, velvety blackness...and you can feel yourself going deeper into that warm...safe... velvety blackness...a feeling of nothingness...total release...floating...and you can feel yourself drifting down...like a leaf carried by the wind...drifting left and right and right and left...down and down...floating and swirling...round and round...down and down…"

All her side thoughts vanished.

Isa heard as if right on cue, "You don't have to think. You don't have to do anything. You can watch any thoughts that come into your mind wander away. They are not important. Nothing is important. My voice is not important. My voice is in the background. It is only a beacon to guide you. It can be the voice of a teacher, a parent, or someone from the past. My voice is the voice you trust. My voice can be the sound of the wind in the winter long ago or the rain against a window in a far-off place on a dark night, or my voice can be the sound of a leaf blowing along an empty street. My voice is anything you want it to be.

"Now, I want you to find yourself in front of a door. When you are in front of that door and ready to go in, I would like you to signal to me by moving a finger or a thumb that lets me know you are ready to go in."

Isa could see the door in her mind's eye. It was a large wooden door worn from the weather and the years. Isa lifted her index finger.

"Please describe the door to me."

"It's thick. It's old and worn."

"Can you open the door?"

"Yes."

"I want you to go through the door."

There was silence.

"Is it daytime or nighttime?"

"The sun is out, but it has been raining. It's hard to believe."

"What's hard to believe?" he asked.

"Everything is so vivid."

"Trust what you see. Look down at your feet. Look carefully and tell me what you see."

"I see leather, black leather, worn from lots of work. They're summer shoes. They slip on. There are no laces."

"Can you tell me what else you are wearing?"

"A long skirt. Not that long, but midway down from my knees. I think it's blue. Yes, it's dark blue. And I have a loose white blouse on. My clothes look worn."

"Do you have anything covering your legs?"

Hesitating a moment, Isa said, "My legs are bare. They're hairy, dark hair."

"What about your head?"

"I'm feeling my head. My hair is tied back into a bun under a cap."

"Do you know how old you are?"

"I think I'm young, but not that young, maybe twenty-two."

"I'm going to count to three, and the year will pop into your head. One, two, three...what year is it?"

Isa said, "1704. I don't know why, but that number just came to me."

"I'm going to count to three again, and you will tell me what country you're in. One, two, three...what country is it?"

"I'm here in the same place, near the Edge."

"Where is this place? The edge?"

"France. I'm in France, this village near the cliffs."

Once again, Father Foley counted to three and asked Isa her name in that lifetime.

"I'm called Dora."

"Is Dora short for something?"

"Dorcel, but everyone calls me Dora."

"Tell me, Dora, what is happening today?"

"The usual."

"What is the usual?"

"I have to take out the chamber pots. I have to get my husband up into a chair. My father comes by and helps me in the mornings before he begins his work. When my son gets older, he will help. Sometimes my mother comes by to help as well. She cooks."

"Why do you have to get your husband up? Can't he get himself up?"

"No, he can't walk. He fell from a tree. Everyone in the village knows that. My son is too young to help. My father and I get him into a chair in the mornings. And I get him a bowl of clean water from the well. He can shave. I try to get him to do things for himself, but he only gives me grief over it. I think he has lost the will to live."

"If your husband can't walk, how do you make a living?"

"His father was rich. Adrien was the only surviving son. There were others, but they died in childbirth. He inherited the house. It's a big house. My husband wanted to make it into an inn. I didn't want to at first."

"Why didn't you wish to have an inn?"

"I wanted to fill the house up with children."

"Why didn't you?"

"I couldn't, not after our son was born. I was pregnant when we got married."

"How would that stop you from having more children? Did your husband's accident prevent you from having more children?"

"Maybe, I don't know. But I had an accident, too—a small one. I fell off the Edge, the cliffs. Not a big fall. I grabbed onto a tree as I went down. I couldn't have any more babies."

"How do you feel about that?"

"Sad," Isa said in a demure voice. A tear ran down her cheek. At this point, she was starting to feel uncomfortable but resisted giving a signal. She was beginning to sink into being Dora too much. She tried to remove herself a bit by remembering that she was Isa. At the same time, she saw similarities. At thirty-three, she had no children, and deep down inside, she feared she was never going to. Dora wanted a house full of children and only had one. Isa recognized the parallels. Was this why she worked at an elementary school? She could hear Father Foley's voice again, far off into the distance.

"Okay, let's move forward in time. Let's go to an important event. I will count to three again, and you will be forward in time. Now, describe the scene."

"I am trying to help my husband. But he won't even try anymore. All he does is complain. Esther came by. It made matters worse. She does that."

"Who is Esther?"

"She is a woman in the village. Her husband sometimes plays fiddle at the inn on Saturday nights. She is such a busybody."

Isa's body tensed up. Father Foley tried to relax her more, telling her just to observe. "Look at it as a motion picture on a big screen." Isa felt the tension releasing.

"Now look at Esther and your husband from a calm perspective. Explain the scene. What is going on?"

"Esther is criticizing. She judges almost everything I do, and she complains to my husband as well. At first, I liked her coming by. She would talk to my husband. It freed me up to get more work done at the inn and tend to customers. But sometimes, I feel like they plot against me."

"Do you know why Esther does this?"

Isa had to think for a moment. "Jealousy." The word sprang from her lips, but Isa immediately saw it as the truth of the matter.

"Why is Esther jealous?"

"She thinks I am having an affair with her husband, and she has told my husband this."

"Are *you* having an affair with him?"

"No, not him. But he has flirted with me, and she has noticed it. She is jealous that we have the inn too."

"Why would she be jealous that you have the inn?"

"Because she is the illegitimate daughter of the judge."

"The judge?"

"Yes, you know, my husband's father."

"Okay, then. You said you were not having an affair with Esther's husband. Have you had affairs?"

"Sometimes."

"Sometimes? Why did you have affairs?"

"Because my husband, like Esther, is always criticizing. Men tell me nice things, not like my husband."

Chill bumps spread over Isa's arms. She felt the afghan being pulled up over the rest of her body. Daniel must have done it. The thought of his presence reassured her. She had forgotten he was there.

"Okay, let's move on." Father Foley said it matter-of-factly, with no judgment whatsoever.

"I will count once again to three. Upon the count of three, you will go to a pivotal moment in your life. It can be forward in time or backward."

Isa heard three and the Father's voice saying, "Now you are there. Describe it."

"I am at the inn, the only one in the main room. A man comes. It is raining, and it's late. I am the only one still up. We are alone together. He talks about the meaning of life. He tells me that he will see me again in another life, that we will be together. I didn't remember what he said until now."

"I am once again going to count to three. You will be at the end of your life. You will see your death. You will see what your life as Dora meant. ***One...two....three***, now tell me what is happening."

"I am at the cliffs. I wanted a break from the inn. My son is running it now anyway. I am still there to help and care for my grandchildren. I want to rest for a while by a tree that is there. It is near the edge. I fell asleep. I wake up and stand. I have one hand against the tree while I put my shoe on with my other hand. As I do, I look over the edge to the ground below, thinking how high up I am.

"I start thinking about my life, my husband who had already died, my son, my grandchildren. Suddenly I start thinking about the man who came that night so long ago. It has been so many years since he came. I'm old, but I still think of him from time to time. He used to be all I thought of. What would he think of me? He would be old too. I thought he would come back, but he didn't. I was bending down, too close to the edge, trying to put on my shoe. I was holding onto the tree with the other hand. But I was too close to the edge. Someone tapped me on the shoulder. It startled me. I scream. I am falling. The woman who tapped me was Esther. I didn't even hear her approach. I was so absorbed in my thoughts.

"She reached out her hand. It was too late. I am lying on my back at the bottom of the cliffs. I don't feel my body. I am floating upward, my spirit, that is. I see my body down below, blood running from my head. I see Esther looking down at my body. She is screaming. I can read her thoughts. She is sorry for what she just did. She didn't mean to scare me. And she is afraid. She looks around to see if someone might have seen her. It wasn't her fault, but still, she knew what people would think. Everyone in the village knew we didn't like each other.

"I forgive her. I try to tell her so, but she can't hear me. I'm hovering over her, not my body, my spirit. I'm trying to comfort her, but she only sees my shattered body below. I see it too, but it doesn't matter anymore. I am feeling this overwhelming love. I think about my son and grandchildren but know they will be fine. I feel so much love. It's indescribable. I see a ray of light. I go toward it. That is all I remember." With this, the chills subsided, and a rush of warmth spread throughout Isa's body.

"Okay, we are going to wrap this up. I want you, as both Dora and Isa, to look at the life you have now and the life you have just experienced. Please tell me what it means from your soul's perspective. Let's start with Dora's husband. Can you see someone or something in your life now that is represented by him?"

"He's Nick."

"Who is Nick?"

"Nick was my husband in this life. We're divorced."

"Can you see any lessons, any similar experiences?"

Isa could feel her body trembling, and once again, she heard Father Foley's soothing voice giving her calming instructions. "There was an accident, a car crash. I was diagnosed to be a paraplegic."

"What happened?"

Tears streamed down her cheeks, but her body remained immobile. "I lay in the hospital and thought of Nick. I thought of our life together. I was unhappy, and he was too. He worked all hours. I saw him less and less. I thought if I had to live my life in a wheelchair, he would have to stay home and take care of me. Maybe our marriage might be better. But then something inside of me said, *No!* And it was a very loud no. That this is not what I wanted. At that moment, I had the power to choose. I prayed with every ounce of strength I had. Then the doctor came in and said they were wrong."

Isa felt herself calming down as if some great weight had been lifted.

"Okay, we have made significant progress. Is there anything else about the life as Dora and how it relates to Nick?"

Isa thought for a moment. "Nick worked all the time, trying

to prove he could be successful, always trying to please his parents. I did the same as Dora. The situation was reversed. And Nick, as Adrien, couldn't walk. I had to take care of him. Nick would have had to take care of me in this life, but the prayer changed everything."

"You were granted a miracle. It was the grace of God. The other person you have talked about is Esther. She must be significant in your soul's journey. Can you see Esther in your life right now?"

"Not now, but once. I see it so plainly. She is Denise."

"What relationship to Denise did you have in this life?"

"I knew her in college. There was a bunch of us who hung out together. We both liked Josh. She was jealous that Josh and I were together. But we weren't together. Not the way she thought."

"What happened?"

"She married Josh."

"What do you see about this relationship from your soul's perspective?"

"Now I am the one who is jealous."

"Are you still jealous?"

"No, I mean I was. I see now."

"What do you see?"

"I was better off without Josh. He didn't stand up for me."

"Didn't stand up for you?"

"Yes, when he saw me with Nick, he didn't even fight for me. He just walked away and went on with his life. I see now that marrying him wouldn't have been any better than marrying Nick."

"And the man who came to the inn. You went to him when I said to go to the most pivotal point in your life. Is this man in your life now?"

Isa could feel more tears welling up, but they were tears of joy. She said without any embarrassment, "Yes, he was, is Daniel."

"Okay, Isa, you have done well. Let's look once again at Dora's life. Look at her life from the soul perspective and tell me what she accomplished and what she could have done differently."

"She was a strong woman. She was able to care for a husband who abused her verbally. She ran a business almost on her own and held her head high even though people criticized and judged her. She raised a child who became a good husband and father. She shouldn't have had the affairs. It didn't solve anything."

"Let's go back to the field where the children are playing. You walk past them. You see the cottage. You are walking up the sidewalk, one you have walked up many times before, and you are comfortable. You are relaxed. You feel the sunshine on your body. As you walk along, think of all the things you have talked about tonight and all the things you have experienced and remembered. You think of the lessons learned. You see your soul's purpose more clearly. You know how you have touched other people's lives and how they have touched yours. You see how these people also had a soul purpose and how you helped each other grow as souls. With this in mind, you can begin to come back to the present. I will count from five to one, and when I get to one, you will be back in the present. You will remember everything vividly. You will feel great.

"*Five...four*...begin to feel the sensation coming back into your body...*three*...stretch....*two*, and ready to come back....*one* and eyes open."

Isa's eyes opened to dim candlelight. It took her a while to focus. She felt wetness on her cheeks. She heard Daniel and Kate move in their seats. At times during the regression, she had forgotten their presence in the room. Everything was surreal. Isa heard Father Foley's voice yet again, but this time she could see him as well.

"How do you feel?"

"Groggy, like I have been awakened from the dead. I also feel sensational, like something has been released."

"Something *has been* released," Father Foley said.

18

$\mathcal{D}$aniel, Kate, and Isa thanked Father Foley. The clock on the desk said they had been there for over two hours. The monsignor would be back soon, so Father Foley gave each of them the sign of blessing.

They walked out into the night in silence, each afraid to speak as if words might break the residual feeling of what had just transpired. Isa looked in the direction of Father Foley's office window to see him blowing out the candles.

The moon was full and bright, illuminating the graves. Only the crinkle of the grass beneath their feet could be heard. Isa's initial feeling of relief was shrinking. Doubt about what had just happened trickled in. What could Kate, with her logical, pragmatic mind, be thinking? Did she even believe it? More importantly, what was Daniel thinking? And did he believe it? Did she even believe it herself? Yet the scenes were vivid, like a 3-D movie in which she had the lead role.

They walked through the cemetery as separate entities until Daniel's hand reached out to hers. The warmth of his palm pressed against hers and melted away her apprehension. He pulled her in close and wrapped his arm around her as they approached the inn.

Kate broke the silence. "It's been a most remarkable day in more ways than one. I'm drained. I can only imagine how you feel, Isa. Goodnight, you two. I'm sure you have lots to talk about."

Daniel and Isa stood together at the door. He looked into her eyes in all seriousness. "Do you want to talk?" He gave her a reassuring smile. "If you want to neck or do some heavy petting instead, I'll understand. After all, I am the man of your dreams if what you saw in the regression is true."

Isa laughed. "That part was for sure true." She was glad Daniel was back to his usual joking self. But after everything that had happened to her on this trip, she wasn't sure if *normal* had a place in her life anymore or what it even meant.

"Honestly, I would like to do some heavy petting, but maybe we should at least talk first." Isa sighed. "Although you might be tired of talking?"

"Never with you," Daniel replied.

They sat in the back overlooking the garden on the bench they had sat at that night. "I feel like I just had my wisdom teeth pulled, and the anesthetic is beginning to wear off."

"I would say that is a good analogy. I wasn't in the hot seat, so to speak, but I was gritting my teeth for you."

"Yes, I know you were, and I appreciate that." There was a pause. "You see the small pond?"

"Yes," he said.

"That was where the tree was that Adrien fell from. Don't ask me how I know that, but I do. Afterward, he hated that tree. He could see it from his room. He had men cut it down and dig up its roots. There was plenty of firewood that winter."

"You didn't say anything about that in the regression."

"Maybe it's a remnant bit of information coming from the regression. Maybe Dora is telling me."

"I think Kate and I sat there, afraid to move a muscle. You were spurting forth so much information. I thought some of it might have come from the dreams. But after seeing the sketch of Dora's son, who both resembled and bore the same name as my son, my mind was open to believing almost anything, even the Loch Ness Monster."

"What about Kate? What do you think her reaction to this is?"

"The look on her face told me she was questioning her clinical thinking. But she *is* rather dogmatic. If I know Kate, she will analyze it to death before drawing a conclusion."

"I can't believe you just referred to your sister as dogmatic."

"Don't tell her that." He winked.

Isa smiled. "I was so glad Dora didn't commit suicide. Maybe just knowing that now, her ghost will rest. We should tell Madame Girard what we found out. And Claire, and of course, Albert."

"We will," Daniel said, his lips edging closer to hers. "I don't know if we will ever have answers. I only know that I am falling in love with the person called Isa in this life."

Isa felt a flush in her cheeks and looked down, trying to hide it, but the full moon would have none of it.

Daniel tilted her head upward and pressed his lips against hers.

$\mathcal{T}$omorrow morning, the three of them would leave after breakfast and catch the train to Paris, where they would hook up with Marc. Kate had planned for them to stay in Paris with Marc for a couple of days of sightseeing. The plan for going to Scotland was to travel on the Eurostar from Paris Gare du Nord St Pancras International to London Kings Crossover and then onto Edinburgh. The entire trip would take eight hours. Isa didn't mind. She relished the idea of seeing more countryside. More than that, she would have more time with Daniel.

Kate said she wanted to spend the day resting and packing. Isa and Daniel headed to the cliffs for a picnic. Isa wanted to see if the place where Dora fell to her death—it sparked any memories. Claire provided a picnic basket. Isa had no clue what might happen after Scotland, even if she would return to the inn.

Daniel carried the basket of food while Isa carried a blanket on the walk to the cliffs. The day was sunny and perfect. They found a secluded spot near a clump of trees that still provided a good view of the vineyards below. Daniel sat the basket down, pulling back the cloth and peering inside. "I don't know about you, but I am rather famished."

"You quit using your cane. How is your ankle?"

"No need to. My ankle is much better."

"I'm glad."

Isa's phone buzzed from inside her pocket. "It's my parents. I forgot to email them last night. They must be worried."

"Text them back. Or should I?"

"You?"

"Yes. You did plan on telling them about me, didn't you?"

"Well, yes. I had thought.... well…" She didn't know how to finish.

"Go on. You thought, what? After all we've been through, me knowing your deepest darkest secrets, I mean deepest darkest past lives, you can't tell me what you were thinking about telling your parents?"

"Okay, well, I thought maybe we could possibly Skype them together. I had wanted Kate to do it with us as well."

"I think it's a great idea, and Kate isn't here. Why do we need Kate?"

"I don't know…"

"I get it. Because she's a psychologist and my sister, she might add some credibility to you falling in love with the first man you meet in France?"

"Well, …"

Daniel grabbed Isa's phone from her hand. He found the Skype app and opened it.

"Now?" Isa exclaimed.

"Why not? There's no time like the present. You will stress about it during our picnic. So let's get it over with and then eat. Besides, I want to meet the couple who produced such a beautiful soul."

"I thought you were famished."

"I want to meet your parents face-to-face. They say look at a lass's mum to see what she will look like when she gets older. I may need to rethink this."

"Daniel!"

"Kidding."

"I look like my father."

"I hope he's not bald?"

"You're insufferable."

"I will assume this is them. It says Mom and Dad." He hit call. Isa heard the familiar tone. Daniel was holding the phone when they answered. Isa could see the shock on their faces. Isa moved over into the picture, not to alarm them. She saw the look of relief.

"Hi, Mom, Dad!"

"Hi, Mom, Dad! I'm sorry. I don't know what to call you. I know Isa as Isa Muir." He looked at Isa. "But that is your married name. You haven't told me your parents' names."

"Mom, Dad, meet Daniel, Daniel Stewart. Daniel, this is my Mom, Gloria Manning, and my father, Steve Manning."

"Hello," they both said somewhat reluctantly. Their faces reminded her of Cartman's surprised look on *South Park*.

"Daniel is a math professor at The University of Edinburgh in Scotland. I assure you that he does not deal in drugs or the sex trade."

Daniel raised his eyebrows in a question mark while looking at Isa.

"I'll explain later."

"We are glad you set us straight on that," Mr. Manning said.

"You met, how?" Mrs. Manning asked.

"Well, Mom, scrolled across a restroom stall in Paris was, FOR A GOOD TIME CALL DANIEL. Things had gotten a tad boring. So, I called. Of course, it was in French. But some things are the same in all languages."

Isa's dad's face turned beet red while her mother rolled her eyes in disgust.

"It's amazing how good this connection is. I can see every vein in your face, Dad." Her dad coughed.

"He doesn't sound French," Mr. Manning said.

Daniel tried to hold the laughter in. "She is joking, of course. I'm rather stuffy, not much of a good time at all, you will be pleased to hear. But let me answer that. We were, are both, staying at the inn, ma'am. I was riding through on a bicycle tour but hurt my ankle. Isa and I became friends. Also, I'm Scottish."

Isa nudged Daniel and whispered, "Don't call her ma'am. It makes her feel old."

Isa had never seen her parents at such a loss for words. Isa could tell they were trying to decide the next course of action.

Before they could say anything, Isa said, "We are just pulling your leg, of course. Daniel likes to joke. I think I assimilated his sense of humor. I met Daniel at the inn, both he and his sister. Daniel is a twin. They had been bicycling across France. Well, only partly across France. Daniel hurt his ankle and stopped riding, as he told you, and Kate is a psychologist and is leaving tomorrow to get back to her practice, and she also teaches at the university."

His face turning back to normal, Isa's father said, "Well, Daniel, as I am thousands of miles away, I can only hope that I can trust you with my daughter."

"You can, sir. In fact, I love your daughter."

Isa punched Daniel in the rib.

Her parents looked astonished.

"Mom and Dad, I hate to cut this short, but Madame Claire, I told you about her in the emails, packed us a lovely picnic basket, and I have no idea what's in it." She held up the basket. "I hope it's nothing that will spoil. So, we will talk again later, okay?"

"Bye, Mr. and Mrs. Manning!"

"Love you, Mom and Dad."

They clicked off. Within half a minute, Isa's text alert went off.

"And that would be your mum."

Of course, he was right. The text read, "Isa, are you really okay?"

Isa texted back, "Mom, I have never been better in my life. Trust me on this."

"Do you realize that was almost as scary as seeing the ghost and having the past life regression?" Isa said.

Her text alarm went off again.

"In love?"

"Mom, Daniel jokes a lot, but yes, we are rather fond of each other. We will Skype again soon. Promise."

"Do you think that assuaged your mum's fears?"

"Probably not. I'll write her tonight."

"Maybe you can send her some of our Nice pictures." He smiled. "She'll see how happy we are together."

"Yeah, maybe that would be a good idea."

Daniel leaned over, kissed her, and dug into the basket. "Okay, we have chicken salad on croissants. It's on ice. We have some grapes and wine. Oh, and something chocolate. Hmmm, I think it may be some of Madame Girard's leftover cakes."

Isa gasped, "Leftover? I'm surprised Albert didn't gulp them down right after saying something sarcastic about them first."

Daniel laughed and pulled out some wine glasses. He uncorked the wine with a corkscrew, also provided by Madame Claire, and poured the wine into the glasses. Daniel put his glass against hers. "What shall we drink to?"

"Oh, gosh, let me see. Love, we shall drink to love. Amore! Daniel and Isa sitting in a tree, K I S S I N G."

"Okay, to all that," They clinked glasses and finished their first glass.

"You said the chicken salad was packed in ice."

"Yes."

Isa pulled him down on top of her on the blanket.

"Mrs. Muir, in such a public place. I'm shocked," he said as he buried his lips into her breasts.

Isa was no expert, but it was slow and more than good, in her opinion. Luckily no one came by, or if they did, she and Daniel were much too involved to notice. Even if someone did stroll by, being in France, they would have either been ignored or applauded.

He pulled his pants back on, as did Isa. Then he began to help her with her buttons. "I love you, Isa, but you already know that."

"I love you, Daniel Stewart, and I think you already know that as well."

"I am definitely famished now."

AFTER LUNCH, THEY WALKED TO THE CLIFF'S EDGE AND LOOKED over at the vineyard.

"It's probably all changed so much now. We'll never know where it happened," she said. Isa noticed Daniel looking at her a little funny. "What is it? Did you get my buttons wrong? Are my breasts too small?"

Daniel laughed. "No, your buttons are fine."

"My breasts are too small?"

"No, your breasts are perfect."

Daniel hugged her. "They're perfect like you are perfect. I was just getting a reaction out of you. I'm sorry. I shouldn't have done that. But no, that is not what I was referring to. Do you see how close to the edge you are?"

"Now that you mention it, yes."

He held onto her hand. "And you're not scared?"

"Wow, I'm not."

"I remember how scared you were the day we were on Castle Hill in Nice."

"It must be knowing what happened. The regression somehow released my fear."

"Kate said that sometimes she used hypnosis to help patients with fears and phobias."

"But she doesn't regress patients back to past lives. What if a lot of our fears *are* from past lives?"

"I guess a lot of them could be."

They walked back over to the blanket and finished off the bottle of wine.

"I think I am maybe a little drunk. I have never drank that much wine before."

"Are you saying my girlfriend can't hold her liquor?"

"Yes, I think that is what I'm saying."

They lay on the blanket, looking up at the clouds, not saying anything for the longest time. Then suddenly, Daniel moved his head toward her.

"You shouldn't worry about your breasts. They're fine with me, but they're going to get bigger with all those children we will have. You do want a lot of children, don't you? Breast-feeding makes your breasts bigger."

"What makes you think I would breastfeed? And how does a math professor know such things?"

"Oh, I'm a widely read man. I will leave that up to you regarding breastfeeding, but you strike me as a natural kind of lass." He laughed. "Ian was breastfed. It was hard not to notice how big Stephanie's breasts got."

THE NEXT MORNING TO ISA'S AND DANIEL'S SURPRISE, NOT ONLY were Albert and Claire downstairs, but Madame Girard and Gromit were there as well. Kate was sipping tea, her luggage on the floor beside her.

They were greeted with *bonjours*.

"Father Foley was here early this morning. He dropped off this disk for you." Claire handed her a padded brown envelope.

"Claire, you and Erma keep it for now. You said you wanted to listen."

With their luggage and bicycles strapped to the back, Albert drove them the short distance to catch the train. Daniel pushed hard to make it all fit. They held the overflow on their laps. Albert handed them a basket for the train before they boarded, kissing them on both cheeks. "Some wine, croissants, and chocolates to eat on the train."

After kissing him on both cheeks, Isa hugged him extra hard. "I can't thank you enough. You have all been real friends, more like my family away from home."

Once again, Isa was Paris bound.

20

*D*aniel and Isa sat behind a couple with three young children who spent more time in the aisle than in their seats. The smallest, who Isa judged to be three, fascinated by Daniel's and Kate's red hair, plopped herself down in the vacant seat next to Kate, offered up her book, and asked Kate to read to her. Kate opened the book and began to read the French words while the little girl pointed to the pictures and giggled.

The mother looked back. "She knows you are twins like her brothers. If Adele is bothering you, please let us know." The mother spoke French but changed to English upon hearing Daniel interpret for Isa. "They aren't identical. This is Charles, Philippe, and Michelle. The boys are in the first year of school and enjoy reading on their own now."

Isa reached into her backpack and pulled out *Tintin,* the book she bought in Nice. "Maybe the boys would like this one to read on the train."

When it was lunchtime, their mother handed Isa back the book, and the family proceeded to the dining car. Daniel, Isa, and Kate took naps.

MARC MET THEM AT THE TRAIN STATION. ALTHOUGH KATE HAD never described him, he was not at all what Isa expected. He was shorter than Kate and sported a goatee. His manner was gentle, indicating a good bedside manner. Both couples walked off hand in hand to Marc's car, parked on a narrow cobblestone lane a few blocks from the train station.

Marc's parents had what Isa would call a mansion in the states. The French chalet was constructed of huge gray stones, the ones so typical in Paris, and was located right in the heart of the city amid all the noise. The city for lovers was one of the noisiest places Isa had ever been. The sounds subsided as soon as the massive front door closed behind them.

Marc's parents were doctors, away for a few days attending a medical convention in Switzerland. Marc showed them to the guest rooms. Kate and Isa would share one, and Daniel was to share one with a bicycling buddy named Michael, who would be up later that night to meet for dinner. Isa thought that Michael was traveling alone since he would be sharing a room with Daniel but wondered if he had a girlfriend or wife, so she asked Marc, who replied, "He's going through a rough divorce, so it's better not to mention the opposite sex to him."

The room with twin beds reserved for Kate and Isa was on the same side of the hall next door to the one Daniel and Michael would occupy. Daniel brought Isa's luggage in, huffing and puffing.

"You have to consider I had to bring enough to last me the whole summer. And I thought as a cyclist, you would be in better shape."

"I just hauled this up a flight of stairs."

Were they already sounding like a married couple? The bicyclists on the train came to mind.

Isa went over to the window and pulled the drapes. She

gasped. "Daniel, you have to come to see this view. We are right on the Seine and look. There is the Eiffel Tower."

He lay stretched across the bed. "I can't move. I think I pulled my back out. Besides, I can see it from here."

"Oh, I'm so sorry. Where does it hurt? She began to rub his shoulders."

"Lower."

"Here?"

"No, lower, really more in the front." He pulled her on top of him.

"Kate will be back any minute," she said.

"She and Marc went out. We have the place to ourselves for at least a couple of hours."

"But I wanted to see some sights. We only have a couple of days in Paris."

"Like what?"

"Well, the Eiffel Tower, for one."

"Open the drapes wider. You can see it while we make love."

"Okay, but tomorrow we'll go there, right?"

"Yes, we'll sit on a blanket and drink wine in the grassy area the way the tourists do. I will even buy a rose for you from one of the hawkers."

"Do the Parisians do it?"

"I suppose they started it, but the tourists have taken over."

After making love, they fell asleep but were soon awakened by voices from downstairs.

"Daniel, get up. Get dressed. They're back."

"Don't worry. They purposely gave us this time alone."

"That was considerate."

"But I'll get dressed. You wanted to see some sights. So where to first?"

After slipping into her floral dress, Isa pulled her phone from her backpack and handed it to him. "Open up notes. I made a list."

"Aren't *you* prepared."

"It's kind of a librarian thing."

He looked at her phone, studying the notes. "Isa, we can't see this entire list in two days."

"I do have the summer here. What do you suggest for the two days?"

"Well, tonight I propose we climb another hill, and you don't even have it on the list."

"Oh?"

"*Montmartre.* You can see the entire city, and the cathedral at the top is magnificent."

"I trust your judgment in these matters."

"We will do that tonight. We have time for one thing until we meet them for dinner."

"Daniel, I didn't have this much sex during my last three years of marriage with Nick."

"No, Isa. I was talking about Notre Dame."

"Oh."

"Okay, Notre Dame it is," he said, shaking his head.

"I'm so glad I have my own personal tour guide, and I'm sorry about the comment about Nick. Did I spoil things?"

"No, it's okay. You were married to him for eight years. Plus, you dated for two years. Right? I'm sure his name will come up from time to time. We both do have pasts, after all."

"Considering my past as Dora, that's an understatement."

He pulled her in close for a kiss.

Daniel and Isa both shouted, "Come in," upon hearing the rap on the door.

"We're dressed," Daniel added. Isa punched him.

"Hi, Kate," he said. "Isa and I were just going out to visit Notre Dame. Do you and Marc want to go?"

"No, we were planning on just hanging out here. Go on without us."

"Okay, Isa, just you and me."

Isa and Daniel were about to leave when Kate, following them down the stairs, walked over to the door. "Just a minute, Daniel. I need something out of your luggage." Kate leaned over and whispered something to Daniel.

Daniel looked at Isa. "Ready, Isa?"

"What was that all about?" Isa asked as they walked out the front door.

"We are embarrassing her. She feels pressured with Marc."

"Really, how? I thought you said they left to give us some time together."

"That was Marc, not Kate. They are at that awkward beginning stage. You know. Do I do it on the third date, fourth date?"

"I figured as her brother, you might not want her to do it at all. I always thought brothers, especially older brothers by thirty-three minutes, were overprotective of their younger sisters."

"There was a time I was, but that stopped after freshman year in college. I can hardly tell her what to do now. She's an adult. Marc's a good guy. I wouldn't mind having him as a brother-in-law. High time she settled down."

"Like you?"

He reached for her hand as they walked down the rue and looked at her. "I want to settle down."

"Now, maybe, but why have you not found anyone up until now?"

"Destiny, I suppose. I was meant to find you."

"There's that word again."

"What word?"

"Destiny or *destin*. Claire used it when she first saw me."

"Claire is a wise woman."

"You've had to have had serious relationships before meeting me."

"I had relationships, and there were times I might have thought they were serious, but for some reason, they never panned out. The reason had to be you, Isa."

"It's just I did the marriage thing for eight years, and you've remained single all this time. Granted, you are a bit younger, but still, it's surprising you were never even engaged."

"There was one woman with whom I came close. We talked about it."

"What happened?"

"She didn't want Ian in her life. She didn't want children at all."

"Do you still love her?"

"No. Why are you asking me this?"

"I guess I'm probing for skeletons in your closet. This thing between us has gone so fast. I dated Nick through two years of college before marrying him, and I still didn't know what I was getting myself into."

"Is this anything like dating Nick?"

"No. Nothing."

"Ian may be the only skeleton in my closet, but I would not label him a skeleton."

"Nor would I," Isa responded. She stopped. "I've seen this bridge in videos."

"So, Isa, recent history lesson number one. We are on the *Ponts des Arts*. It dates back to 1801, but in France, that is recent history."

"I love the wooden floor. It's something like a pier back home. Rick Steves talked about the sides of the bridge covered with locks?"

"Rick Steves?"

"He does lots of travel books and videos. I studied them before coming to Europe."

"Tourists started the locks. Parisians hate them. They are symbols of love. But they weigh down the bridge, so the city is replacing sections with these plastic panels to stop people from putting them on."

"So I won't suggest we do it. I wouldn't want our love to be the last straw that brought a landmark of Paris down."

He pulled her closer. They rested against the railing.

"It was a nightmare in many ways, especially for our families. So maybe, in a sense, I've paid my dues. And you paid yours with Nick. Like Father Foley said, who's to say that the time wasn't right until now? Maybe we had to have the life experiences we did before we could appreciate each other. Maybe we had karma to experience."

"You believe in karma?"

"Karma is only cause and effect. It's mathematical, logical, and if you study history enough, you will see it playing out."

"Why didn't you and Stephanie marry?"

"We almost eloped when Steph told me. I wanted to do the right thing, but her father caught wind of it. When her family found out she was pregnant, all hell broke loose. Our families were friends. Her parents called my parents. Then more hell broke loose. We, Steph and I, and the bairn on the way were caught in the middle. I think that was the only time that Steph and I didn't fight. We banded together against our parents who were deciding all our fates."

"You and she fought?"

"A lot."

"I can't imagine teenagers fighting or *you* fighting for that matter. It doesn't seem in your nature."

"I was an unruly teenager. We had little in common except for sex. But then, what teenage boy doesn't put that on his priority list? I hope I've grown up a wee bit since then."

"What happened next?"

"Our parents held council. Steph's mother wanted her to have an abortion."

"What stopped it?"

"My mom was brought up Catholic. She put a halt to talk of abortion. The thing is, Steph's mom loves Ian to a fault."

176

"And you? We've never talked about religion. Maybe we should."

"Me? I've attended mass plenty of times. You know, on those special occasions. But my mom is more of a nonpracticing Catholic than a practicing one. Still, she went to a Catholic school. Their teachings are ingrained in you."

"So, what do you lean toward?"

"The truth, whatever that may be."

"Then we practice the same religion. What happened next?"

"What do you mean?"

"With the bairn, Ian? I assume bairn means baby."

"Yes, bairn is baby. Both our parents wanted more for us than to marry right out of high school. They planned that we would both go to college as we had originally intended. Then if it was right, and both of our families, including us, knew on the deepest levels that it wasn't, we would marry after college.

"We went to separate colleges to avoid further conflict. Still, there was a lot of tension during the pregnancy. Steph had Ian before enrolling. After Ian was born, the tension melted—at least for a while. We all agreed that Steph's parents would keep the child until Steph completed school. My family shared the fiscal responsibility, and we had unlimited visiting rights. I owe my family a lot."

"But it all worked out in the end? Ian is doing well?"

"Yes, I think extremely well. Of course, he knows nothing about the controversy surrounding his birth. He only knows we were too young to marry, and if we had, life would have turned out very different for all concerned, probably not in a good way. We told him this early on."

"I can't wait to meet him. Do you think meeting me might mess him up?"

"No, not at all."

"It's just, well, working in an elementary school, I saw children growing up in all kinds of conditions. I don't mean that…"

He cut her off. "I know you don't. I may teach older kids who are more like adults, but the effects of broken families have a lasting impact, no matter the situation. And it can be just as bad even if their parents stay together and they fight all the time or if they just have a terrible home life for whatever reason."

"You're right. When I look back on it, it was better that Nick and I didn't have kids. I'm ruining this tour of Paris."

"No, you're not." He smiled and bent down and kissed her. "It's good that you know the situation with Ian before you meet."

Daniel cupped Isa's face. "I know we only met days ago, but I feel like I've known you forever."

"I feel the same. I also feel I can ask you these questions."

"You should."

"Nick and I never talked like this. It's been like a fairy tale meeting you—a rather weird, eerie, unnatural fairy tale. I don't want it to end, but I know real life will find us at some point. But for now, you are my prince."

"I'm not sure I can live up to the demands of a fairy tale prince, but I will stand against all the ghosts of the past that I can for you and any that may appear in the future."

A mustached man in a beret playing the accordion strode past them. Isa laughed. "So perfect. Are we close to the cathedral?"

"About fifteen minutes. Come on." He reached for her hand.

"Walking along the streets of Paris with my prince. What more could a girl ask for?"

He pointed. "See it? We are almost there."

"It is so tall. Granted, it's no skyscraper, but for the period in which it was built, it's magnificent. The buildings here amaze me. And the doors. They're all so tall. When exactly was it built?"

"It was started around 1100 AD. But it wasn't completed until sometime in the 1800s."

"It boggles the mind."

"The stained glass is even more impressive from the inside."

They walked single file with the other tourists. At the entrance was a well of water. "Holy water," he said. He dipped his finger in and touched Isa's heart. Isa did the same.

Daniel dropped a couple of Euros in a box and took two candles, handing one to Isa.

As they walked outside to the bright sunshine after an hour inside the cathedral, he said, "One day, we'll do the top."

"What do you suggest I get Ian for his birthday?"

"Going to his party is enough."

"No, an eleven-year-old expects gifts, and rightly so."

"Anything concerning football."

"I know nothing about soccer. I mean football."

"Oh, no, no, no!"

"Oh, no?"

"Isa, that is such a deal breaker."

"What do you mean a deal breaker?"

"We may have to call this relationship off or give you a crash course in football, and then you must love it."

"Really?"

He laughed. "No, but if you want Ian to like you, you might want to pretend you love it."

"Excuse me," Daniel called out. The young Japanese man stopped. Daniel held out his phone. "Do you mind taking our picture in front of Notre Dame?"

The man held the camera, letting Daniel and Isa see the result.

"Thank-you. It's great." The young man nodded and walked away.

"I think this is our best picture together yet. Don't you think?"

"Yes, except maybe for the gargoyle in the background."

"Hmm, you might have a point there, but still, it is an excellent picture. Better gargoyles than ghosts."

"I think I liked the stained glass windows the best at Notre Dame and the statue of Joan of Arc."

"Did you know that Notre Dame professes to have the crown of thorns?"

"No, I didn't. I'm learning caboodles with you."

"Caboodles?"

"Lots."

"Where to now? We still have some time before we meet for dinner."

"You're the tour guide."

"We could walk along the river. Or we could go underground."

"Underground? I do want to see the Catacombs."

"They're too far away. I was talking about Paris before it was Paris. It's right beneath our feet."

They walked several feet from Notre Dame and down some stairs and toured an underground area that was once the Roman baths.

"What do you think?" Daniel asked.

"Other than the Romans were everywhere? It's okay, interesting, a good bit of knowledge to have, but not as fascinating as Notre Dame Cathedral."

They walked along the Seine until coming to the chalet. They kissed and went their separate ways to freshen up before meeting Michael for dinner. Isa opened the door to her bedroom and saw Kate sitting cross-legged on the bed, reading.

She looked up from her book. "So what did you two love-birds do?"

"We saw Notre Dame and the Roman baths beneath the city and walked across *Ponts des Arts*."

"Oh yeah?"

"Yeah. And you and Marc?"

"We talked."

"Really? Just talked?"

"Okay, more. But our relationship isn't as advanced as yours and Daniel's."

"Kate, do you mind if I ask for some advice?"

"Are you asking my professional opinion?"

"Maybe I am?"

"Shoot. I will even give you a family discount." She laughed. "I think of you as already one of us."

"Do you think Daniel and I are moving too fast?"

"Normally, in my professional opinion, I would say a definite yes, but I've seen you together. And how do I say this without it sounding trite? You seem to have spent lifetimes together."

Isa smiled. "I feel that way too, but after an eight-year-long marriage that failed, I am a bit hesitant. It is easy to get wrapped up in a whirlwind fantasy in Paris, the city of love. Things change with real life."

"Isa, you are wise. They do change. I've never been married, but even I know that. Sadly, from experience. I've had several failed relationships."

"That is why you are being so cautious with Marc?"

"Yes. But hey, I've seen what you and Daniel have, and I would bet my career that it is the real thing. Has Daniel told you much about Steph?"

"We did a lot of talking on our way to Notre Dame."

"Daniel's been through a lot. It has also taught him a lot. I trust his judgment when it comes to you. Besides, I would love to have a sister in the family. And we look to be the same size."

Isa hugged Kate. "Thank you. If I don't do some laundry soon, I may have to borrow some clothes."

"You can wash them at my apartment. Or wash them here. I'm sure Marc wouldn't mind."

"You wouldn't have any ideas for a birthday present for Ian, would you?"

"Anything football."

Isa laughed. "That's what Daniel said."

"You will like Ian. He is a good kid. I know he would like for his father to settle down. In my professional opinion, you as Daniel's wife would be good for Ian."

"He hints at marriage, but there has been no proposal. It's way too soon for one, don't you think?"

"I have seen couples who have dated for years and still gotten a divorce. I've also known couples, one in particular, who married after two weeks, and they now have children in college and are as happy as ever. Follow your heart. It won't lead you astray."

"Good advice."

"One more piece of advice. To ensure a happy relationship, you should learn to love football."

"I gathered as much. So what should we wear?"

"Something casual. I think we are just going for pizza. Is that okay?"

"I love pizza."

21

"*K*ate, you look beautiful. You both look beautiful," Marc said, seeing the two women come down the stairs.

"Doesn't she, though? All that dental work paid off." Darts flew from Kate's eyes.

"Your brother is a riot, Kate."

"Isn't he? I'm afraid all those therapy sessions were a total waste," Kate quipped.

Isa looked at Marc, smiled, and said, "Get used to it."

Marc got back to the business of being a host. "We will take the Metro part of the way if that's okay. It's crowded this time of night. But walking is too far."

As the four of them walked out the door together, Marc said, "Isa, Daniel says this is your first trip abroad. Have you been to the Champs-Élysées yet?"

"I stayed in Paris on my first night here and ate at one of the restaurants, but I haven't explored it. So far, I've seen Notre Dame, the Roman baths beneath the city, Orsay, and Giverny."

"A good start. But there is so much more to Paris. You have to get a feel for it. I'm a native, but I'm always wondering about all those souls who made it, what it is, and all those who came here for inspiration—Van Gogh, for instance. So many painters came here, Dali and Picasso, and many others. Your American writers, too—Hemmingway, Stein, and Fitzgerald. They came here to breathe in its aura. Paris is the nectar that draws anyone with a deep yearning of the soul to create."

"I hear what you are saying. The paintings at Orsay took my breath away and the clock—I love the clock. It stands as a time portal overlooking the city's panorama, what is past, what is now, and what is to come. As I stood there enamored by it, I couldn't help but imagine the hands suddenly moving backward and the view changing."

"Or perhaps moving forward in time," Marc said. "On the subject of time, it took quite a bit of time for the impressionists to be accepted. I do believe we are all impressionist lovers. Kate told me the impressionists were her favorite." Kate smiled as Marc squeezed her hand.

"And don't forget Nice," Daniel said.

"I could never forget Nice," Isa said.

"I detect Nice has some special place in your hearts," Marc said.

"It was where they went on their first date," Kate said.

"I love Southern France. Michael is coming up from Nice. He has been working there on an archeological dig."

"The Castle?" Isa asked.

"Yes, that's where he has been working."

"We watched them for a while."

"We are here," Marc said as they approached the steps to the Metro. "We had better speed it up, or we will have to wait for the next train. We don't want him to have to wait long for us. Lots of good places to eat although some will be touristy. I thought pizza might appeal to everyone. It's a staple of bikers, and I think it's Michael's favorite food. He said when he was in college, he used to deliver pizzas. I told him to meet us at George V's. It's easy, close to the Metro."

"I do admire France's transportation system. I wish we had the same in America," Isa said as they ran down the steps.

Daniel maneuvered the Metro tickets like a pro. Marc had a pass. The trains came in and out every few minutes like clockwork. They boarded only to be squished in like the cheese inside a grilled cheese sandwich. They came out right at George V's.

"I don't see him. Oh well, we'll get a table." Marc turned to the maître d. "Four please, a bottle of pinot if you please?" He spoke in French. Daniel interpreted. Marc changed to English. "Is that all right with everyone?"

"I was going to say if you ordered merlot, I was out of here," Isa said, laughing.

"What?" Daniel asked.

"It is from the movie *Sideways*. Loved that movie. I like your girlfriend, Daniel," Marc said.

"I'm not much of a drinker. My puns may get worse through the night."

"I don't think any of us is a match for Daniel when it comes to wit," Marc said.

The waiter brought out the bottle and four glasses. "Merci," Marc said, promptly standing. "Here he is! One more glass if you please."

They rose to their feet. Isa felt faint before even tasting the wine. He recognized her. That was evident. Isa saw Daniel looking at her. She saw Daniel looking back at him. She felt her face either flushing or turning white. She couldn't tell which.

"Michael, this is Kate, Kate's brother, Daniel, and his girl-friend, Isa."

"Isa, how have you been?"

"Okay, Josh. You?"

Isa took one of those deep breaths Father Foley told her to

take during the regression and tried her best not to appear nervous at seeing him.

"I can see us knowing each other has caught everyone off guard. Isa and I were in college together. I went by my middle name back then, Josh."

"I remember now. I saw you at the dig in Nice. I saw you looking at Isa," Daniel said.

"I thought it might be her, but what are the odds? I thought it must be someone that looked remarkably like her. Besides, I heard she had married Nick, and you weren't Nick."

"We divorced," Isa said flatly.

"It's a small world," Marc said.

"You go by Michael now?" Isa asked, not knowing what to say.

"My first name and the name on my resume, the one people used when I got hired. Denise called me Josh, my middle name." Michael looked at the others to explain. "Denise is my ex. Another reason I go by Michael now."

Isa could hear the awkwardness in his voice.

"We should all sit," Marc said. Isa ended up across from Josh. Daniel sat on her left. Marc picked up his glass. "To friendship!" Everyone took a drink. Isa needed hers.

"So, *how* is Denise?" Although Marc had warned her, Josh had already brought her up, and Isa couldn't resist. She took another drink.

Kate kept a professional decorum.

"I guess Denise is okay. Haven't seen her for a year. Just waiting for the divorce to go through."

"I'm sorry it didn't work out," Isa said. "Really." She felt a stab of pity for him. She leaned sideways, her shoulder touching Daniel's.

"Don't be. It wasn't much of a marriage. So, are you and Daniel…?"

"No, we only met since I came to France," she said before he finished.

"It's gone way beyond meeting. Daniel is taking Isa to Scotland to meet his son and our parents," Kate said. "Oh, Daniel and I are twins," Kate added.

Did Kate know this was the Josh in her regression? Of course, she did. How could she not?

Daniel looked at Isa and winked and then back to Josh. "This astounds me that you two ran into each other like this."

"Me too," Kate echoed. "But then, a lot of strange stuff has been happening lately."

"Oh?" Josh asked.

"Too long to go into right now," Daniel said.

"I guess it was *destin* in a way that we should run into each other," Isa said.

"Destiny, fate," Josh echoed. He spoke French or knew what that particular word translated to in English.

"If you don't mind me asking, how is Nick doing, or do you keep in touch?" He looked at the others. "Nick was my room-mate in college."

"It's been three years since the divorce, but he has moved on, remarried, well, that is what I heard, still lives in Lexington, works at his father's company. Not that I've kept up with him. I suppose he is still there. I can't imagine he would be somewhere else."

"You two didn't have children?"

"No," Isa said, taking another drink.

Marc motioned for the waiter. "Could you bring us another bottle?"

"It's my turn to say I'm sorry. I remember once you saying you wanted a house full of children."

"It's not too late for that," Daniel said, squeezing her around the waist.

"Don't be. I might have never met Daniel if I did have kids by Nick."

The maître d stood at their table, white cloth over his coat sleeve as he uncorked another bottle of wine and poured.

"What should we drink to? Relationships that work out?" Marc suggested.

"Sounds like a good thing to drink to," Daniel said as they clinked glasses. "I, for one, have found a relationship that I am most confident will work." He turned to Isa and kissed her. Isa smiled. Did she detect somewhat of a grimace on the part of Josh? Maybe some of Denise's jealousy rubbed off on him. They do say couples, after a while, begin to act alike. Perhaps she might become as witty as Daniel and be in control of every situation.

To Isa's relief, the conversation took a sudden turn to cycling —equipment, their bikes, what roads were best, the steepest grades, and their best times. Not knowing much about bicycling, Isa's mind drifted. Here she was. Less than a month ago, she was just leaving the states, her house, her career, and everything familiar to her. Now she sat in a foreign country with a new man in her life while sitting across from the man she had once hoped would be in her life. He looked subpar compared to Daniel.

"Are you okay, Isa?" Kate asked

"It's the wine."

"I learned early on Isa cannot hold her liquor," Daniel said. "Maybe we had better order, get some food in you."

Both Isa and Daniel knew it was more than the wine. It was seeing Josh here of all places. And Kate knew it too. Would she tell Marc? Marc was the only one out of the loop. Should she ask her not to? It didn't matter. Josh was part of her past. In a way, the hands of the Orsay clock *had* turned back time just enough to give her closure.

One of the things Father Foley had said before they said their goodbyes to him was how things from the past would return until they were resolved, if not in this life, in the next. She was glad Josh came up again in this one. Maybe she could get some kind of clean slate in the next life.

Josh turned to her. "Isa, do you bicycle?"

"No, Josh."

"I'm not used to hearing you called Josh," Marc said.

"Should I use Michael?" Isa asked

"No, Josh is fine."

"We may change that as well as getting her interested in soccer," Daniel said.

"I'm more into football myself, American football, that is. Sometimes baseball, The Atlanta Braves, of course. I have to be true to my turf. I did play soccer in middle school, if that counts. I was in Belgium at the time."

"I remember. Your family was military. You traveled a lot."

"Good memory."

"So, Josh, or Michael, tell me why soccer isn't as big in America," Daniel said.

"I would say the lack of commercials. Everything is money in America. Football, baseball, and basketball bring in the big bucks with advertising. Soccer doesn't work that way. For that reason, it will never happen in America, at least not in a big way."

"I will try not to get off on America since we have two Americans present here," Marc said.

"I don't mind," Isa said. "There are good things, but we could improve so much. I have seen lots of things in France that I would love to emulate in America."

"What would you change, Isa?" Marc asked.

"I would change what Josh, or Michael, sorry, said about money. Money or corporations run America. Many people think it is the politicians. But corporations rule the politicians. For instance, there is a battle about GMOs in our country. Your country, along with other European countries, has banned them. I wish it were so in America. The French speak up much more than Americans do. Our protests are rather pathetic compared to yours. And the ones we do have are just a bleep covered by the press because the corporations own the news agencies."

"Also, our prison system is the biggest in the world. We imprison people for minor offenses like marijuana but let the real culprits go. The bankers have the politicians in their pockets. The pharmaceutical companies keep cures from people because cures would mean no more business," Josh said.

This was the Josh she remembered. These were the conversations she remembered. He always loved a good conversation. Josh was a closet activist, one who spoke a good talk but didn't act. But she couldn't judge. She was the same. Josh was the same in relationships. What did Daniel say about things becoming crystal clear in Nice?

"Josh, did you ever join the Peace Corps like you talked about in college?"

"No, and I sometimes regret that. Denise and I ended up getting married. Denise wasn't the Peace Corps type."

"I had no idea that you and Denise were a couple." Did he remember kissing her? Of course, he did. She took a bite of her pizza.

"It just sort of happened. It was more Denise's idea than mine."

Isa thought, what a cop-out. He was weak. Then she thought of her own weakness. She knew marrying Nick wasn't right, but she just went along with it to please. The regression was having a lingering effect. The lessons were revealing themselves. Could she have walked away and never married Nick? Or was it in her karma? Father Foley said her prayer kept her from being a paraplegic. He said it was God's grace. Maybe she could have stood up for herself and walked away from her karma with Nick. She would never know. One could be a lifetime student of this stuff.

Marc broke her thought process as he poured more wine and asked, "What does America have over France?"

Isa looked to Daniel and Kate, "You have both been there. To New York, you said. What do you think America has over France? And Marc, I'm sure you have been there, right?"

"Yes, I think maybe one of the things I liked best was the diversity of culture. I love my country, but most of the French can be lumped together. We tend to think alike but not Americans. Your country is more colorful."

"I will agree with that," Josh chimed in.

"As for colorful. America sure has some colorful personalities," Daniel said.

"Forgive me. I'm thinking of something more mundane. Clothes," Isa said.

"No, clothes are not mundane," Kate said. "Paris is the fashion capital of the world."

"All the colors in France are muted. I've passed enough people and windows to know. The main color or noncolor is black. I stick out like a sore thumb."

"You won't in Scotland," Daniel said.

"Black is also the primary color in New York," Marc said.

"Agreed, and redheads don't look good in black," Kate said.

"Isa is a natural in black with her dark hair and dark eyes. But she also looks great in colorful things," Daniel said. Isa kissed him on the cheek.

"Kate, what else would you say America has over Europe?" Isa asked.

"I'm having a hard time coming up with something. But then, America is only a little over two hundred years old, and Europe is thousands of years old, so maybe we should give it some time." After a slight pause, Kate exclaimed, "Movies! I do love American movies."

"Yes, we do like American films. You will notice all the billboards for them in the Metro," Marc said and laughed.

"I definitely know what the best thing about America is," Daniel said.

"What?" Isa asked.

"You," he said with a kiss.

"Cheers," Marc said. They clanked glasses again.

The conversation continued for another couple of hours, somewhat reminiscent of the movie *My Dinner with Andre.* They sipped wine and offered solutions to the world's problems. Josh talked about the archeological dig he was helping with at Castle Hill in Nice. Isa hadn't even noticed him there. Funny, Josh wasn't even on her radar when she was with Daniel. The time wasn't right. That's what she remembered the stranger saying in the dream. The time must be right *now.* She felt her past slipping down the garbage disposal right behind the journals she kept during her marriage to Nick. And it all felt so light and easy, or maybe it was only because she was lightheaded from the wine. Darkness had descended while they ate pizza, drank a third and fourth bottle of wine, and finished off with crème brûlée and tea.

Daniel looked at his watch. "It's eleven p.m. Isa and I want to catch the Metro. We have a date at Montmartre. You are all welcome to join us."

Everyone begged off, not wanting to intrude. Daniel and Isa feigned disappointment but weren't fooling anyone.

"Then we will see you in the morning at breakfast unless you are still up when we get back."

After getting off the Metro at Abbesses Station, they began the ascent to Montmartre. It was easy enough to find, even for Isa. You only had to follow the people. There were no secluded romantic spots in Paris, for everyone had the same idea. The steps went on and on.

"Is your ankle okay?" she asked.

"Healed long ago. I can prove it to you. Do you want me to carry you?"

"Do you think you could?"

"I carried your suitcases. They might weigh more than you."

"I wish."

They looked up to see the *Basilica of Sacré-Coeur*, a beacon watching over the city. After maneuvering through the people-packed stairs, they lodged themselves about a third of the way down from the cathedral, far enough from the entertainment, positioned a third up from the base of the steps. Speakers and equipment were off to the side, on the grass. A man played guitar and sang American songs, James Taylor, a little James Blunt, all easy listening. Street hawkers sold wine and beer along with miniature Eiffel Towers. You couldn't get away from them. Sometimes the gendarmerie would come by and run the peddlers off, but Isa saw none tonight. Isa thought selling alcoholic beverages to be a strange custom on the grounds of a church, but hey, they were in France. The long climb had caused the wine from dinner to wear off. Paris below them was an array of lights. Midnight in Paris, and everyone was teaming with life.

People sang along. They all knew the American words. Daniel could not carry a tune, but that didn't stop him. The singer interwove some French songs throughout his repertoire. Daniel sang along to the French versions as well. Then the singer sang *Storybook Love* by Mark Knopfler from *The Princess Bride*. Daniel and Isa looked at each other. Tears came to her eyes. He wiped them away and smiled. From that moment, it was their song. They kissed again from another spot on top of the world, or what felt like the top.

They walked on, reaching the cathedral. From below, the songs had become more upbeat—something in French.

"And they say New York City never sleeps. Come on, let's go inside the church," Daniel said.

"We can? At this hour?" Isa asked, but she saw the church doors were wide open. A nun handed out programs at the door while a choir of nuns filtered in for midnight Mass.

Daniel and Isa passed the fountain containing the holy water.

To their dismay, there was but a muddy drip left, thanks to their predecessors. Daniel dropped some Euros in the box, and once again, he lit two candles for them. Her prayer was the same as it had been at Notre Dame, that she and Daniel find love and happiness together with a house full of children, except this time, she added that they might find each other life after life.

They made their way down the stairs, to the Metro, and back to Marc's house. The house was quiet. Everyone was asleep.

A note with Isa's name scribbled across it was on the foyer table, in direct view of the entrance. It caught Daniel's eye before Isa saw it. He handed it to her. "Do you need privacy?"

A note for her. It seemed odd, but then she knew as obviously as Daniel did that it was from Josh.

Neither of them had brought up Josh after leaving dinner. They had already been rehashing things from their past. It needed a rest, and Isa didn't want to spoil the romance of their trek to the basilica.

"I want no secrets between us." She opened the note as he stood over her shoulder. They read silently.

Isa,

I wanted to say goodbye this time. I don't know if it will make up for the fact that I didn't say it those many years ago. Maybe I should be doing it in person, but under the circumstances, this seemed best. I hope you still don't think of me as the coward I was back in college. The odd thing is that when I saw you and Daniel in Nice, I wanted to say something, call out to you, but still, I was a coward. And what if it wasn't you? Would it have mattered? But I looked up, and there you were. I wasn't sure at first. It was too unbelievable. Maybe what stopped me from calling out your name was seeing how wrapped up in each other you were and still were tonight at dinner. At Nice, I observed you for as long as I could. You disappeared around the corner. I shrugged it off as my eyes *were deceiving me. Maybe it was someone that just looked like you.*

And then there you were again in Paris, the two of you staying with Marc. For some reason, our paths were meant to cross. Maybe it was just so I could say goodbye. I confess. I did know you had married Nick and that you had no children. Nick and I kept in touch for a while. I doubt he told you. Nick was like that. I didn't know about the divorce but figured as much upon seeing you and Daniel together. I wasn't sure if it had anything to do with Denise. I suspected all those trips she took up to Lexington were to see Nick. Nick never deserved you. For that matter, neither did I. I hope my saying this is not out of line. I figured you must have known, divorcing Nick and all.

Maybe things would have been different if I had made a move back in college. I have no excuse. I was lazy regarding matters of the heart, but I had feelings for you. I more or less let Denise call the shots. She wanted to transfer and talked me into going with her.

As you know, she was outgoing. Okay, obnoxious. I see that you have opened up a lot more. I'm glad.

Maybe if things were different, we could have made it work this time. But no, it is clear that you have found the man of your dreams in Daniel, and I can tell that the guy loves you with all his heart. I wouldn't stand a chance now. But it blew my mind that we crossed paths after all these years, and of all places, in France. I don't know if it was awkward for you, but it was for me. You seemed as cool as a cucumber. I have some other bicycle buddies in Paris I can stay with, so I took off after dinner.

I wish you and Daniel all the best. Maybe I'll quit being so lazy in love now and take some action. You and Daniel inspired me. Denise has been waiting for me to sign the divorce papers. You see, I'm even a coward when it comes to that. There has to be someone out there for me.

Best wishes, and may all your dreams come true with Daniel. I hope you have that house full of children you wanted.

Josh

Isa stood frozen. "Nick and Denise?"

"Something you didn't know?" Daniel asked.

"No, I didn't. But it does explain Nick wanting me to ask Denise to be a bridesmaid at our wedding."

"Are you okay, Isa?"

Isa folded the note and stuck it back in the envelope. "He's right. He wouldn't stand a chance now. Also, both Nick and Josh are in the past. None of it matters. Do you think Marc has a garbage disposal?"

"What? Why?"

"So I can put this note down it, the same way I put my old journals down mine before leaving Nick."

"You can't put paper down a garbage disposal."

"You can't?"

"No, it would turn to pulp and clog it up."

She laughed.

"Why are you laughing?"

"I think I left Nick with a really big plumbing problem. Anyway, moving on."

"Yes, moving on. I'm happy to let you know a vacancy just opened up in my room."

THE FOLLOWING DAY JOSH WAS ONLY MENTIONED CASUALLY. Marc said he decided not to spend the night, wanting to hook up with some other cyclists. Isa could tell from Kate's face she suspected it was an excuse not to be around Isa and Daniel. One day, Isa would possibly tell her about the note but not today.

Since it was their final day in Paris before leaving for Scotland, Daniel and Isa debated over touristy locations versus quaint off-the-beaten paths. They chose the latter. Isa agreed she had the whole summer. She would save The Louvre, Versailles, and the Catacombs for later but not Shakespeare and Company.

IF ISA HAD TO PUT THE ECSTATIC FEELING OF WALKING INTO THE famous bookseller into words, she would sum it up as bohemian, eccentric, and warm. Oh, and small and cozy *and* English—she couldn't leave those out. Besides books, every nook and cranny housed something spectacular, notes or drawings, all having to do with books. This bookstore had everything: heart, soul, *and* romance. Isa had read that up to one hundred married couples had met here.

She rubbed her fingers over the different textures of the covers and took in the essence of the aroma coming from the pages. Who could have held these books before her? And there were the Tumbleweeds upstairs. The next equivalent of *Harry Potter* or *The Great Gatsby* could be in progress right over her head while she walked between the store's bookshelves—someone at a keyboard or even an ancient typewriter pouring out the next great masterpiece.

Daniel settled into the part that housed first editions while Isa explored every facet of the shop, lingering wherever she heard a conversation about a book, even if it was in French, trying to decipher a word here or there. But for the most part, she found English was the native tongue of the bookstore.

"Has Ian read the Harry Potter books?" Isa asked Daniel.

"No, he has only seen the movies."

"Would the complete set be a good gift?"

"Definitely. I've been encouraging him to read more."

After several hours, they were outside, each carrying Shakespeare and Company bags. At a café, they indulged in a typical Parisian lunch, watching the other tourists. Isa thought herself smug to believe she was no longer one of them.

They meandered through cobblestone alleyways exploring small boutiques with offerings ranging from tea to vintage clothing to *boulangeries* to wines and cheeses.

To make good on his promise, Daniel took Isa to the lawn adjacent to the Eiffel Tower, where they spread a blanket and uncorked a bottle of wine they purchased at one of the wine shops along with some aged cheddar and crackers before making their way back to Marc's to turn in early by Parisian standards.

PART II

22

"*P*lease call us Kathryn and Colin," Daniel's mom insisted while she and her husband hugged Isa.

Isa spent a good portion of the initial meeting apologizing for her two overstuffed suitcases that both Daniel and his father worked up a sweat wedging in behind the van's back seat.

"Not to worry, Dad. Maybe Isa can ride on top with the bicycles."

"Now, Danny, I reckon if anyone needs to ride on top, it will be you." Mr. Stewart winked at Isa.

Danny? No, she much preferred Daniel. Besides the same blue eyes, Isa also noted both father and son had the same propensity for winking. In studying their features, Isa could see both Daniel and Kate in their parents, but the red hair undoubtedly came from their mother. There were streaks of gray, but the auburn color was still predominant. Colin's hair was a receding, thinning gray, making Isa wonder if it was a sign of Christmas future.

After arriving at Daniel's parents' house, there was a bit of hesitation regarding which vehicles the luggage was to be reloaded in. In other words, what were the sleeping arrangements? Colin made a joke, which led Isa to believe they regarded their thirty-year-old children as adults capable of deciding their relationships and sex lives. Also, there had been a new development between Kate and Marc. Those two said their goodbyes, driving off to Kate's apartment, leaving Isa and Daniel free to head to his cottage but not before Colin insisted on giving Isa a tour of the house while Daniel curiously disappeared upstairs with his mom.

After checking on his grandfather, who was sound asleep, Daniel said, "Isa, we should get going to the cottage. It's a wee bit of a drive, and I want you to see the countryside before it gets too dark."

DANIEL'S COTTAGE WAS ABOUT A HALF-HOUR DRIVE FROM HIS parents' house, which was in a suburb of Edinburgh called Morningside. Would it even be called a suburb in Scotland? So many little minor differences to learn, like which side of the car to get in.

"Oh, do you want to drive?" Daniel asked when out of habit, she went to the driver's side instead of the passenger side of Daniel's white Prius. Isa laughed and proceeded to the opposite side, where Daniel stood with the door open for her.

"I'll never get used to how you drive on the wrong side of the road," Isa said as he closed the door behind her.

"We'll save that argument for later," Daniel said with a wink.

The car was immaculate. She had expected a back seat full of fast food wrappers, something she thought might be typical for a bachelor and busy university professor.

"I would give you a tour of Edinburgh and show you where I work, but since it will be dark soon, we'll save that for another day."

Daniel maneuvered through side streets and roundabouts

with ease while Isa took in what appeared to be well-established businesses in old stone and brick structures. There was a lot of stone in Scotland. Whereas in America, trademark signs abounded, a building simply said Pharmacy in bold letters, not that the American way of life hadn't reached its tentacles into the land of Robert Burns. They passed the all too familiar logos of Domino's Pizza and Mcdonald's, among others. There was even a Thai nail salon.

"A702, a straight shot to West Linton," Daniel said as they left the last vestiges of the city.

"West Linton?"

"Where I live," he said, reaching his left hand for hers. Both of their hands clasped together over the center console. At that moment, everything seemed right in the world. It was like all of those moments of childhood when she felt secure and loved, her mother tying the hood of her parka snuggly around her neck before letting her go outside to play in the snow and warm chocolate chip cookies fresh out of the oven when she came back in the house. But this was a different kind of contentment one rarely finds in adult life. She looked over at Daniel, his eyes straight ahead on the road. She observed his rugged jawline and the trace of beard stubble and slightly upturned lips conveying the same happiness. There was no need for words. She turned her head toward the window taking in the sights. They passed a lot of sheep grazing in pastures, houses that appeared to have been handed down through the generations, and a lot of stone walls. There were also golf courses appearing out in the middle of nowhere, a fixture along with the sheep and stone.

Daniel withdrew his hand, navigating some side streets before slowing and coming to a stop. "This is it, home sweet home."

This cottage wasn't as idyllic as the one Isa envisioned in her regression. It could use some fixing up. Daniel insisted on carrying her over the threshold for good luck. He flipped on a light switch, illuminating something in definite need of a woman's touch.

A leather couch faced what kind of coffee table was anyone's guess as it was cluttered with books, magazines, an empty pizza box, an empty Guinness bottle, and an unwashed coffee mug.

"I'm sorry. If I had any idea I would have been bringing you back with me, I would have cleaned. I guess I did have some idea or hope but didn't know for certain until returning to the inn."

"I think I might have been worried if it had been cleaned."

She flipped through the math textbooks, history books, and bicycling and sports magazines on the table. Finding nothing of a sexual nature reassured her Daniel was who she thought he was, but then, he probably wouldn't put them on display in his living room.

"Are you looking for anything in particular?" he asked.

"Only seeing what interests you."

"Oh," he said, drawing the letter 'o' out. "Those are under the bed. And the bodies are buried in the garden under the zucchini."

Her eyes grew big.

"You know I'm kidding. Do you think I planted a garden?" He drew her close and kissed her forehead. "You have nothing to worry about. You did not come home with a sexual pervert or axe murderer. Are you hungry?"

Hungry? That was certainly a change of topic from sexual pervert or axe murderer. "No, but possibly some tea, something relaxing if you have it."

"Are you nervous?"

"I guess a little. So much has happened since I've been in Europe."

He laughed. "Aye, but it's been good, right?"

"Yes," she said and smiled.

"The kitchen is this way. Follow me. I doubt if there is

anything to eat in the house. We will need to go food shopping tomorrow. Are you feeling domestic?"

"Should I get used to feeling domestic?"

"I don't know. Somehow I didn't picture you as being domestic, more of a bookworm." Daniel opened a cabinet. "My tea cupboard."

Isa pulled out a box of chamomile. The teakettle rested on a stove burner. "This is gas. I'm used to electric."

"It's easy," he said. He turned the knob on high, and a blaze shot up. "No matches these days. Well, the one I had previously took matches, but I replaced it."

Isa looked around. The kitchen was small but surprisingly clean.

"How come your kitchen is so clean, and the living room is such a mess?"

"I don't want to attract rodents. I would get a cat, but I'm afraid Samantha doesn't like cats."

Isa's widened eyes betrayed her surprise.

"My dog, a chocolate lab. Come on. I will introduce you to her." Daniel walked down a hallway from the kitchen, passing a side pantry. He opened a sliding glass door and called out, "Samantha, where are you, girl?"

A moment later, a wet dog jumped all over Daniel. "Meet your new master. Ah, look, she's wagging her tail. She likes you."

Isa bent down to pet her, looking up at Daniel. "You didn't tell me you had a dog."

"I was saving her as a surprise."

"Who takes care of her when you're gone?"

"Mrs. Ferguson, the next-door neighbor. I'll introduce you to her tomorrow. She's a godsend. I'll be honest. She's the reason my kitchen is so clean. She has a key for when I'm away. She knows better than to go through my books or magazines, though. She took the liberty of rearranging one time, and I had a heck of a time finding things. I hope she doesn't break down when she meets you."

"Break down?"

"Aye, I think she's been in love with me for the longest time."

"You said, Mrs. Ferguson. Isn't she married?"

"A widow. Aye, I did consider it once but had to let her down easy. I told her it wouldn't work with us."

"Why not?"

"As you know, I like older women, but when I told her I was looking for someone to have my babies, she wouldn't hear of it."

"You talked to her about having your babies?"

"Ah, Isa. I'm kidding. She's eighty, if not a day. I don't ask her age. It's not polite. She'll love you. She's always nagging me to find a good woman and settle down."

Daniel filled Samantha's bowls with some food and water.

"I usually eat in the living room, so that's another reason my kitchen is clean."

"I noticed you don't have a dining table, or is there a dining room somewhere?"

"No dining room. I did have a small table in the kitchen, but since I mostly eat in the living room, I moved it upstairs for a desk. I'll move it back down if you want. Do you want to drink your tea before Samantha and I give you the grand tour?"

"Sure."

They settled on the couch. "I have been meaning to make some improvements on the cottage. It belonged to my grandfather, well, actually my grandmother. My grandfather was from a village called Smailholm. He comes from a long line of postmasters. When he met my grandmother, he moved here and took a job at the post office. Always said he preferred the post office in Smailholm, though. He said you got your mail on Saturday. If you went early, you got last week's gossip. If you went late, you got this week's gossip. You didn't meet him because he turns in early. He lives with my parents now since the heart attack. He's been in assisted living for the last three years. Didn't want to live in the cottage after my grandmother died. I was to inherit it anyway, so I moved here when my lease was up on my apartment. You'll meet him tomorrow at the party."

THE NEXT MORNING, ISA HAD A BETTER VIEW OF THE COTTAGE. It was in a small residential neighborhood, but the front lawns were big, and the houses were well-spaced. There was even a sizable fenced-in backyard. The uneven stonework set Daniel's home apart from the more modern structures of the neighborhood. A shaggy lawn greeted the slate stoop in the front. Large shrubs encompassed a good portion of the front of the house.

Isa moved through the house, examining every corner in the light of day. Daniel had told her on the train to get used to rain and dreary days in Scotland. They hadn't even discussed it, but she thought he was already moving her in with him. When she checked out of the inn, she didn't know what to tell Claire. She had stuttered, saying, "Claire, I don't know…"

Claire cut her off with a smile and said, "*Destin.*"

Isa stood barefoot in her pajamas beside Samantha just outside the back door. She looked down at the rain puddle and saw her reflection. Samantha barked. For an instant, she thought she saw Dora staring back at her. Chill bumps rose on her arms. Daniel came up from behind.

"What's wrong, girl?" He reached down and petted Samantha. Her barking turned into a whimper. He wrapped his arms around Isa. "Scotland can get mighty cold in the winter. Sometimes even the summers can send a chill through you."

"I see you have a fireplace to handle it and a good stack of wood out back."

"It can make the living room a cozy place in winter. Nice for reading," he said and smiled. He knew the way to her heart.

A drip from the gutter caused a slight ripple in the puddle. For a brief moment, the yard changed. Isa saw a swing set over a green manicured lawn with kids playing. Daniel was grilling. Isa was placing paper plates on a picnic table.

"I think I'll be able to handle the cold winters," she said.

"I just put on some coffee. Want some?"

"Yeah, that sounds good."

Daniel returned, handing her the cup. "What are you thinking?"

"I think that your yard could use mowing."

"Ah, it is rare when the lawn gets dry enough to run a mower over it. I hope you packed a rain slicker in your overstuffed suitcases and a decent pair of boots. If not, they're in plentiful supply here."

"Like the miniature Eiffel Towers in Paris?"

"Aye, like those."

"I do have a rain jacket but no boots. Will I be staying that long? You talk as if I'm moving in with you."

He took the empty mugs. "Stay right here. I'll be back. The sun is coming out for a change. We don't want to waste a moment of it."

Isa obeyed.

"Just half a cup for me this time," she said in his wake.

He returned but not with the coffee. Instead, he bent down on one knee.

"Isa, Isabella, would you do me the honor of marrying me? I know we have only known each other a few weeks, but we've packed more into this time than some people pack into years, and I just know that you are the one I've been waiting for. This isn't what I had planned for a proposal. Well, I hadn't planned anything yet. I kept mulling over in my heart how to do it. During the train ride, different proposal scenarios played out in my mind. But somehow, everything about this morning seems right. Please forgive me if this is not the kind of proposal you wanted, but I couldn't wait. Besides, I've been a little nervous about it."

A tear rolled down her cheek.

"Isa, I would wipe that tear from your face, but I'm still on bended knee waiting for an answer."

Another tear rolled from her other eye. "Please get up because the answer is yes or aye." She laughed.

"Are you disappointed?"

"Disappointed?"

"That the proposal wasn't more elaborate?"

"No, this is perfect. You caught me off guard, is all."

He pulled a ring from his robe pocket, took her hand with his other hand, and placed the ring on her finger.

"It's beautiful. It looks old. Daniel, when did you have time to get a ring, and how did you know my size?"

"It belonged to my grandmother. The size was just lucky."

"Or maybe *destin*." She examined the ring with a smile. "The grandmother in Spain?"

"No, my mum's mum, the one who lived here before. She had been saving it for me when I found the right someone. That is what we went upstairs for when my father showed you around."

"So your parents know. Do they approve?"

"Aye, they can tell how much I love you. Also, they are happy to see me settle down."

"What about Ian?"

"I did think about having him meet you first, but then thought maybe he should meet you as my fiancée. Besides, I know he will love you as I do, well, not exactly, but you know what I mean. And now, we had better get dressed, grab breakfast, and plan a party. Mum has probably cooked up a feast this morning. And then we'll plan a wedding."

Samantha nudged up beside them. Daniel said, "Look, Samantha approves. She's wagging her tail."

Isa laughed. "That dog hasn't stopped wagging her tail since you returned. Daniel, there is one thing I have to know."

"I'm listening."

"Children?"

"No more than four, Isa."

She smiled. "Hmmm, well, the cottage isn't that big."

"We'll make it work. You can see we have room to build on."

"I'm thirty-three. You do know we'll have to get started right away."

"That's fine. I'll do my part."

23

*I*an inherited Daniel's freckled complexion and mop of red hair. He was a well-adjusted kid, if ever there was one, and also a typical boy who was inside playing video games when he wasn't playing football.

Ian had taken to her right off, as did Kathleen, Colin, and even Gramps, who Isa surmised was where Daniel got his wit. The only hesitancy about such a short engagement came from Isa's parents, one reason Daniel insisted on a honeymoon in New Orleans with a side trip to see her parents.

Vows were exchanged at a register's office in Edinburgh with Kate and Marc as witnesses. Besides them, Kathleen, Colin, and Ian were present. Isa wanted no fanfare, the opposite of her first wedding. Adorned in the dress Daniel bought for her at the antique market in Nice, they were married by a state registrar. "The money we save can be used for travel," Isa insisted.

The highlight of their honeymoon was not the plush hotel, Le Pavillon, where Daniel so boldly swam naked in the hotel's rooftop swimming pool, which they had all to themselves. Nor was it the French Quarter or the gumbo. It was a colorful character by the name of Carl who gave them a tour of the Edgar Degas House.

Thoughts of France lingered heavily in the air as Daniel and Isa sat in a coffee shop they discovered to have once been the Cotton Exchange building, a subject of one of Edgar Degas's paintings. It had once been a cotton office owned by Edgar Degas's uncle. This aroused Daniel's historical curiosity. Neither Daniel nor Isa had thought of Edgar Degas as having been in America. This little-known fact led them on a trail that ended up with them meeting Carl.

Daniel and Isa were the only ones to show up for a tour of the house where Degas had lived with his maternal relatives from 1872 to 1873. The woman at the main desk, the only one who appeared to be on the grounds, made a quick phone call to secure a guide. A short time later, a stoutly built man in khaki shorts, not much taller than Isa, shuffled in. He literally waddled like a duck.

It wasn't long before Daniel and Isa concluded Carl epitomized Mr. New Orleans. The charm of the city radiated from his core. Adding Daniel's Scottish flair to the mix was like setting off fireworks on the Fourth of July. Unfortunately, Daniel and Isa's trip to America had just missed Independence Day.

Being the only customers that morning, they received a private tour of the house. To be exact, it was two houses, although originally, it had been one. An early twentieth-century developer thought it would be more valuable if he were to have two houses. So half of the house was moved to the lot next door. It astounded Isa that this could be done during this era. But compared to Notre Dame, dividing and moving a house a few yards was a small feat. The two structures doubled as a museum and bed and breakfast.

Degas wrote five letters while he was there. He did four drawings and eighteen paintings, some of which were *Children on a Doorstep, A Cotton Office in New Orleans, Woman Seated on a Balcony, Portrait of Estelle Musson,* and *Cotton Merchants in New Orleans.* It was the latter that led them to the house. His paintings took a different turn after he returned to France. It was then that he began the ballet paintings she had viewed at Orsay.

Daniel found that telling people you were on your honeymoon brought certain favors. It was no different with Carl. Carl immediately started laying out a must-see itinerary for them. His top recommendation was *Café Du Monde*, famous for their beignets, square pieces of dough that are fried and covered with powdered sugar. Since they had taken the trolley to the Degas House, Carl insisted on dropping them off there. Daniel and Isa followed him across Esplanade Avenue to an old Ford jalopy that had seen better days. He apologized for the mess, pushing aside a mountain of papers, and discarding take-out boxes and soda cans to make room for them. After a few attempts at igniting the engine, they were off. Along the way, he pointed out various buildings and their history. It was the tour that didn't end.

Before departing the vehicle, he handed them a folded-over card that read more like a resume than a business card. Carl gave about any type of tour that was to be had in New Orleans, including ghost tours. He also did dry walling and plastering. But what caught their eye was that he was also a priest. Father Foley was from New Orleans. Yes, Carl knew him. Carl knew most anyone worth knowing in New Orleans and vice versa. They told him they had met Father Foley while in France, omitting details. They weren't sure if they should be talking to anyone, least of all another priest, about their past life regression experiences. Carl might have believed in ghosts, even possession, but past lives might be another matter altogether.

Carl instructed Daniel and Isa to meet him in a few hours in front of Antoine's Restaurant for a free tour, a honeymoon special. Antoine's was not on the usual New Orleans tour list. It was a behind-the-scenes tour. Being a fixture of the city, Father Carl had connections. He encouraged them to go on a ghost tour, but after giving each other the newly married telepathic signals, they declined. Even though they opted to spend their honeymoon in a town inhabited by ghosts, they wanted to leave them behind, concentrating on romance.

At *Café Du Monde,* with white powdered lips, they discussed the amazing synchronicity of meeting Carl, who knew Father Foley. On a phone call to announce their marriage to Claire and Albert before their honeymoon, Claire advised her to pay attention to synchronicity. "Maybe there is unfinished business with Dora's ghost," she had said.

They met Carl and several others in front of the restaurant at the appointed time. He had ditched the shorts for pants. He started the lecture about the buildings on the street. It seemed every local that passed by knew Carl.

Antoine's started in 1840 and boasted of being the oldest family-run restaurant in the city. The two-story structure consisted of a maze of rooms in which almost anyone famous had dined at least once. Antoine was from France and returned there to die on his native soil. Before they left, Daniel made reservations for later that night.

It was on the lower floor of the restaurant while seated in the center of a sea of white tablecloths and black-attired wait staff who swam like schools of fish around them, Isa first heard Daniel referred to as her husband by someone other than the official at their small intimate wedding ceremony. Daniel had gone to the restroom when their waiter came by and asked Isa if her *husband* would like horseradish with his Oysters Rockefeller. It was a simple enough question, but it struck Isa that she didn't know if Daniel liked horseradish. It was a minor thing, but there was still so much to learn about each other. There were all those little intricacies that conjoined them as man and wife that hadn't transpired between them yet.

Daniel sat back down. "Everything all right?"

"It couldn't be better. You should give that man a good tip."

"Oh, I think that goes without saying in this place. Do you know the waiters here make as much as I do at the university?"

That night at the hotel, their lovemaking was the most intimate, tender, and uncomfortable with such full stomachs. If Isa could pinpoint the moment she conceived, it would be on that night.

It was also the night she dreamed they were at the inn asking Claire and Albert to be the godparents of their child. The hands on the Orsay clock moved forward. Isa saw everyone together one last time, except for Ian, who was away at college. Albert and Claire were showing a boy and a girl the flowers in the garden. The girl had dark hair like Isa. She looked up, revealing rosy cheeks and dark eyes. The little boy, younger than the girl, ran around the garden like a child who could find nothing but mischief to get into. He tilted his head of red curls upward. Isa saw sparkling blue eyes before waking up.

*D*aniel and Isa were greeted with *bonjours*, hugs, and kisses from Claire and Albert. It was March and spring break at the university when Daniel wheeled their one small piece of luggage into the inn.

"You both look so well. Marriage agrees with you. Isa, you are glowing. I hope you don't mind that I put you in room eleven?"

"*Merci,* Claire. I will need all the extra space I can get. She rubbed her beach ball of a belly."

"You'll be happy to know we put a bigger bed in that room," Albert added.

"*Merci,* Albert," Daniel said with a wink.

"Do you have a date yet?" Claire asked.

"Next month, April 11. I can't wait. I stay uncomfortable."

"Oh, maybe it's twins?" Claire exclaimed.

"No, only one, a girl. That's what the ultrasound shows."

"A girl. Girls are so much easier to buy for. Such cute clothes they have for little girls." She paused. "Erma and Pare Foley will be joining us for dinner tonight."

"We will be happy to see them," Daniel said.

"Yes, we have a surprise," Claire added.

"A surprise? Okay, well, this should be interesting."

"It is," Albert said.

"You will want to freshen up before we eat. Dinner will be in about two hours."

Isa walked up the familiar steps, much slower than all the other times, with Daniel behind her pushing her along with one hand and dragging the luggage behind him with his other hand.

"Wait," he cautioned. "I will inspect first for ghosts." Daniel quickly perused the room before announcing, "All clear. Isa, I would carry you over the threshold for luck, but…"

"Are you telling me I'm fat?"

"Only in a good way."

Isa settled on the new bed and eased back against the pillow. "This mattress feels much better than what was in here before. My back is killing me. What surprise do you think they have for us?"

"I have no idea. You're the one with the ESP."

THEY ENTERED THE KITCHEN TO FIND FATHER FOLEY AND ERMA waiting for them. Albert uncorked a bottle of wine and opened a bottle of sparkling water for Isa.

"We must toast to this new baby," Erma said.

It was no surprise to Father Foley to hear about Carl. "God works in mysterious ways," he said.

"I can't help but think that all this is fate waiting to happen. But I don't know what," Isa said.

There were some mixed looks passed around. Erma broke the silence. "We also have some news for you."

"Yes, Claire said that earlier," Daniel said.

"One of the rocks on the hearth has been loose for the longest time. You know the fireplace is original to the inn," Claire said.

"I think it's one of the inn's most endearing features," Isa said.

"I love it," Daniel said.

"I've been after Albert for years to fix that loose stone. Finally, he broke down and started the repairs. He pulled the stone out to fill it with cement and well…"

"We found something," Erma chimed in.

"Found something? What?" Daniel asked.

"Something quite astounding," Erma said. Isa remembered Erma's propensity for keeping you on the edge of your seat with a story.

"Claire, tell them," Albert said.

"We found the letters."

"*The* letters? You mean the journal? The one that Dorcel kept?" Isa exclaimed.

"Yes, the letters or diary, the one I told you I had found when we tore out the bookshelf but then they disappeared. I thought I put them aside for the move. Someone didn't want them to leave the inn," Erma said.

Daniel and Isa looked at each other in disbelief.

"There's more," Albert said. "We found a coin, an old coin, dating back to sometime in the seventeenth or eighteenth century."

Isa thought back on her first dream about Dora and the stranger. She gasped. Daniel reached over to hold her. "Are you okay?" Claire poured her some more water.

"Maybe we shouldn't have told you with Isa's condition and all," Claire said.

"It's too much," Daniel agreed.

Isa took a sip of water. "No, no, don't worry. It's not so much the letters. Well, it is the letters, but I dreamed about the coin. That is what I reacted to. I had forgotten about it until you mentioned it."

"We don't want you to get too agitated over this. We have

been so excited. We thought about sending them, but when you called and said you were coming, we had to tell you in person. Also, we only found them a few days ago," Claire said.

"Yes, I thought I might transcribe them to English for you," Erma said.

"Sadly, some were ruined from smoke seeping in from the hearth," Claire said.

"Isa, do you need to lay down a bit? Maybe I could help you to relax with some hypnotic suggestions," Father Foley said.

"No, no, I'm okay. All of you are too overprotective."

"What news has your doctor been giving you?" Claire asked.

"The pregnancy is going well. Oh." Isa jumped.

"What?" Daniel asked, startled.

"A kick. A rather strong one." Isa rubbed her stomach. "See, a sign. She is telling me she is doing fine."

"I thought she had stopped kicking," Daniel said.

"I thought so too, but obviously not. It might not have been a kick, maybe an elbow or knee jab."

"Can you explain about the coin? What you dreamed?" Pare Foley inquired.

"It was in the first dream I ever had about Dora. I mean, Dorcel. I'm sorry, I never told you about the dreams. I started having them right after arriving here before seeing Dora's ghost. The stranger who came to see her had given her coins for payment. She had saved one in a hiding place. I might have known it was hidden in the fireplace in my dream but couldn't remember at the time."

They looked at her, stunned.

"Can we see the coin and the letters, that is, if there are no more shocks that might upset Isa?" Daniel asked.

"I will go get them," Claire said. She slipped off into the next room and came back with a box. Daniel opened it to find stuffed within a worn book holding a stack of yellowed, fragile papers, brittle letters, written more than likely with a quill pen, of course in French. With the softest touch, Isa ran her fingers over them. Shivers ran through her. She touched her belly. The baby seemed content.

"Do you want me to read them? Translate them into English?" Erma asked.

"No, not now," Isa said. "Somehow, I don't feel the time is right."

"Do you want to take them with you when you leave? I feel as if they are rightfully yours," Claire said.

"No, I think they belong to the inn," she replied.

"After you leave, I will write them out in English and send the translations to you," Erma said.

"Yes, yes, I think that would be good. I would like to read them back in Scotland. I don't know why. But for some reason, that might be better. After the baby is born. There is so much going on right now. We only got the nursery finished. Dora had faded from my mind."

Claire reached for Isa's hand, clasping it. "Yes, I agree. You can read them when you are ready at your leisure and when Daniel is there with you if that is what you want."

"I would love to see the coin, though."

"Sweetheart? Maybe you should wait on that one too."

"No, Daniel, I'm all right. I would like to see it."

"You're sure?"

"Yes, I'm okay. The baby is fine. I know it. Remember my dream? The one I told you I had on our honeymoon?"

"Aye, okay. Albert, please show us the coin."

Albert pulled a pouch from his pocket and, from it, a copper coin about the size of a US half-dollar. Isa held it in her hand. She felt the coin's warmth. Possibly, the heat came from being in Albert's pocket. She knew it was something more.

"It *is* unique," Father Foley said.

"I can see that," Daniel said. "Do you know what the picture on it is?"

"I think it might be Ezekiel's wheel. It is mentioned in the Bible," Father Foley said.

"I'm sorry, Father. I'm afraid we are not up on the Bible as we should be," Isa said.

"Some think Ezekiel was describing a flying saucer. Some could interpret the picture on the coin to be this."

"The writing on it appears to be Latin. Father, you know Latin," Isa said.

"The legend written in Latin around the rim is also mysterious. 'OPPORTUNUS ADEST' translates as 'It is here at an opportune time.'"

Daniel looked at Isa. Isa looked back with a puzzled expression. "I'm afraid I don't know what that means."

"All things will be revealed in the end. It's nothing we should worry about," the Father said.

"Do you mean we should have faith, Father?"

"Yes, Isa, we should have faith."

"I want to think all this means something good. I was drawn to France for some reason. To this inn. I think the pull started when I was small. My grandmother was originally from France. She always wanted to come back but never did. It's like I fulfilled that wish for her. I listened to my heart about coming here, and when I did, everything happened like boom, boom, boom. Everything that has happened since I came to France has some sequence. Daniel hurt his ankle. If that hadn't happened, he would have been on his bicycle instead of sitting by the hearth where I met him, the very hearth where the letters were waiting for us to discover them." Isa reached for Daniel's hand. He clasped it tightly. "It was the same morning after seeing Dora's ghost. And there was seeing Josh again."

"Josh," they questioned.

"Yes. Father, I don't know if you remember, but he came up during my regression. We ran into him in Paris. It was fate, or *destin,* as you put it, Claire, giving us both some type of closure.

Dora has never done us any harm. I can only think she wanted us to find the letters and coin for some reason and that it must be good."

DINNER ENDED. ERMA HUGGED THEM GOODBYE. FATHER FOLEY heaped blessing after blessing upon them and the baby.

The following morning, they sat with Claire and Albert, loading up on croissants and tea.

"Now we have something we want to ask you," Isa announced.

"Aye, we would very much like you to be godmother and godfather to our child," Daniel said.

Isa couldn't help but smile, noticing the tear that escaped from Albert's eye, running down the creases on his face.

"You have made an old woman and old man very happy," Claire said, hugging Isa and Daniel.

Albert locked the inn's door, and he and Claire drove them to the train station. Claire handed them a basket with a couple of baguette sandwiches for the train. The basket also contained a bottle of wine for Daniel and a bottle of Perrier for Isa. They watched both Claire and Albert waving from the train window. Isa relished in one of the many moments of contentment she had been blessed with since coming to France as she and Daniel waved back.

After they shared the lunch, Isa melted into Daniel's arms and slept, dreaming of a house full of children.

25

*J*t was a crisp spring morning in late May. Frost, hopefully the last of the season, covered the ground as Isa pulled the package from the mailbox. She had just finished breastfeeding Danielle Claire before putting her down in the nursery.

It had been less than a year since Isa had made such a dramatic change to her life by deciding to make the trip to France. Who would have thought so much would happen due to that trip—a ghost, past lives, moving to Scotland, a husband and a baby?

Isa didn't have to read the return address to know the package came from Claire. It was the letters. She hadn't thought of them since that day. As usual, her life was moving at a rapid pace. Danielle Claire came two weeks early—not on the eleventh, the date predicted by her doctor. A baby in the house changed everything. Besides falling in love all over again, this time with this tiny miracle who was the spitting image of Daniel except for Isa's dark hair, her life consisted of dirty diapers and breastfeeding as Danielle had an insatiable appetite. Exhaustion and when she could catch a catnap were how she spent the remainder of her time. She couldn't complain, though. When not at the university, Daniel did his part, even to the point of holding Danielle Claire up to her swollen breasts when she was dead tired. It was plain to see from the start Danielle would be a daddy's girl. And Daniel was right about her breasts becoming bigger.

Isa checked on Danielle in the nursery, set the box on the coffee table, and brewed a pot of tea. The coffee table was a beautiful oak. She smiled, thinking about the first time she saw it, or rather the first time she *didn't see* it with all the clutter on top.

Should she wait for Daniel? No, she thought. Seeing the box lying there was too much of a temptation and would haunt her all day. Haunt. She laughed out loud at that particular word choice. The fire that Daniel started before leaving for work was still burning. Danielle Claire was soundly asleep. Samantha was also asleep, curled up on the couch at her feet. Except for the occasional snap of the fire, all was quiet in the cottage. She ripped the package open, covered herself with the Stewart Clan throw draped over the back of the couch, took a drink of her tea, and carefully removed the contents out of the box.

A letter from Claire was on top.

Dearest Daniel and Isa,

We hope that both you and the baby are in good health. By all means, protect that godchild of ours. Albert and I send a prayer your way every day, as do Erma and Father Foley.

We know you must be busy. Although Albert and I weren't fortunate enough to have children, we know how much work a baby takes.

I have enclosed copies of the letters in their original French as you thought the actual originals should remain at the inn. Also enclosed are the translations. Perhaps we will frame the letters and display them in the main room. Albert suggested that we even update our website, making reference to them. But we would not do so without first receiving your permission. He has decided that he now likes the idea of the ghost and thinks it would bring us more business. God knows we could use more business. At the same time, I fear we couldn't handle it at our age. Erma also agrees with Albert, thinking framing the letters would be a good idea. Those two agreeing on anything is a first. Ha Ha!

Something in the letters floored us all, even Father Foley. You will see when you read them. It is something we kept from you when you were last here. But trust us. We all feel that it is something that will please you. Father Foley called it the hand of God. We all agreed that we would wait a while before sending them—after the baby was born.

I don't think you will find anything in them that is disturbing. In fact, they might be somewhat comforting to you. Father Foley agrees as he has read them too. He said they might bring any lingering past life concerns about Dora to a close.

With all our blessings and love. Erma sends hers too.

Claire

P.S. You said nothing about the coin staying at the inn. I know it's valuable being as old as it is, but in Albert's heart and mine, we feel it should be yours.

Isa opened the manila envelope. The letters were arranged from the earliest writing to the last.

16 October 1722

My Dear Confidant,

I have decided to keep a diary of sorts, and I will address it to you, not the parchment that takes the scribble of my pen, but to you, whose name I do not know. For you see, I have more time on my hands now, and I decided what better way to use it than to write out my thoughts. Only last week, we buried my husband, Adrien, in the church cemetery. His legs had become so shriveled in the end that Adrien agreed a surgeon should remove them altogether. His final demise came from an infection that set in after their removal. The undertaker said there was no need for a normal size coffin. I did not protest as it saved some extra coins in payment.

I wear black as I write this, although I feel little in the way of mourning. My mourning lasted a decade as I watched his crippled body suck the life out of him. And almost me, but I persevered. I have always had the will to forge on in life. Had I not, I would not have been able to run the inn, care for Jean, and be a nursemaid to Adrien.

I have no regrets in that respect. I cared for him well. I cannot say I have no shame in other areas of my life. Oh, that I could go back and somehow change things. I would, like so many would do if they could and would have the chance to do so. I would beg Adrien not to climb the tree. Maybe our lives would have been different. But alas, it can't be made right. If there is a heaven, and as each day passes, I believe it is so, I wish for him to be happy. Perhaps he will smile down upon me, seeing I did care for him, and forgive me for my indiscretions.

Jean is now grown and has taken a wife. A baby is on the way. They now bear most of the burdens of running the inn. I am glad of it. I am so weary of it all.

I look forward to many grandchildren. I once looked

forward to a house full of children of my own, but it was not to be. I will now find solace in my child giving me what I couldn't give myself, a house full of children.

Yours most truly,

Dora

20 October 1722

My Dear Confidant,

I took leave of writing for a few days. We had a scare. Amine had some pain and took to bed. The midwife came and relieved us of our fears. She was working too hard at the inn. I have taken up the slack. It comes easy enough for me. There was a woman. I may as well tell you about her. I think it was she, Esther, who gave Amine some upset. She is always meddling. She said some things about me to Amine. I do not deny that they are true, but they are only true in the most exaggerated scenario. One would think that Esther would have the sense not to throw such aggravation on a girl with child. But then, no one ever said Esther had much sense. She has always been a thorn in my side. I have always done my best to shrug it off, but this time I gave her a piece of my mind. I have no guilt. It was for Amine's sake, but most importantly, for the good of the soon-to-be child. I have forbidden Esther to show her face here again.

All is getting back to normal now. Amine's rosy cheeks have reappeared. She became bored with taking to her bed and has once again started doing light work around the inn. I even heard her singing the other day.

Yours most truly,

Dora

1 November 1722

My Dear Confidant,

I almost forsook this diary, thinking it to be of a frivolous nature. There is still so much to do around here. Granted, we have help, five employees all together, but still, running an inn is a never-ending task.

Someone from a far distance walked into the inn today. I watched as Jean poured him some ale. He had crimson locks like your own and blue eyes. Yet, they did not sparkle the way I remember yours doing. Nor was he tall and slender like you but short and stocky. Another man followed after him, a bit older. He walked with a cane. I thought it might have been you had you aged. I heard the stocky man call the man with a cane Daniel. I hope you don't mind that I use that name for you, for I have no other. Daniel is a good strong name, one whom God favors. More and more, I believe in God.I thought the two men were a sign, perhaps from God. Do you believe in signs, Daniel? Do you believe in God? I don't know.

Most truly yours,

Dora

CHILLS TRAVELED THROUGH ISA'S BODY. THIS, NO DOUBT, WAS what Claire had referred to. Isa snuggled deeper into the throw and sat in silence, staring into the flame of the fire for what might have been a half hour. She listened for any sounds from the nursery. There were none.

Maybe she should have waited for Daniel to return home before opening the package. He would be holding her at this moment if he were here. A tear of happiness ran down her cheek. It would be so good to feel his arms around her, now that he *could* get them around her. Breastfeeding was shrinking her body to how it was before she became pregnant.

There was a note on the next bunch of papers, which were paper-clipped together. It read,

> *"I'm sorry that these were too faded or damaged from the hearth to translate. So rather than try to piece together something that may or may not be, I went on to the rest in good enough shape."*

It was signed, Erma. Isa counted ten papers, still in French, the ink disappearing into the copies. She went on to the next.

1 March 1723

Daniel, regarding the shooting stars that appeared in the sky a fortnight ago, I have come to the conclusion that they might have been a forerunner of something grander. For last night, I saw as others did something most strange in the sky. The lights were still, then shot upwards in one swift stroke and disappeared from sight. Church attendance was greatly up this morning, as were the clinks of coins in the offering plates.

I see them as some kind of omen. I don't know of what. I think if you were here, you could tell me. Still, on so many days, I long for your return. You did say you would. Or did I build more into your words than you meant?

You praised my eyes. I fear they have grown dull with age.

Most truly yours,

Dora

5 March 1723

Dearest Daniel,

Little Andre is doing well, taking to his mother's nipple with much heart. I see both Jean and Adrien in him. I am glad that Adrien lives on in him. One day he will carry on the inn if it continues. I could not say for certain, but maybe Jean and Amine will fill it up with so many children that there will no longer be rooms for the patrons.

Now on a sad note. I had the unfortunate experience of seeing Esther today. It was entirely accidental. Our paths rarely cross. I saw her eyeing over produce at the market. Sometimes I feel guilt over her. But I know it is for the best I stay away from her. I started to walk away before she saw me, but I'm afraid I lingered a bit too long. She gave me the most sinister look, causing chills to swell on my body. But then, chills are not something new for a woman of my age.

I did confide in the local priest about the situation. Yes, it is true. I have been more inclined toward warming a pew now and again. I always sit far in the back. Esther sits as close to the front as possible. The priest gave me ten Hail Marys to say but also gave good counsel on my decision to part ways with Esther. It implied he knew something I didn't.

I do try not to be bothered by such things. Life is too short.

Most truly yours,

Dora

20 March 1723

Daniel, once again, I have been neglectful of the pen. But an odd set of most curious dreams has caused me once again to resume this writing, which after much thought, I have concluded is not frivolous at all. For it soothes my soul. For, other than a priest, who else can I share my thoughts with?

Last night, I dreamed of a woman in the oddest of clothes, indecent even by French standards. She looked like me in the face yet younger in appearance. The strangeness of the dream roused me from my bed. I saw her in the inn. You and she were together. You appeared quite happy, as did she. I saw the two of you laughing. The inn was also different in the dream. Some things were much the same, but some things I didn't recognize at all.

There was another time, before this latest dream, I dreamt of the same woman. It is not correct in saying it was a dream, though, because it happened while I was awake. I was going about my usual chores. I was in the library tending to the fire. I turned. I saw myself as the woman in the dream. I was clutching tight to a pillow while sitting up in bed. The woman in the bed disappeared. I let out a scream. Amine heard me and ran up the stairs.

Both incidents, the dream and the vision, were most strange, but the dream was most pleasant since I saw you again, laughing and quite happy. Is this how you meant you would return?

Most truly yours,
   Dora

ISA READ THE DATE ON THE NEXT ENTRY. OVER A YEAR HAD passed. Isa surmised that many indecipherable letters might have been written during this time.

10 June 1725

Daniel,

Once again, I have been neglectful of the pen. My letters to you have been sparse. I hope you will forgive me. Adrien, on many occasions, accused me of starting things and not following through. It was with good reason I did not take pen to paper so often. My spirits have declined. A healing woman came. She prepared herbs which put me on the mend. I am pleased to announce that I am now in much more agreeable form.

I am also most jubilant to proclaim that Amine is again with child. Andre is now into so much mischief that it wears us out chasing after him. That is yet another reason I have not kept up my penmanship.

Tomorrow I have planned an outing to the cliffs by myself to rest, reflect, and catch some fresh air. I have grown quite reflective in my old age. I have also grown quite accepting of life and am as happy as one could be. My health is doing better. A jolly old fat woman is what I am with one grandchild and another on the way. I have much to look forward to.

I vow a renewed interest in keeping up this correspondence in the most verdant manner from this day.

Most truly yours,

Dora

ISA PUT DOWN THE LAST LETTER. SHE THOUGHT THIS MUST HAVE been the day before her last day on earth. She would have died on June 11, 1725. The eleventh. Isa smiled. She took comfort in knowing that she died with peace of mind. This entry also confirmed that Dora was in good spirits and in no way was bent on taking her life.

Isa opened the smaller envelope and pulled out the coin. It was wrapped in another note.

If you do not keep the coin, you might decide to sell it. Being so old and different, it must be valuable. We thought it would be an excellent start to our godchild's college fund.

With our love,

Albert and Claire

Tears welled up in Isa's eyes.

Isa looked at the picture on the coin, trying to decipher it. For some, it might look like a UFO. She thought how absurd and laid it back down. Then she put everything back in the package just as she had received it and placed it on the oak coffee table. Once again, her mind whirled, but her heart was filled. She reached down for her tea, now cold.

She checked on Danielle Claire, who was waking from her nap. The stink of a dirty diaper brought her back into the reality of her world.

After getting Danielle Claire cleaned up, she took her into the living room, popped *The Princess Bride* into the DVD player, loosened her top, and put Danielle Claire up to her breast.

26

*I*n two years, Isa found herself pregnant again. Albert entered the world with a wail as loud as a set of Scottish bagpipes. He was a train wreck of charm and the spitting image of his father.

It was one of those atypical hot summer days in Scotland, so warm that beads of sweat formed on Isa's arms. Isa was hanging laundry on the clothesline while Albert zoomed around her feet with a toy fire engine. Danielle Claire ran around the garden, pretending to be a fairy princess. Through the sheets, Isa could hear her speaking to someone.

"Danielle, sweetheart, who are you talking to?"

Danielle Claire walked over to Isa but didn't respond. So Isa asked again, "Danielle, I heard you talking. Were you playing make-believe?"

"No, Mummy, I was talking to the lady."

"What lady? I don't see a lady."

"I am the only one who can see her."

"What does the lady look like?"

"She looks a lot like you, Mummy. But she doesn't dress like you."

A cold chill went through Isa. She bent down, hugged, kissed, and held onto Danielle Claire without saying anything. Albert's whine broke the hold she had on her daughter.

"What's wrong, Mummy?" her daughter asked meekly.

"Nothing, Danielle. Everything is fine. Let's you, me, and Albert go inside. How about some cookies?"

Albert threw his fire engine down. "I want a cookie."

"Yes, we will have a nice little tea party with cookies," Isa said.

"Yea, a tea party!" Albert cheered.

"Can we invite the lady?" Danielle asked.

Isa looked around. "Is the lady still here?"

"No, she left when she heard you call to me."

"Well, let's just the three of us have a tea party, for now, okay?"

"Okay, Mummy."

IT HAD BEEN A YEAR SINCE THE REPORTER HAD SHOWN UP AT their door wanting to write a whole feature article on Isa and the ghost. Claire and Albert were so shaken up over it that they wanted to take the letters that hung in the inn down and off their website. But Dora's ghost or the chance of seeing Dora's ghost had brought in a new group of clientele, and Albert was finally able to put in that insulation. Isa told them, "No, leave everything as is." She didn't want to spoil the success they were finally having with the inn.

How the reporter discovered it was Isa who had seen the ghost was a mystery. They all racked their brains as to how it might have happened. Claire, Albert, or Erma would never give anyone Isa's name in a million years. Father Foley revealing it was out of the question. The only theory Daniel and Isa could come up with was possibly someone working for Kate might have seen her notes. She dismissed publishing the paper early on, but Kate was meticulous in keeping files on everything, and student interns regularly went in and out of her office.

Isa politely turned the reporter away as well as the two other paranormal researchers that contacted her a few weeks later. She did not want fifteen minutes of fame as the woman who saw her own ghost. Nor did she want the wife of a prominent university professor, who taught something as down-to-earth as mathematics, to be known as someone so totally off the wall and as one who dabbled in ghosts and past lives. And she certainly didn't want Danielle Claire and Albert to suffer for it at school. Kids could be cruel, and the parents of those kids even more brutal if they thought their mum, who was active on every school committee, was a threat to the kids. She now had a responsible job as a librarian, and Daniel was working on his doctorate and a year away from tenure. Between all that and the renovations to the house over the last few years, making room for Danielle, Albert, and Ian, who was there for most of the summers and off and on during the rest of the year, had been stressful enough.

When Daniel got home, Isa didn't bring it up. They had never kept secrets from each other, at least none that she had known, but things had just started to get normal with the renovations complete and the children no longer keeping them up all hours of the night. This would undoubtedly cause a kink just when things were settling down. Ironically, the ghost that had brought them together, Isa thought, in this stage of their lives might be their undoing.

Once or twice a year, they had always taken the train down to the inn to visit everyone, but there had never been any more appearances from Dora. Nor had there been any more dreams. Isa hadn't thought about Dora in a long time.

Daniel came through the door and set the groceries on the counter. The children both ran to him. "Daddy, Daddy!" He picked them up, one in each arm, and kissed both of them.

"Have you been taking care of Mummy while I was gone?"

Albert smiled and raised his arms in glee. "Yay, take care of Mummy!"

"Daddy, Mummy's been sad," Danielle Claire said.

Daniel put the children down. "Danielle, you and Albert go in the living room and play, and Danielle, watch your little brother."

"Come on, Albert." Albert followed a few steps behind her, falling once.

Daniel turned to Isa. "Is something wrong?"

"No, everything is fine." She began unloading the groceries. "Daniel, where are the chips? You know Ian will want chips and not potatoes. This cookout is for him, after all."

"Isa, don't get so upset. I still have another bag out in the car."

"It's the onions. You know they always make me cry. I had to reapply my mascara." It wasn't a lie, even though it had happened earlier in the day.

"I've told you a zillion times. Save the onions for me. Besides, you don't need makeup anyway. You are beautiful without it."

Isa took a deep breath and realized how she was acting. She folded up the grocery bags, went over to Daniel, and put her arms around him. "I'm sorry. I want everything to be right for the cookout. It *is* for Ian's graduation, you know."

Daniel looked at her, relieved. "Isa, it will be okay. It's just a little cookout. I've never known you to get upset over something so small. Are you sure there's nothing else?"

She lied again, not wanting to bring up the Dora business after all this time. "Yes, I'm sure."

DANIEL HAD JUST GOTTEN THE GRILL ALL FIRED UP WHEN THEY heard voices coming through the gate to the backyard. It was Kate, Marc, and the baby. Danielle Claire ran up to them. "Mummy and Daddy have been fighting."

Isa raised her eyebrows, looking over at Daniel while swooping the baby from Kate's arms. "He has grown so much!"

"Okay, Danielle, we will have a little talk later about Mummy and Daddy business. In the meantime, won't you help me set up the playpen for Little Marc and Albert?"

"Okay, Daddy." She acted undisturbed.

"Hope there isn't trouble in paradise," Kate said with a laugh after Daniel returned from putting Albert and Marc in the playpen.

"Hardly, Kate. Are you telling me that you and Marc never fight?"

Marc took the beer that Daniel handed him. "He has us there, Kate."

"And it wasn't even a fight," Daniel said.

"Okay, I'll save my professional opinions if anything big ever comes up, and I hope it doesn't. I always use you two as the perfect example of a happy couple."

Ian, Kathryn, and Colin popped in about that time. Isa missed Gramps at these little get-togethers. He had passed at ninety-two, long enough to see his great-granddaughter come into the world.

THE SUMMER PASSED. ISA WAS RELIEVED DANIELLE DIDN'T report any more sightings of Dora. Children grew out of these things, she told herself.

Daniel was back at work. Isa was proud of him. He had been working on some big project that brought in lots of grant money for the university, an added stress, another reason the issue of Dora needed to stay in the background. Albert was back at nursery school. Danielle Claire had settled into her class, and Isa was reading the classics, books like *Little Women,* to several of the classes at school in the library, one of them being Danielle's.

It was months later that Isa took a personal day to stay home with Albert, who had a slight fever.

Daniel didn't say anything until they had put the kids to bed and were both in bed themselves. "Isa, we need to talk about Danielle."

"Is there something wrong?"

"Now, don't get alarmed, but she has been telling her teacher about a lady that sometimes helps her with her homework. She also eats with the lady sometimes in the cafeteria."

"What?"

"She told her teacher the lady looks like you, except that she wears old-fashioned clothing. We both know she is referring to Dora. You have never mentioned Dora to her, have you?"

"No, of course not. Maybe she means me. I help her with her homework when she needs it, and you know I sometimes sit with her in the cafeteria."

"Yes, her teacher asked her if it was you, and she said it was an invisible lady that only she could see. She went on to describe her."

The instance in the backyard was looming over her as she said, "Well, all children have imaginary friends."

"Yes, Isa, but they are not usually grown women in old-fashioned clothing who look like their mums."

"Who was the teacher who told you this?"

"Mrs. Buchanan. You know she is not the kind to make something like this up."

"Why did she call *you*? I mean, I work at the school. Why didn't she wait to tell me? I would be back on Monday."

"She said she knew Albert was sick and you were home with

him and didn't want to trouble you. My number was on the emergency form in the office."

"Emergency? Did she think this was an emergency, something that couldn't wait until Monday?"

"I don't know, Isa. That's kind of beside the point now. What do you think we should do about it?"

"I don't know?"

"We could have Kate talk to her."

"Kate? Do you really think that's necessary?"

"Okay, that might be extreme. Tomorrow's Saturday. We will sit down with her and talk to her about imaginary friends. Discussing the ramifications with her may be all she needs." He reached for the light and turned it off. "Goodnight, Isa. I love you." He reached over, kissed his wife, and rolled over, ready to sleep.

"Daniel?"

"Yes?" he responded, his voice already groggy.

"This isn't the first time."

He rolled back around. "Isa, what do you mean."

"Do you remember the day of the cookout, the one we had for Ian for his graduation?"

"Aye."

"It was before you came home. If you remember, I was upset. I heard Danielle talking to someone. I asked her who she was talking to. When she described her, I knew then it was Dora."

Daniel sat up in bed and turned the light back on. "What? Why didn't you tell me?"

"Daniel, calm down. You will wake the children."

Daniel changed to a softer voice that wasn't any less agitated, "Isa, how could you keep something like this from me?"

"I thought it was a one-time thing. And it was, at least as far as I knew. Danielle never brought her up again."

"Isa, you should have told me."

"You're right. I should have. We will sit her down and talk to her tomorrow."

"Isa, it may be beyond that. Kate is a professional. It's an hour later in Paris. Kate may already be in bed. I'll call first thing in the morning. We'll make the trip to Paris this weekend if she says it's okay."

"Daniel, do you really want to bring Kate into this? Do you think it's that serious? I've seen Dora, as have Erma and Claire. She never did anyone any harm. Dora has always been a friendly ghost."

"Isa, this is not Casper we are talking about. Maybe she is friendly, but do you want this to be happening? It's one thing to have this happen to an adult, but a child is a different story. The other kids will think her strange."

"Daniel, I saw Dora. Do you think me strange? You seemed to think it was all a big adventure when we first met," Isa said as she grabbed a pillow, holding it close to her chest with a tear welling up in her eye.

Daniel let out a sigh and reached for his wife. "Isa, I'm sorry. I didn't mean it that way. Please, please don't think I did."

"I can't take Albert. He is just getting over the virus."

"Danielle and I will go." He turned the light back off and rolled over. Isa lay awake for what seemed like hours. She almost wished Dora would appear and give her some guidance.

27

*E*verything was returning to normal, not that Isa had a definition of normal. Their lives together had been anything but normal when she looked back on it. But by normal, she meant there had been no sign of Dora since Kate had talked to Danielle.

By all accounts, Danielle was doing well in school. She had a best girlfriend, Rebecca, who had almost become a permanent fixture at their cottage. There was no need for a ghostly friend. Both Isa and Daniel exhaled sighs of relief with no reported ghost sightings by Danielle. They theorized Dora had transcended to the light or whatever happened in these cases.

BY HIGH SCHOOL, REBECCA HAD BEEN MORE OR LESS EDGED OUT by David. David was the big-eyed puppy dog everyone kept tripping over. Ironically and sadly, Samantha had been put down a month before David came into the picture. Isa didn't mind David's constant presence saying, "They're both here where we can keep an eye on them. Plus, he's a good influence on Albert. Be glad Danielle's type isn't the 'bad' boy."

Isa knew Daniel agreed even though he put up the front of the annoyed father, often complaining within earshot of David, "Doesn't the lad have a home?" David seemed impervious to Daniel's mumblings.

Isa reminded Daniel, "David is Danielle's first crush. She will tire of him eventually, or he of her. She'll go through a broken heart. And believe me, that will be rough for everyone concerned since I'll be worried you'll do physical harm to the boy."

"I forbid any lad to break my daughter's heart," Daniel declared.

"Danielle Claire has a good head on her shoulders. She's smart. Her teachers are always praising her. A broken heart at some point is inevitable, and they're worse for smart girls, but she'll bounce back because she *is* smart," Isa said.

"Like her mother." Daniel smiled.

ALBERT, ON THE OTHER HAND, HAD ALWAYS BEEN A HANDFUL. They didn't get many glowing reports on him. When they did, it was a cause for celebration. Mostly, they wrote it off as he was his father's son. Albert excelled at soccer, or football, rather. It had taken Isa a long time to call it football.

THE HANDS OF THE ORSAY CLOCK SEEMED TO BE MOVING FASTER, not that Isa had seen the clock in years. Last year, she had started covering the gray cropping up in her hair. Daniel's red mop thinned out like his father's, and he began wearing spectacles.

Isa told him he finally fit the picture of a stuffy old Ph.D. at a university.

They didn't end up making as many trips to the states as they had planned in their early days of marriage. Fortunately, after Isa's parents retired, they were free to travel and spent most of the holidays in Scotland. Ian always looked forward to her parents' visit, and even though he and his wife Carol lived in Glasgow, Ian always made time to hit the golf courses with her dad when he visited. Daniel, along with Marc, for one week each year, continued to meet up with his old cycling buddies. They never reported seeing Josh anymore after that one time they all met for dinner in Paris. Isa hoped he had found someone and had a full life like her.

When Danielle and Albert were both in college, making trips to the inn became easier. Danielle, a senior, majored in accounting, while Albert, a freshman, still hadn't decided on a major.

Daniel never succeeded in running David off. He and Danielle became engaged and planned to marry as soon as they graduated.

It had been a couple of years ago that Erma passed. Daniel and Isa went to her funeral. Both Albert and Claire were growing frailer. How they still managed the inn, Isa didn't know.

Right before Christmas break during Danielle's final year, they received a phone call from Claire. Albert had passed peacefully in his sleep. This time, the whole family went to the funeral. Father Foley was no longer there, having been transferred back to New Orleans. Isa thought maybe one day if she and Daniel ever made the trip again, they would look him up. They had heard that Carl had died sometime during Hurricane Katrina.

After Albert's funeral, everyone gathered at the inn to celebrate Albert's life. Claire had their usual room waiting, although they could have had their pick. It was the off-season; their business had been going down for several years. The musty smell of the inn had become more pronounced. It brought back memories of her grandmother.

Claire, Daniel, and Isa sat at the kitchen table after those who came to pay their respects had left, and the children had turned in. It was so strange without Albert, Erma, and Father Foley there. Isa missed Albert and Erma's bickering. "I've been saving this. I think Albert will look down on us with a smile," Claire said.

The year on the bottle read 2002, the year Isa and Daniel had met at the inn.

"To Albert," Daniel said.

"And to Erma," Isa added.

"I think they are finally getting along," Claire said.

They sat silent for a while before Claire announced, "I will be closing the inn. At first, I thought about moving into Erma's house. Her son kept it, and the last renters moved out. It sits vacant. But then I thought, no, it would be easier to close most of the rooms in the inn and live in the part I live in now. That way, I could open some of them back up whenever you and the children want to visit."

Daniel and Isa both agreed that might be a good idea.

"Albert and I had been discussing retiring anyway before he died."

"Do you hear from Father Foley?" Isa asked.

"From time to time. He has his hands full after Katrina. He says there are still signs of it even after all these years."

"We always said we would return to New Orleans, but life always got in the way." Isa sighed.

"Well, dear, you've had your children to keep you busy. Albert and I," she paused, "we were just never blessed in that way. We've always considered you and Daniel and our godchildren the closest we've had to children."

"And both Isa and I have always looked upon you and Albert as our second set of parents," Daniel said.

"There is something I want to discuss with you."

"What is it, Claire?" Isa put her hand over Claire's wrist.

"Albert and I made out a will. In the event of our deaths, we wanted the inn to go to the two of you."

"Claire, we couldn't accept that," Daniel said.

"No, Claire, we couldn't. You have already been so kind to us over the years. Besides, what would we do with it? We both have our life in Scotland."

"What am I going to do? Sell it? I am all that is left, other than Erma's son and grandchildren. They don't need the money. Nor would they want the inn. I would like to see it go into good hands."

"But Claire, we teach. We have never thought about running an inn."

"What about Danielle?"

"Danielle?" Daniel asked.

"Yes, I think maybe she might want to take it over."

Daniel and Isa looked at each other, a bit startled. "But, Claire, she's still in college and plans on getting married after graduation," Isa said.

"Well, after college."

"I don't know, Claire," Isa said.

"But it's what she wants to do."

"Claire, why do you say that?" Isa asked.

"Because she and David visited this past summer. Both Albert and I discussed it with them. It's what they both want to do."

Daniel and Isa looked at each other, stunned.

28

*I*sa's phone went off. Carol called to say that Ian was in an accident and that he was in the hospital for evaluation. He was driving home after work. The roads were icy, and he had veered off the road, hitting a tree. Somehow, he was thrown free of the car. No one seemed to know what happened. A truck had come around the corner, hitting the same icy spot, and rammed the vehicle. It would have meant certain death if Ian had still been in it. Ian was unconscious. The truck driver wasn't hurt and called for an ambulance.

By the time Daniel and Isa got to the hospital, the doctor was already looking at the MRI results. Ian had escaped with only bruises and sprains and a slight concussion. He would be on either crutches or a cane for a while.

Ian was groggy from painkillers but smiling when they entered his room. Carol was by his bedside. His head was bandaged. Seeing their concerned expressions, he said, "Don't worry. I think it looks worse than it is. The doctor said it was just some cuts and scratches on my head."

"I hear you will be hobbling around on a cane like an old man," Daniel said.

"Don't let your dad tease you. He was walking around on a cane on our first date."

"Oh, yeah? You never told me about that."

"It's true. I twisted my ankle on a bicycling trip."

Danielle and David walked in. "How's it going? You gave us quite a scare."

"Ah, I'm okay. I had a guardian angel looking out for me."

"Your mum and I are just glad you are going to be okay."

Albert was the last to arrive.

"It was the strangest thing," Ian said.

"How so, Ian?" Danielle asked.

"I may have had something like one of those near-death experiences."

They all looked at each other curiously.

"Aye, I was leaning against the steering wheel in the car, and the front windshield was broken. The next thing I know, I'm lying outside the car in the snow. I looked up to see the back of a woman walking away."

"Did the police know who she was?" David asked.

"They said I imagined it. The truck driver didn't see her, and there were no footprints in the snow."

Danielle's face lit up. "Who do you think she was?"

"An angel. She was otherworldly. She even had strange clothes on."

Daniel clasped Isa's hand. Then Albert chimed in, "I've seen her before."

"Albert, you never told us about this!" Isa said.

"No, and I wasn't about to. I was in my last year of high school. Some boys and I were out skinny-dipping with some girls." Danielle broke the seriousness with a laugh. Albert continued, "It's okay to talk about it now, considering I don't think I can get into trouble over it."

Isa looked at Daniel with a smirk.

"Well, my foot caught on a tree root in the water. I couldn't reach the surface. I couldn't break free. My short life was literally flashing before my eyes. Like, why did I not bang Kathy MacGregor when I had the chance?"

"Albert!" Isa gasped.

"Mum, I was drowning, and you're worrying about decorum?"

"But you didn't drown," Isa said.

"Surely you and Dad did something outrageous when you were young. You were young once, weren't you?"

"Okay, are we playing Truth or Dare? On our honeymoon…"

"Isa!" Daniel cut her off.

"How did you get free?" David asked.

"A lady, like the one that Ian described, freed me. One moment I saw her in the water. The next moment she was gone, but I was free. At first, I thought it was you, Mum. But she was younger, and she was wearing the weirdest clothes. I couldn't understand why she wore all those clothes instead of a bathing suit. Later, I thought maybe I imagined the whole thing, but how did I get free?"

"You were skinny-dipping with girls? Why was I never that lucky?" Ian said.

"You do know that Carol is right outside the door with the twins and can probably hear you, don't you?" Danielle said.

"There is obviously a lot you have kept from us," Daniel said.

"Well, while we are confessing, I would often see Dora from time to time."

"Danielle, I thought you never saw her anymore after Kate talked to you," Daniel said.

"I just knew it was better not to bring it up anymore. Don't look shocked. Dora has always helped. She has saved both Ian's and Albert's lives."

"How did you know her name?" Isa asked.

"When I got older, I read the letters at the inn."

"You're right. She has always helped us. And she brought your mum and me together."

Isa smiled, and Daniel encircled his arms around her.

"Do you mean you know who this woman is?" Ian asked.

"Yeah, why haven't you ever told us about her?" Albert asked.

"It's a long story," Isa said. She looked at Daniel. He winked. Isa thought about the first time he looked at her with those blue eyes. They were the same eyes. Only now, there were more wrinkles around them.

"Maybe you should tell them about it," Danielle said.

"Danielle, you know?"

"Both David and I know. After I read the letters at the inn, I asked Claire and Albert about her. Claire didn't want to tell me. Said you should be the one to do it, but Albert spilled his guts."

"I hope you're not mad at Albert," David said. "Truth be known, we forced the issue with them."

"Since we are on the subject, Claire tells us you want to run the inn."

Danielle looked at David. "We've been discussing it."

"Why have you never mentioned this to us?" Daniel asked.

"Dr. Stewart, we've been meaning to. We were actually going to bring it up over the holiday."

"Sis, does this mean I would have a free room whenever I wanted?" Albert laughed.

"Maybe a family discount," Danielle said.

"Dad, I think she is already making a good businessperson," Ian said.

"I've always loved that inn, ever since you and Mum took us there as kids. It's where I first met Dora," Danielle said.

"You saw her there?" Isa exclaimed.

"Every time we went."

"I'm beginning to think Dora is one of the family," Daniel said.

"You have to admit that she has been watching over us," Ian said.

"He's right, Daniel," Isa said.

IAN WAS RELEASED FROM THE HOSPITAL THE NEXT DAY. THE whole family gathered at the cottage on Christmas Day for dinner. It was there that Daniel and Isa told them the complete story of how they met, about her ghostly encounter, the past life regression with Father Foley, and how Kate, Daniel, and Isa, along with Claire, Albert, and Erma, worked together to solve the mystery.

Daniel disappeared into their bedroom. When he returned, he was carrying a box. Daniel pulled out a key from a space behind the hearth and opened it. They took turns passing around the photocopies of the letters.

"I always wondered what was in that box," Albert said.

"I suspected it had something to do with Dora," Danielle said.

"You children knew about the box?"

"Of course we did. Didn't you think we ever searched the house for hidden Christmas presents?"

"Don't let the twins hear you say that," Carol said.

"We would have opened it, but it was locked. Don't think it wasn't from lack of trying. We looked but couldn't find the key."

"When you were young, I kept the key in my desk drawer at school," Isa said.

"Darn, I never thought to look there," Albert said.

"I think Dora's presence at the inn will be a plus," Danielle said.

"I think you're right," Daniel said. He hugged Isa.

"So why all the secrecy?" Albert asked.

"Your mum and I discussed it early on. Your mum was pregnant with you, Danielle, when your godfather, Albert, found the letters. Something like this might have drawn the wrong kind of attention had we divulged Isa's dreams, the ghost, and finding the letters. Then there was Father Foley. We could hardly bring to light a Catholic priest had done a past life regression on Isa. And last, but not least, there was the coin."

"The coin?" Ian asked.

"David and I know about the coin too," Danielle said, "but we've never seen it."

Isa reached inside the remaining folder in the box, unwrapped it, and pulled out the circular piece of copper.

"Wow, looks old. What's all the strange stuff on it?" Albert asked.

Daniel explained what Father Foley had told them.

"Claire and Albert were gracious enough to give it to us," Isa said. "We had thought about using it but always resisted the urge. Again, we felt it might draw unwanted attention."

Isa looked over at Daniel, who nodded approval.

"Danielle, maybe you and David should take it. It belongs to the inn. Or, if you decide, you may want to get it appraised and use it for renovation to the inn. We're sure Claire *and Albert* would be pleased if you used it for that."

"Don't forget, Dora. I think she would approve of that too," Danielle said.

Isa and Daniel laughed. "Yes, she would," they agreed.

The following summer, Danielle and David got married. After a honeymoon in the states, where they also took some time to visit Danielle's grandparents, they returned home to the inn, moving in with Claire.

29

"I got a letter today at the university."

"Oh?" Isa said while turning the page in the book she was reading.

"I've been invited to a special conference."

"Oh?" Isa continued to read.

"Yes, by the United Nations."

"United Nations?" Isa put her book down. She raised her eyebrows in the form of a question.

"It's a great honor. Scientists, environmentalists, teachers, professors from universities worldwide, not to mention world leaders, will be there."

Isa got up, walked over, and hugged him. "Oh, Daniel, I am so proud of you. Where will this conference be?"

"Honestly, I don't know. Because of all the bigwigs attending, it will be held at an undisclosed location. We only know somewhere in the North of France."

"Isa, I wish Claire and Albert were still alive. We could run down to the inn after the meeting, make it like a tenth honeymoon or something. I've lost count. What honeymoon are we on now?"

"I think it would be the eleventh, but I won't be mad that you forgot. How many wives are lucky to get that many? We could still go. Danielle and David would be happy to have us."

"I don't think it would be the same—honeymooning at the inn with your children?" he said.

"You're right." She laughed.

"When is the conference?"

"It will be in June, right after school lets out."

"Daniel, I can't go then. That's around Danielle's due date."

"That's right. What was I thinking? It's just not an opportune time. I will write and say I can't go."

"Not go! But it's such an honor. You have to go. Danielle and David will understand. You have to go. I'll still be at the inn for as long as Danielle needs me. You can come and join us as soon as the conference is over."

30

$\mathcal{P}$lace: Australian Astronomical Observatory Sydney, Australia

First man: "This is big!"

Second man: "What is it?"

First man: "Something coming at earth at an incredible speed. It appeared out of nowhere."

Everyone leaves their desk to gather around the first man's screen. There are various murmurs and sedated screams.

Third man: "How big do you estimate it to be?"

First man: "It's hard to say at this point, but rest assured it will hit the earth, and it's going to make a dent."

One woman says: "What is it? A UFO? Meteor? Asteroid? What? What should we do?"

First man: "We could start calling leaders, but I think it's too late. It's moving fast."

Second man: "Still, it's protocol." He picked up the phone.

Another woman: "Can you pinpoint exactly where it's headed?"

First man: "Hold on—I'm calculating. By its trajectory, it

appears to be somewhere in Europe. Maybe to the north of Paris."

Another man: "Oh my God! Isn't that where that big meeting is being held? A reporter leaked it. Anyone who is anyone in the academic field is there."

Third Man: "Not to mention most of the world's leaders."

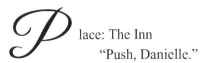

lace: The Inn

"Push, Danielle."

"I *am* pushing. You try this if you think it's so easy."

"Come on, Danielle Claire, I did the hard part," David said.

"You…" She stopped what she was about to say, letting out a scream instead. Calming back down, she said, "I can't say. I don't want to bring our baby into this world using foul language."

"I see the head. You're almost there," the midwife said.

"Come on, Danielle. You can do it."

There is a thunderous cry. "And you have what appears to be a healthy baby girl!" the midwife said.

"David, please go tell Mum that Dora Isabelle has arrived."

"Right after I kiss my wife."

The midwife weighed Dora at seven pounds and one ounce. She cleaned the infant up, wrapped her in a blanket, and put her up to Danielle's breast.

Isa came bursting into room number eleven. "I must call your dad and tell him the news."

"Isa, did the baby come?" Daniel asked before even saying hello.

"Yes, Daniel. A healthy girl, Dora Isabelle, all seven pounds and one ounce of her, arrived at 11 a.m. on June 11. She has your eyes, Daniel. Blue."

"Isa, babies start out with blue eyes. They will probably…"

"Daniel, Daniel? We're breaking up."

Danielle and David averted their eyes from their newborn to Isa.

"Mum, what happened? What did Dad say?"

"I don't know. We lost the connection. I'm sure he'll call back. He sounded ecstatic."

The electricity flickered and went out.

32

*I*sa was tired—more tired than she had ever been in her life. All she wanted to do was sleep and dream of Daniel, about when they first met, about the day they had in Nice, and the time they had in Paris. The locks on the bridge. Why didn't they write their names together on a lock and put it on the bridge? It wasn't the weight of the locks that finally destroyed the bridge.

Then there was their honeymoon. She remembered the nice man they had met. What was his name? Oh, yes, Father Foley. No, no, Father Carl. That was his name. It was so hard to remember these days.

The world has become so broken. Maybe in time, it could be fixed. She could feel the warmth of the blanket that Dora put over her. It was familiar. She was in an overstuffed chair in a priest's office. No, no, she wasn't there now. She was at the inn. Yes, in her old room. Number eleven. Eleven, that number kept coming up. On June 11, the day Dora was born, everything changed.

"Do you need anything, Grandma?" she heard a voice ask.

"No, is that you, Dora?"

"Yes, it's me, Grandma."

Isa opened her eyes. "You're too young. You're not Dora."

"Do you mean *her*, Grandma?"

"Yes, *her*. Do you know about her?"

"Of course I do. I was named after her. Mum has told me all about her."

"Yes, your mum *would* tell you."

"Grandma, drink your tea. It's getting cold. Mum told me it's the tea that Grandpa liked. I wish I could have known him."

Isa's lips turned upward. "Yes, it's strong, the way Daniel liked it. He was drinking that tea on the day we met. Oh, but it was always too strong for me," she said, laughing, "But I never told him that. Do you keep secrets, Dora? You won't tell him, will you?"

"I don't know. I guess sometimes. But don't worry. I won't tell him, Grandma."

"We all keep secrets. Your grandfather and I said we wouldn't keep secrets, but I kept a few."

"What were they, Grandma?"

"Now, if I told you they wouldn't be secrets, would they?"

"No, Grandma, they wouldn't."

Isa coughed for a full minute.

"Are you okay, Grandma? Should I go get Mum?"

"No, no, I'm okay. I think I *will* have some of that tea."

Dora placed the cup in her hand and helped her grandmother hold it up to her mouth. "Here, Grandma."

"Thank you, dear. I guess I can tell you now. The secrets don't matter in the end. I told your Grandpa I never saw her again after that first time."

"Seen who, Grandma?"

"Dorcel."

"Dorcel? Do you mean Dora?"

"Yes, Dorcel, the ghost. Dorcel was her proper name. I would see her from time to time, almost always when we visited the inn, sometimes at the cottage where we lived. Do you know this was the room where it all started?"

"What all started?"

"Where I saw the ghost. Then the next morning, I met your grandfather."

"I wish I could have met Grandfather Daniel."

"I wish you could have too, dear."

"Tell me about him, please."

"He had a wicked sense of humor. You got your red hair and blue eyes from him."

Dora smiled. "Yeah, that's what Mum tells me. You have a wicked sense of humor too, Grandma."

"I do? Well, if I do, I learned it from your grandfather. He took me on the train to Nice. It was so romantic. We dipped our feet into the Mediterranean and almost sank into the rocks. The beaches are different back home."

"Back home?"

"America."

"I've never been to America, Grandma. Mum told me about it. That was before—when we had plane travel across the ocean. Maybe someday. They say all the planes will be back soon. The grid is coming back on all over the world."

"Yes, dear, in time. Time rules everything."

"What else did you and Grandfather do?"

"We spent our honeymoon in America. In New Orleans. It is a bit like France. That is because the French settled it. We even skinny-dipped there."

"Gosh, Grandma, you were wild in your day." Dora giggled.

"No, not really. Your grandfather taught me wild too. Your grandfather taught me a lot. He was always telling me the history of places and things. In Nice, we climbed to the top of Castle Hill. That is where he first kissed me."

"One day, a prince will come and kiss me, Grandma."

"I'm sure one will. But don't kiss any frogs."

"I won't, Grandma."

"I know you won't. You're smart like your mum. Your grandfather was my prince. Up until him, there were only frogs. We had a picnic by the cliffs. He made love to me. Oh, oh, what am I saying? I forgot myself. You're too young to hear that."

"No, I'm not, Grandma. I know about sex."

"You do? At your age?"

"I *am* eleven, Grandma."

"He took me to the cliffs. It was so romantic."

"The cliffs, Grandma? Do you mean the Edge? Where the spacecraft crashed when the solar flare hit? When the grid got knocked out? On my birthday."

"Yes, now it's the Edge, part of the Edge. The Edge in my dreams was much bigger." A tear trickled down the side of her face.

"Grandma, you should rest now." Dora adjusted the chair for her grandmother.

"I don't remember this chair in this room."

"Don't you remember, Grandma? We got it for you for Christmas."

"Oh, yes. I remember."

Isa closed her eyes briefly, then opened them again. "Did you know there used to be wall-to-wall bookcases in this room?"

"I didn't know, Grandma."

"Yes, I liked to come in here and lock myself away. I would read, and sometimes I would write. I wrote letters I never sent."

The teacup dropped to the floor.

I drift off to sleep. But I'm not asleep. I look down. I see an old, frail body in a chair.

"Grandma, Grandma?" Dora ran out into the hall and shouted, "Mum, come quick!"

I hear the creak of the steps as someone runs up them. I see Danielle. She is feeling for my pulse. She wipes a tear from her eye and turns around to Dora.

I turn away. I can no longer see them. I see a light. I see a woman standing in the light. I recognize her. She was in my room, standing at the fireplace. I say, I know you.

She says, and I you.

She reaches out her hand to me. I take it. It seems so natural. Our ethereal bodies merge. I understand every-thing now, the dreams, what they were about.

We, I—look ahead. There is a man, a young man, with waves of chestnut hair and sparkling blue eyes. He beckons me toward him. I take his hand. My world is no longer broken.

ACKNOWLEDGMENTS

Susanne Larssen went above and beyond when it came to the historical accuracy of France in Dora's time. I thank her immensely.

Philippe Georgel and Liliane Najm were extremely helpful with the French phrases used in the book.

Bill Leroy helped me with all things Scottish.

Then there were my faithful beta readers: Kim Daniels, Barbara Chambers, and Melissa Woods.

Thanks to my editor, Lisa Binion, who has taught me a lot.

And thanks to my husband for supporting me in my writing career.

ABOUT THE AUTHOR

J. Schlenker, a late-blooming author, lives with her husband, Chris, out in the splendid center of nowhere in the foothills of Appalachia in Kentucky where the only thing to disturb her writing is croaking frogs and the occasional sounds of hay being cut in the fields.

For more information:
https://www.jschlenker.com/
jschlenkerauthor@gmail.com

facebook.com/J.SchlenkerAuthor
twitter.com/athursdayschild
instagram.com/jschlenkerauthor

ALSO BY J. SCHLENKER

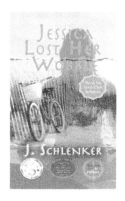

Jessica Lost Her Wobble

A Novel Tea Book Club Selection, 2017 Wishing Shelf Book Awards Finalist, 2014 William Faulkner-William Wisdom Writing Contest Finalist, and recipient of a 5 Star Readers' Favorite Award.

At mid-life, Jessica, after many upsets, moves to an island for contemplation of her life and to make a new start. While there, she reflects back on her beginnings in the early twentieth century in England, her move to New York City, and marriage at a young age, while making friends with a girl half her age. This friendship opens up a new world for her and helps her explore her own soul. Jessie becomes a part of the island otherwise known as a local as she reinvents her life there and finds love. But all is not as it seems.

"Jessica Lost Her Wobble" is J. Schlenker's first novel.

Review Excerpts: "Let me get this out of the way... Buy this book and read it!!" "Exceptional book. I would give it 10 stars if they were available." "This is a book that must be read to the end, meaning all the way through the last big surprise epilogue. I didn't see it coming and it changed the whole texture of looking back on this well-written novel."

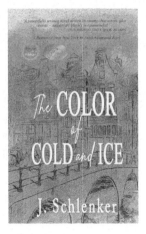

The Color of Cold and Ice

A recipient of the IndiBrag Medallion and 2018 Wishing Shelf Book Awards Finalist

Sybil has dreams; the prophetic kind, although interpreting them correctly is another matter. Her latest dream involves her sister Emerald, who wants to pursue her art once more and move on with her life after losing her husband. John, once felt he was making a difference as an ER doctor, but finds himself slipping away in his Manhattan practice as well as in his marriage. Allison, 's wife wants to change her ho hum existence with into something spectacular. Mark, Allison's brother, a struggling musician, wants to quit rambling in life and find his purpose.

The cold changes everything.

'A powerfully written novel driven by strong characters, plot twists—and color! Highly recommended.'

This has been written by a very talented writer; I will be keeping my eyes peeled for her next book too.

— A 'WISHING SHELF' BOOK REVIEW

A 5 Star Readers' Favorite, 2018 William Faulkner-William Wisdom Writing Contest Bronze Winner, IHIBRP Reviews 5 Star Recommended Read, 2018 Bronze Winner of Wishing Shelf Book Awards

Sally

Michelle, a white woman stumbles upon her grandmother's journals that have lain dormant in the attic for fifty years. There is a picture of her grandmother alongside an African-American woman. It is inscribed: Sally, born into slavery—my ancestor. The journals relating Sally's story end abruptly. Michelle makes it her mission to find out more about Sally. The quest brings up more questions than answers. Just when she thinks she has come to a dead end, she uncovers the most startling fact of all.

Based on the life of Sally Ann Barnes 1858 to 1969

'The powerful story of a black woman in the American South and the astonishing life she lived.'

Powerfully written and populated with well-developed characters, I would recommend this book to anybody interested in American history. Or to anybody who simply enjoys a gripping story.

— A 'WISHING SHELF' BOOK REVIEW

Review Excerpts: "Sally by J. Schlenker has touched me with a strength, a grace, and a beauty that belies the sadness that the pages hold." "Mesmerizing Story. Superbly Written." "A Compelling Read." "Should be taught at schools."

The Missing Butler and Other Life Mysteries

A Collection of Short Stories. A 5 Star Readers' Favorite.

Sometimes life is absurd. Sometimes life is serious. Sometimes life is sad. Mostly, life is a mystery. This collection of short stories, along with the author's whimsical art work, humorously explores the absurdness, the seriousness, the sadness and the mysteries of life, or at the very least causes us to pause and think, and maybe even laugh at ourselves.

Review Excerpts: "Great collection of short stories!" "A brilliant collection of outrageous, people in a variety of situation." "Whimsical and Well Written"

A Peculiar School

What if all animals got along?

Miss Ethel Peacock, who lives at a nature preserve, has the brilliant idea of starting a school for all animals. She musters up her courage to take her idea to Mr. Densworth Lion, principal at Cub Academy, who thinks the idea is preposterous. He roars, "Animals have a pecking order. Getting along isn't in an animal's nature."

Ethel is disheartened until her friend, Luce Pigeon, tells her about a tiger, hyena, orangutan and polar bear who live together in the tunnels under the city after escaping from the zoo, and about the badger who helps them.

The two set out to meet the animals. What Ethel finds when they arrive is beyond her imagination. Animals with distinct personalities are working together but barely surviving. She and Luce must help them escape their underground prison.

The night of the escape is chaotic. The animals scatter amid the blare of police sirens. What happens next motivates Ethel even more to open the school. Her plan gets a big boost when the owls, keepers of the sacred knowledge of the forest, give Ethel their blessing.

But, the owls are hiding something about the nature preserve that could change everything.

Right after graduating high school, Alice escapes the grip of her clinging mother and leaves Queens with a Columbia law student and four others to live primitively in rural West Virginia. Called back home by her ailing mother, she seeks answers to why her father disappeared. Her mother takes the secret to her grave. Alice is ready to move on until a visit from a plain clothes detective and cryptic messages from fortune cookies appear.

https://www.jschlenker.com/

Works in Progress

Birds of a Different Feather

The Imaginary Life of Abigail Jones

Down the Rabbit Hole

Made in the USA
Las Vegas, NV
04 January 2023